# The Dolphin Pool

# THE DOLPHIN POOL

## Yvonne West

**VANTAGE PRESS**
New York / Los Angeles / Chicago

Lyrics of "The Music Goes Round and Round" used by permission. 1935, Intersong Music, Inc. (renewed). All rights reserved.

FIRST EDITION

All rights reserved, including the right of reproduction in whole or in part in any form.

Copyright © 1989 by Yvonne West

Published by Vantage Press, Inc.
516 West 34th Street, New York, New York 10001

Manufactured in the United States of America
ISBN: 0-533-08551-9

Library of Congress Catalog Card No.: 89-90194

1 2 3 4 5 6 7 8 9 0

For Cecil
and Ben, Charles, Jean-Claude, Cecily

# Contents

| | |
|---|---|
| Prelude to War | 1 |
| The French Village | 55 |
| Caldaquès | 137 |
| The Numbered Days | 191 |
| German Time | 237 |

# The Dolphin Pool

# Prelude to War

# 1

"Wake up, Ma-ree-ee."

Marie-Claire jerked her head off the pillow. She winced at the mockery of her French name.

"Didn't you hear the whistle?" Joan's shadowy figure had emerged from under the curtain that separated their beds, and she was hissing in her ear.

"Who didn't?" muttered a still groggy Marie-Claire. Now she realized what had cut through her dream, just as she saw the dolphin—the first shrill whistle announcing an air raid drill. And in the middle of the night this time!

"Get ready," Joan admonished her, before she disappeared under curtain pleats into her own cell.

Inside the white-curtained cells, bed springs creaked, clothes rustled. The entire English convent school dormitory stirred. When the second whistle blew, the girls were on their feet. Bundled in eiderdown, stockings and gas masks dangling around their necks, they formed two straggly columns under the alert eye of Sister Aloysious. *She must lie on top of her bed in her black habit,* thought Marie-Claire. *How else can she dress so fast?*

"Your flashlight, Marie-Claire," called her drill companion.

"Hush, I have it."

Gold halos from twenty flashlights bobbed across the floor as the columns advanced.

"Stay in pairs, girls," Sister Aloysious admonished them.

Marie-Claire trudged along, shivering despite the heavy comforter around her thin shoulders. She'd forgotten to put on her bed socks last night and through her felt slippers the linoleum was cold. They didn't turn on the radiators till November at Saint Ethelred's. Colder still were the stone steps the girls descended in silent procession and the interminable corridors of the school, which had once been an archbishop's palace in the Middle Ages.

*The corridors smell of yesterday's boiled cabbage*, thought Marie-Claire, wrinkling her nose in disgust.

As they passed the current events' bulletin board, Joan poked her in the back.

"What now?" asked Marie-Claire, Joan's breath hot on her neck.

"Did you see that picture of the little marching boys, Mar-ee?" Joan referred to a newspaper clipping of a contingent of Nazi youth at a parade, in shorts and neat, long socks.

"Yes," answered Marie-Claire, her eyes intent on the shuffling feet ahead of her.

"They all look like my little brother, Charles," said Joan.

Mother Eulalia awaited the schoolgirls at the entrance to the basement passageway that was to serve as an air raid shelter in case of war. The Munich Agreement of September '38, when Britain and France had narrowly averted war with Nazi Germany over Czechoslovakia —otherwise known as The Munich Scare—had prompted the neccessity for air raid drills.

The passageway was located directly under the school concert hall. Folding chairs, music stands, music scores, little used instruments, such as a beautiful golden harp, were stored in rooms off the long, sloping corridor. Every month before distribution of conduct cards and once a year at prize-giving, nervous musicians and actresses waited there—backstage. Soon it would be Halloween and the corridor, festooned with damp sponges and nose-tickling threads, would become a ghost train and echo with screams of delight.

Now, hand-holding couples slid down the brown linoleum. *Into the subterranean cages of the Roman Coliseum,* thought Marie-Claire, *like sacrificial animals before a fight.* They stood in front of their assigned seats.

Joan stepped on the heel of Marie-Claire's slipper, and her drill companion lurched forward without her, nearly pulling her arm out of its socket.

"Jo-oan."

"Sorry."

"Keep moving, please," Sister Aloysious said.

At last they plopped onto their chairs, lined up against the walls, and Mother Eulalia called the role.

Under drooping lids Marie-Claire stared at the gas mask opposite her. Mentally she placed it on the girl's face. *She looks like an anteater,* Marie-Claire thought.

"Twenty-five minutes from start to finish," said Mother Eulalia, towering above them in her black habit. "Next practice we must move faster. Still calm, you understand, but faster." She clasped her white hands and smiled at the anxious faces. "If this were a real air raid, we would have tea and sandwiches for you and a gramophone."

"S-s-s-shall we get a rest tomorrow morning? I mean today. Or do we still have to get up early for chapel?"

The question came from a small, mousy girl five chairs down.

"If you absolutely need one, Letitia, you may have

my permission to pull out the string next to your name on the rest card. Otherwise, we must carry on as usual."

*Lucky girl, I wish I'd thought of that.* Marie-Claire sighed. She glimpsed her sister down the line. Just her presence comforted her. Colette leaned against the wall as if she were basking in the sun, eyes closed, lips curled in that Mona Lisa smile of hers. Her long blonde hair gleamed, even in lamplight. Colette had inherited their American mother's fair looks. At fifteen she moved graciously, like the princess in the fairy tales.

At thirteen Marie-Claire had inherited the worst Gallic traits from their French father—dark hair and a prominent nose—although on Victor Lavalette the nose looked aristocratic; kings and noblemen always had long noses.

"Let us pray," said Mother Eulalia.

The girls pressed the palms of their hands together.

Marie-Claire closed her eyes. *If only she and Colette could have stayed in France with Uncle Mo in his village and not returned to this draughty old prison, separated from civilization by a stone wall, tall trees, and clumps of rhododendrons as high as a man.* Randonette smelled of cheeses and warm bread and wine sauces. English villages—what little contact you had with them—smelled flat. Of course, Colette and she would never have been whisked out of Paris to Randonette if it hadn't been for the war scare and the fear of gas bombs. And there was no old palace in Randonette, only castles. (And their American grandfather had insisted on an English school.)

But history really came alive in the Roman pool Uncle Mo was excavating in the countryside, in his off hours from the pharmacy. She had picked up mosaic squares over a thousand years old, squares that had made up the bottom of the pool. Once they had formed pictures of frolicking dolphins, as in Pompeiian frescoes! "Entirely probable," Uncle Mo had said.

"Amen," intoned Mother Eulalia.

"Time to go, Ma-ree." Joan punched her in the ribs. "Don't forget your flashlight."

"Course not."

Marie-Claire yawned. Clumsily she tugged at her eiderdown, which had slipped off one shoulder, pulling with it the sleeve of her bathrobe and exposing her gown and her flat breast.

Without further prodding she marched up the corridor.

# 2

When the reveille nun came through the dormitory in the morning, she knocked on the bedposts. "Blessed be the King of Kings . . . The King of Kings," reiterated the reveille nun.

She poked her arm through the curtain and shook Marie-Claire's feet.

"Now and forever more, amen," responded Marie-Claire.

She'd hardly gone back to sleep after the air raid drill and it was already time to get up again. Automatically she reached for the photographs of her parents on her washstand and a tiny picture of Our Lady, made of blue butterfly wings, and a coral rosary with a silver cross—her most treasured possessions—and slipped them into the drawer underneath her washbowl. At night the washstand became your personal altar, after the bed curtains were drawn and the door curtain tied and you were ensconced in the privacy of your cell at last.

She grasped her water pitcher and followed the line to the faucets in the hall washroom. You filled your pitcher there and returned to your cell to wash. Morning ablutions before early Mass, then breakfast, classes, gym, lunch, outdoor sports, classes, tea, study hall, music practice, chapel, dinner, study hall, recreation, evening prayers, evening ablutions, and then to bed. Every single day of the week, except for Saturdays and Sundays.

"I wish we'd stayed in Randonette," she muttered to Colette, as they left the refectory after breakfast.

"You're not serious?"

"Ab-so-lute-ly, Sis."

Colette shook her head. "That air raid drill must have upset you terribly."

"No, it wasn't that, although I hated getting up in the middle of the night. . . . " How could Colette understand her feelings about Saint Ethelred's, how she hated the regimentation? Colette had lots of friends. She was a whiz at gym and hockey, while Marie-Claire was clumsy and too scared to participate in any activity that involved physical contact.

"What then?" asked Colette.

Marie-Claire shrugged.

Colette resisted further prodding and put her hand on her sister's shoulder. Together they walked down the corridor toward the classrooms.

"Don't forget Grandpa Sterling's declaration," said Colette.

"I won't have them growing up without a proper command of the king's English!" the girls blurted in unison.

Grandpa Sterling's voice had exploded like party crackers that fateful day two years ago. It had happened during one of his annual visits to Paris.

To Marie-Claire's astonishment her father did not object to Grandpa Sterling's financing his granddaughters' English education, although his long nose quivered as he stared at the carpet. Her father was an artist. She knew artists were not rich, but still . . .

Her mother sat, hands crossed on her lap; she never raised an eyebrow. She was probably glad to see her daughters leave home, she was so busy practicing her piano for the many concerts she gave.

The news had infuriated Aunt Monique.

"You allow your daughters to be shipped off to a foreign country," she sputtered, "where the people are cold and stuffy?"

"The English live under a stable government," Victor had meekly replied.

*"Merde au roi d'Angleterre!"* exclaimed Aunt Monique.

Now Marie-Claire pressed her sister's hand. Without Colette she couldn't have stood it at Saint Ethelred's. Colette, and Mother Genevieve.

"Give my love to Miss James," said Colette as they parted at their classroom doors, where girls in blue tunics congregated.

Marie-Claire smiled wryly. Algebra was a subject she detested. Thank goodness English was first on the agenda. She loved English poetry. Poetry evoked marvelous images that she felt every bit as strongly as she did the plant specimens she collected for botany class on nature walks through the woods, velvety clumps of moss sprouting clusters of tiny white mushrooms, like buttons. They were more luxuriant than the mustard sprouts that grew on blotting paper in the classroom.

Eagerly Marie-Claire lifted the heavy wooden lid to her desk and removed poetry book, paper, pencil, and pen box. She dipped her pen in the inkwell recessed in the desk top. AMDG she wrote at the top of the paper—*ad majorem Dei gloriam* (to the greater glory of God). She opened her book of Shakespearan verse. When a rustling of skirts announced the teacher's presence, Marie-Claire stood up with the other girls.

Under her algebra book, Marie-Claire concealed her Shakespearan verse. English class had passed too rapidly and she was still savoring the beauty of poetry from *A Midsummer Night's Dream.* Miss James usually spent the hour expounding on her subject and rarely quizzed the girls orally. She sprang to the blackboard, waving a piece of chalk, and scribbled some equations.

Marie-Claire lifted her algebra book.

I know a bank whereon the wild thyme blows,
Where oxlips and the nodding violet grows,

Her lips moved in silent recitation.

"The solution of problems concerned with areas," said Miss James, "requires the ability to multiply polynomials. What is a polynomial, class?" she asked without turning around.

"An expression consisting of two or more terms," responded everybody except Marie-Claire, who cocked an ear as she continued her study of poetry.

Quite overcanopied with luscious woodbine
With sweet muskroses, and with eglantine.

Marvelous. The whole verse evoked masses of color on a canvas; and Marie-Claire could smell every blossom, too.

"In analyzing such problems," said Miss James, "you will find sketches especially useful." The chalk squeaked across the board and everybody winced.

"Here are two rectangles, one contained within the other."

Marie-Claire stared out the window at the gnarled, bare branches of a lilac bush; clusters of lavender the blooms had been, the perfume so heady they intoxicated bees.

Miss James suddenly lifted her chalk and swung around to face the class. "Miss Lavalette, what is a polynomial?" she snapped.

Marie-Claire blushed redder than a tulip. She crossed her hands on her books.

"What is a monomial?"

"A numeral? a . . . " Marie-Claire racked her brain for some vestige of knowledge, and the other girls covered their mouths to contain their giggles.

Miss James advanced on her like a wolf on the fold. If Marie-Claire had been a boy, she would have had to extend her palm and receive twenty lashes. But corporal punishment had never existed at Saint Ethelred's.

"Mademoiselle Lavalette, if you were in a French school," blurted Miss James, "you would go without supper for a week. You would not be allowed off the premises for a month. I can't say you couldn't play hockey, because the French don't believe in fresh air and outdoor sports." Her voice quivered with indignation, and wispy strands of hair around her face stood out like a medusa. "Thanks to the Magna Carta, I will simply give you a bad mark."

Marie-Claire looked down at her algebra book. Try as she would, she could not grasp all this abstract reasoning, and the numerals swam before her eyes. Miss James had wounded her, had run her through with a rapier and insulted her French blood. She couldn't wait for the bell and the chance to run upstairs to the clothing room, to Mother Genevieve.

"Greetings, my child," said the old nun, who sat at a long wooden counter patching uniforms. "Hand me that crest."

Marie-Claire reached for the embroidered crown with the underlying motto *Rex Regum Christus Rex* (Christ the King, King of Kings). She sidled up to Mother Genevieve, who placed her long black veil around the child's shoulders.

Theirs was a special bond. Mother Genevieve had lived for several years in France. Rumor had it she had been in love with a French count. He had been killed in the Great War and she had joined orders after that.

"Tell me about the castle again and the dinners and the balls," said Marie-Claire. She laid her head on the black bosom, marveling at the heartbeat. Nuns in their austerity, she thought, were made of different stuff. Covered from head to toe in their flowing black habits, they had no hair, no waists, no legs, and the narrow white caps that encircled their faces were so tight they seemed an extension of their countenances.

Gently Mother Genevieve withdrew her veil. With a flick of her wrist, she threaded a needle. "I thought it was time for gym," she said.

Marie-Claire sighed. The morning was not yet over and the worst was still to come. Today she was in need of gratification.

"*Ma Mère*," she asked, using the French term of address, "were you ever in love with anyone besides Christ?"

"I am the bride of Christ."

"I know."

"All earthly passions have long been extinguished. But I'll tell you a secret." Mother Genevieve winked. "He wasn't a count, he was a duke, the person I gather you are referring to, eh?"

Marie-Claire blushed.

"And I was an English girl and a Protestant in those days. Now, hand me a button before you leave."

A Protestant! So Mother Genevieve was a convert. That in itself proved her passion for the duke, since all Frenchmen were Catholics. But the conversion must have occurred after his death; she had mourned him so, she decided to enter Holy Orders. How romantic! Marie-Claire couldn't wait to tell her sister.

Marie-Claire did not see Colette again till tea time.

Gym had been a failure as usual. She could not vault over the horse, that wooden trapezoid that tested your mettle, despite its padded top and the mat on the other side of it that cushioned your fall. Obediently, she ran behind Joan, but on reaching the inert mass her legs failed her and she had to turn away.

And after lunch, while Colette played wing on the hockey team—there not being any tennis during the colder weather—Marie-Claire joined other stodgy girls in the usual "walk," three by three; battalions marching along the same hedge-lined country road.

Thank goodness she had redeemed herself during Ancient History, when she gave a report on the Battle of Thermopylae and waxed so poetic on the bravery of the Spartans that the teacher announced Marie-Claire's report would be published in the school paper.

"I saw Mother Genevieve today," Marie-Claire confided to Colette, as she munched stale bread and butter and sipped tea the color of dishwater. "Those rumors about the count are true, although he wasn't a count, he was a duke."

"Really?"

"Duke?" queried a girl from the other end of the table.

"Don't pick up fag ends, Moira," Colette said, smiling at the interruption.

"Sorry."

"And Mother Genevieve is a convert," continued Marie-Claire.

"That raises her in my estimation," said Colette.

"She's a wonderful person, Col."

"She's a kind old lady, but you shouldn't isolate yourself up in that clothing room."

Marie-Claire cupped a hand over her sister's ear. She didn't want the other girls at the table to hear what she was going to say. "I'm not isolating myself, just getting away from the crowd, for a little bit," she told Colette, "they're so . . . British."

But the other girls were discussing last night's air raid drill. "Say, that was bloody exciting, don't you think?" asked one.

"Oh, stop talking like an army bloke."

"I wonder what sort of sandwiches they'd feed us if it was the real thing."

"Can you see Mother Eulalia winding up the gramophone? hee hee."

# 3

During convocation on Friday, when Mother Eulalia announced to the assembled students that Saint Ethelred's was taking in a little refugee boy, a ripple of half-contained laughter spread through the ranks.

"They're going to teach us about the birds and the bees now," chuckled Joan, beside Marie-Claire.

Marie-Claire tried to punch her in the ribs but inadvertently poked a plump breast. No way to stop Joan; she was too fully insulated.

"Girls . . . Please listen, girls," pleaded Mother Eulalia. "For many people these are very trying times. When you hear what I am about to tell you, you will thank Our Savior for the many blessings he has showered on our land, on ourselves, and on our families."

Mother Eulalia's imperious demeanor now commanded full attention. "As you know, last March Nazi Germany formed a union with Austria. Some people consider it was a forced union and opposed it politically. Franz Dollbein's father was one of these. He paid for his resistance with his life." Reverently Mother Eulalia placed a hand on the crucifix that lay on her broad bosom.

"Ohhhhhh . . . " murmured the horrified girls.

"Franz Dollbein's uncle is a prince of the church," continued Mother Eulalia, "which places Franz and his family in a precarious position. So they fled their country to seek asylum in ours. We have been requested by the mother house in Rome to let this eight-year-old child and his family rest here for a little while."

Mother Eulalia paused to observe the effect of her speech.

"Special dispensation," whispered Joan to Marie-Claire. "What will our parents think?"

Marie-Claire looked around desperately for another station. She didn't want the girls to think that she shared her partner's levity. But the blue tunics pressed so tightly around Mother Eulalia and the upturned faces were so still she dared not move.

Never, never in the history of Saint Ethelred's had a male student inhabited its precincts.

Once a year, in early summer, boys from a London orphanage were bused through the gates to picnic on the gym lawn, and for the remainder of the afternoon they were permitted the use of the gym facilities, under the aegis of Augustinian friars. The Saint Ethelred's girls could watch them from the gallery, as if they were monkeys in a zoo. (Despite these precautions, two girls were caught last year on their way to a rendezvous—Heaven only knows how they had been able to communicate with the boys—and for this escapade they were expelled.)

"I want everyone of you to treat Franz with the utmost courtesy," said Mother Eulalia. "Because of his age, I am placing him in the junior section."

Marie-Claire sensed the general disappointment. Franz would be out of reach. Juniors went everywhere in line: to chapel, like everyone else, of course; to the refectory; to their own little classrooms upstairs. In their green pinafores and with their sweet, innocent little faces they were like marching dolls, always shepherded by a young, white-veiled novice.

"An eight-year-old boy can be quite mischievous," Joan assured her after convocation was over. "Charles would raise moths on damp towels in the bathroom and Mother wondered where all those flying creatures in her closet came from. He would tie strings to frogs' legs and hold them upside down until their eyes fell out."

*He's no monster*, thought Marie-Claire as she watched the distinguished visitor, in grey shorts and long white socks, leading a green-pinafored column into the refectory at tea time. He stood ramrod straight behind his chair until the girls sat down, then he ate his bread in silence. His short blonde hair was slicked with water, such short hair his ears stuck out from rosy cheeks.

Before music practice he showed up alone with his violin case and quietly stepped aside to let Marie-Claire pass with hers.

"My name is Marie-Claire," she told him. "My sister calls me Claire, but here I'm known as Marie. It's more French, the nuns say."

"Franz Dollbein," he said, extending his hand, and they walked into the music wing together.

"My cubicle is on the right," she felt compelled to tell him, "just knock if you need help."

As soon as Marie-Claire had tuned her instrument, she heard the excitement in the hall and turned to see five girls grouped before the glass door of Franz's cubicle. Even the nun, whose duty it was to supervise music practice, stood there, enthralled at the sight of Franz attacking the strings. (He must have tuned his instrument ahead of practice time.) Then he put down his bow and glared at the onlookers.

The group promptly dispersed: girls to their respective rooms; the nun to commence her customary shuttling in the hall; and Marie-Claire to lose herself in the lyrical strains of a French folk song, until a rapping on the wall reminded her the nun had taken her twenty-minute break and it was time for a Gargoyle Club meeting.

Marie-Claire sneaked onto the roof and squatted next to Caliban. The gargoyle was the last of its kind at Saint Ethelred's, a medieval relic overlooked by archaeological vandals. Half man, half dragon, it cocked its head toward the sky with a frightening leer, stone teeth as jagged as a saw's edge but worn smooth from many years of spitting rain water. Caliban provided grotesque relief in a day otherwise filled with religious fervor.

Marie-Claire paid little attention to the group prattle. She'd joined the club because if she hadn't, she would have been considered a poor sport. Girls with brothers discussed male physiology in terms she couldn't understand, not having brothers of her own.

She gazed at the flaming leaves of an elm tree, breathtakingly etched against a grey, autumn sky. When the meeting was over Marie-Claire was the first to creep back to her window. The gravel crunched under her leather soles.

As she swung a stockinged leg over the sill, her tunic up around her hips, the door to the cubicle opened and in came Franz. He was holding his instrument by the neck, trailing a broken string. He stared at her openmouthed, his blue eyes astonishingly haughty for a boy his age. Marie-Claire felt as if Franz had walked into her cell at night, during evening ablutions, and caught her with one nude limb dangling above the wash bowl.

"I did not know the girls wore blue bloomers," he said at last, as she remained suspended on the sill.

Marie-Claire jumped down, like a frog into an empty well of a summer's noon. Her face burned up to her ears. "What do you want?" she snapped, as she pulled her blue tunic down over her stockinged knees.

"Do you have an E string, Marie-Claire? If not, I shall have to go to Sister Teresa." His tone was menacing. Already the boy was taking advantage of his privileged situation.

"Are you going to tattle on me?" she asked.

"Tattle? tattle?" The boy looked puzzled. Obviously, the term was not yet part of his English vocabulary.

"Never mind," said Marie-Claire, "just sit down a minute."

"But there isn't much time left for practice," he replied.

"Oh yes, there is." She rummaged frantically through her violin case, spilling rosin, pad, and pitch pipe.

"Just like Eva," muttered Franz behind her back.

"Eva?"

"My sister. She's always losing things."

Where's Eva? Marie-Claire was tempted to say, but she decided not to pry; it would be discourteous and she had already snapped at the distinguished visitor.

Franz sat down on the piano bench. All practice rooms had pianos, for most of the music students at Saint Ethelred's only studied piano. "In Vienna," he reminisced, "everyone plays violin. We like violin better than soccer."

Marie-Claire turned around, giving him her full attention. She kept one hand on the string she had finally located.

"Eva and I used to go to the park Sunday afternoons to hear Strauss concerts. In the park were big red flowers growing in the form of a treble clef, so big." Franz's face brightened. "The musicians sat in a little house in the middle of the lawn. We sat on the terrace and had pastry and hot chocolate with cream."

"Yummy," exclaimed Marie-Claire. "Go on."

"The band played waltzes, naturally. People danced and had a good time."

"I can imagine."

"Then at the end came the march." Franz paused. His eyes were at the level of Marie-Claire's knobby knees, but he was merely reflecting, she realized.

Nervously, she glanced out the cubicle door. *Thank goodness the nun has not returned yet,* she thought.

Franz raised his head and started to hum, in a sad, little high-pitched voice, "Tadedum, tadedum, tadedum-dum-dum," his bow keeping time to the march. "Tadedum, tadedum, tadedum-dum-dum . . . " He was off in time and space.

"You must miss your country very much," Marie-Claire said gently. She thought how much she missed her own and she could not imagine what it would be like to have to run away from home.

"No, I don't," Franz replied, drawing himself up very straight all of a sudden. "I shall not return until the Nazis give my country back."

Without hesitation Marie-Claire handed him the E string.

She watched as Franz removed the broken string and expertly poked the new one through the peghole and wound it up. As he tuned his instrument, she stared. This scrubbed, blonde boy with the determined air looked just like the boys pictured in the newspaper clippings of Nazi parades that the nuns pinned to the current events' bulletin board: boys in shorts and long socks, marching in neat rows like miniature soldiers.

With his violin tucked under his arm, Franz stood up; bowed to Marie-Claire, thanking her for the string; and returned to his cubicle not one minute too soon. The nun walked in.

Franz wasn't present at evening prayers. Juniors never were. They supped on bread and milk and went directly to bed. *Franz has probably returned to his mother . . . somewhere in the mysterious labyrinths of the old palace, where Catholics hid during times of persecution,* thought

Marie-Claire, as she shifted her weight on the stone floor. With the other girls, she knelt before the statue of the Little King. Only this evening she happened to be five rows back, next to the bulletin board.

High in his alcove the Little King smiled down at her. While her lips moved in the prayer intoned by Mother Eulalia, Marie-Claire decided to address God inwardly. *O God, who createth us in your image and likeness, why did you create Franz in the image of the enemy?*

"Glory be to the Father and to the Son and to the Holy Ghost," pronounced Mother Eulalia loudly, and Marie-Claire sensed she was looking at her.

"As it was in the beginning, is now, and ever shall be, world without end," she muttered aloud, bowing her head.

When she looked at the statue again, Marie-Claire realized that the Little King, in his long red cloak trimmed with ermine, resembled photographs of the English king in his coronation robes: they both wore gold crowns and carried the orb in one hand.

*So is that the answer, God? We are not supposed to question your manifestations?* she thought.

Next to the statue the votive candles in their red cases suddenly flickered brightly.

"Glory be to the Father and to the Son and to the Holy Ghost . . .

"As it was in the beginning, is now, and ever shall be, world without end. Amen."

# 4

After Halloween, grey skies set in for weeks. The once shiny rhododendron bushes turned limp from the cold; lawns crusted over. Evenings, the wind howled around the turrets and arches of the old palace.

"There goes the banshee," said the Irish girls. "Listen to the old witch moan. For sure she's mourning the death of some prominent person."

Marie-Claire shivered and tugged at her eiderdown. Through the tall dormitory windows above the horizontals of her cell, she watched black treetops shake their skeletal fingers, watched their eerie dance until her eyelids closed. And then she dreamed she and Colette were on a ship crossing the Channel in such a storm that the ship rose higher than a mountain and the French coast was always a pencil line on the horizon.

"Pay no attention to that banshee legend," said Mother Genevieve. "The Irish have always been superstitious."

"They say the banshee mourns the death of someone in the house," Marie-Claire said, nodding emphatically, "someone prominent."

"Poppycock." Mother Genevieve reached for the scissors that hung from her girdle, revealing a tiny skull dangling next to her rosary.

"Why do you wear that?" asked the horrified girl.

"To remind me of the transience of all mortal creatures," Mother Genevieve replied.

"It's so gruesome," Marie-Claire said.

"Death is part of life."

"I never thought of it that way."

Mother Genevieve's old face creased into a smile. "This is not a mystery, but you are still too young to understand.

"Here is your sister's veil. I changed the elastic, too." She handed Marie-Claire the waist-length white netting that all Saint Ethelred's girls wore to chapel. Mother Genevieve never let conversation interfere with her work.

"Thank you, *ma Mère. Ma Mère*, do we have a prominent person at Saint Ethelred's?"

"The only prominent person at Saint Ethelred's lies in her grave." Mother Genevieve was referring to the founder of her order, whose sepulchre adjoined the chapel.

"What about Franz?"

"Franz? Franz is a little boy, my child!"

"Mother Genevieve is right," said Colette, as she folded her veil and placed it inside the cabinet under her washstand. "The Irish are great storytellers and don't you get to thinking something will happen to your friend, Franz."

"We're not really friends, we're just violinists," protested Marie-Claire. "He's only eight and I'm thirteen."

"He confided in you, didn't he?"

"He didn't tell me any secrets. Just talked about the Sunday concerts in Vienna, that's all." Marie-Claire sighed.

"What is the matter, Sis?"

"They're teasing me about him in the Gargoyle Club," Marie-Claire admitted.

"I wager I know who's putting them up to it," Colette said.

"They're asking me all kinds of disgusting questions such as, did I know that boys had wet dreams? and—"

"I'll talk to that Joan, I will." Colette's blue green eyes flashed.

"Oh no, no don't, Col. She's likely to play some prank

on me, put a dead mouse in my bed or nose drops in my Ovaltine."

"Then I'll ask for a conference with Mother Eulalia."

"That's worse. The whole school would know I'd tattled." Marie-Claire paled so with fright that Colette tried a different tactic. "Franz hasn't spoken to any of the other girls," she said. "I know."

This revelation did not astonish Marie-Claire. Girls in the upper classes knew just about everything that was going on in school, because the nuns confided in them.

"This proves he considers you a friend," Colette continued.

"But—"

"Concerning the age difference between you and him, think of Mother Genevieve. You're lots younger than she is and she must consider *you* a friend."

Marie-Claire pondered her sister's words. Colette was so logical. Their father had once said that if she had been a man, Colette would have made a good engineer.

"See," said Colette, "it works both ways."

"And she confided in me," exclaimed Marie-Claire. "She told me about the duke."

"There you are, Sis."

"Oh, Col, you're so right." Marie-Claire hugged her sister. "I'm going to write Mother about my new friend, Franz. Do you think Mother will understand?"

"She knows Saint Ethelred's has taken in a refugee."

"I'm going to write her a long letter. I wish she would write me one, instead of a postcard," said Marie-Claire wistfully.

"She's very busy with all her concerts," was all Colette could reply.

During darning and letter-writing hour on Sunday,

Marie-Claire chewed on her pen and stared at the hunched shoulders of the girl in front. Sunday morning and her parents were probably leaving the house for late Mass and then luncheon in the Bois de Boulogne with their friends from the elegant Avenue Henri Martin (on the other side of the wood). Her father would be descending the narrow stairs of their little townhouse, holding his siver-tipped cane like a scepter. Her mother would be following at her usual leisurely pace, adjusting the veil of her blue hat, coquettishly tipped over one eye. The front door—a heavy glass door ornamented with wrought-iron arabesques—would slam. Now, arm in arm, they would descend the porch steps, past the lilac bush. The bell would tinkle on the courtyard gate, just a tiny, stone court, surrounded by an ivy-covered wall. Nothing as grand as Saint Ethelred's. But the ivy-covered wall set the courtyard apart from the other stucco houses in their modest neighborhood. . . .

Putting pen to paper Marie-Claire wrote at last:

*December 4, 1938*

Dear Mother,

I have been practicing very hard and Sister Teresa says I shall soon be able to work on Kreisler's Liebesleid, which is a romantic piece about his native Vienna.

We are all sad about Vienna because of Franz. You know, Franz had to leave his country because he wasn't safe there anymore after his father had been assassinated. Franz told me about the beautiful park in Vienna, and the wonderful time he used to have during the band concerts on Sunday.

We learned in convocation on Friday that Blessed Manfred, who is an ancestor of Sister Teresa's, will be canonized. Blessed Manfred was an English martyr. He has produced three miracles at last.

At Mass this morning, in honor of Blessed Manfred, Sister

Teresa wore a red ribbon on her sleeve and it so happened, since today is December 4 and the feast of the virgin and martyr, Saint Barbara, Father Woodruff wore red vestments. You know, Saint Barbara is one of those auxiliary saints. She will protect you against lightning and sudden death, if you pray to her.

Please get us a *bûche* for Christmas dinner this year. I am so tired of puddings. All we have for dessert is suet pudding.

I hope Father doesn't finish the portrait of the marquise before Colette and I get home. I can't wait to see it up on the easel and Father in his big apron scraping off his palette, and I want to smell those brushes soaking in turpentine.

I hope he will allow me to use a little canvas again, because I am thinking of painting you some flowers for Christmas. I know how much you love flowers. Don't ask me which ones. For Father's Christmas present I am going to Sennelier to buy him a new brush tin, if you will let me.

Only two more weeks until the holidays!

I have to end this letter now, because I haven't darned my stockings yet.

> Your loving daughter,
> M.C.

P.S. If you would like to know what I would like for Christmas, I'll tell you, it is *The Last Days of Pompeii*, by Lord Bulwer-Lytton.

Marie-Claire carefully folded her letter in half and inserted it into a pink envelope lined with rosebuds. The stationery had been a gift from Colette on Marie-Claire's last birthday.

She sighed as she picked up her wooden darning egg. She had wanted to write a note to Uncle Mo, but she had spent too much time daydreaming and the hour was half over. How could one help daydreaming when it wasn't class time and the room was so quiet you could hear the pens scratching? But there was still that heavy pair of cotton stockings to darn, with holes as large as brussels sprouts. Ugh!

She threaded the big needle. Whenever she balked at darning Marie-Claire thought of Mother Genevieve's advice: "Darning is a womanly discipline, and you had better learn to weave properly, as flat as possible, no knots, please—knots cause blisters—because when you grow up you will have to mend your husband's socks."

*Lucky Franz,* thought Marie-Claire, *boys don't have to learn all that boring stuff.*

# 5

"Good Lord, it's Franz!" exclaimed Marie-Claire as she trudged up the hill in Sunday's navy-coated, navy-hatted, white-gloved column. The whole school went for a walk on Sunday. *Franz with wrinkled socks and wind-blown hair,* she thought.

"Prince Charming's out to meet his fair lady," someone said, snickering.

"Oh, what can ail thee, knight-at-arms, alone and palely loitering?" another recited.

"Please," Marie-Claire pleaded.

"Oh, what can ail thee, knight-at-arms, so haggard and so woebegone?"

"Shut up, do you hear me?"

"Getting sensitive now, are we?" asked Marie-Claire's neighbor.

"Remember what Mother Eulalia told us in convocation," retorted Marie-Claire.

She broke rank without permission to join Franz, who stood alongside the cabbage patch. She knew Sister Anastasi wouldn't mind. All the nuns adored Franz; in their eyes he was the son of a modern Christian martyr.

"I have something to tell you," whispered Franz to Marie-Claire. He leaned over to pull up his socks, a nonchalant gesture probably intended to throw off any spies while he divulged a secret of diplomatic importance.

They waited for the rest of the column to pass by and, inwardly gloating, Marie-Claire spotted the freckled faces of the Irish girls.

In the evenings, during that magical time when curtains surrounded each cell in white anonymity and before the dormitory nun came to bed, the Irish girls would brag of cousins in the Irish Republican Army, a group outlawed by the British. She did not take them seriously anymore. Besides the banshee legend, the Irish girls also related stories about fairies and hobgoblins in every dell, in the greenest country in the world, so they said.

With Franz's secret she would be one up on them at last. Of course, she would only hint of superior knowledge, never give the slightest clue as to its origins.

"I'll wait for you on the swings," whispered Franz.

Heart pounding, Marie-Claire ran inside and removed her hat and gloves. Her muddy walking shoes she placed in the carton for postulants to polish. *What a shame Franz was no older than he was. The whole affair could have taken on romantic proportions.*

"Ouch." Sliding into her Sunday shoes returned Marie-Claire to the world of grim reality. Poorly darned stockings had rubbed blisters on her heels.

At the appointed meeting place in the center of the

graveled playgound, she joined Franz, who was seated on one of the little wooden swings.

"After Christmas," said Franz, "I am going to public school, like the other British boys."

"Yes?" queried Marie-Claire.

"You are the first student at Saint Ethelred's to learn this," Franz replied.

"Is that all you had to tell me?" she asked.

When she saw the hurt look in Franz's eyes, Marie-Claire regretted her insensitivity. The words had come tumbling out.

"You are my friend, Marie; we practice together. I thought you should be the first to know. Don't you like me?" he asked.

"Of course, of course, I do." *It's uncanny how he always has the upper hand,* she thought. "Thank you very much for telling me. I shall miss you." She appeared genuinely sad. Then she thought of what Sister Teresa had told her once. "But I know you will be happier with boys your own age, Franz." Marie-Claire said, nodding graciously.

"You don't know how it feels to be stared at all the time," confided Franz.

It's just because you are a boy, Marie-Claire wanted to say, which was the truth. But the truth wasn't always polite, so she remained silent.

"I am like an object in a glass case in the Kunsthistoriches Museum in Vienna." He stood up and whispered in Marie-Claire's ear. "There is a guard outside my door at night."

Marie-Claire thrilled at that piece of news but "Really" was all she could think of to say under the circumstances.

"I know I am very precious," Franz now said, "or the nuns would never have allowed such a thing as a boy in a convent. They don't do it in Austria, it is upsetting to everybody, even to you."

Marie-Claire shook her head no. "I don't mind practicing with you at all."

She looked straight at Franz. *He is so wise,* she thought. *How can a little boy make such pronouncements?* "Where is Eva?" she suddenly asked.

"In the guest house with Mother."

So it was in the guest house the nuns kept their special visitors. No wonder she hadn't seen them. The guest house nestled behind cypresses and tall rose bushes across from the chapel. It was normally reserved for visiting clergy: bishops, cardinals, archbishops, and the like.

"Eva has been sick ever since we left Austria. She cannot swallow properly and Mother has to feed her." He swiveled around and pointed a finger at Marie-Claire. "Don't you tell anybody. It is a big secret."

"Of course not, I would never betray you." Marie-Claire really meant what she said. For once she felt important. Scrawny little Marie-Claire, whose chest caused scarcely a ripple in her flannel underwear, was the only student to learn Saint Ethelred's biggest secret.

The swing ropes creaked as she and Franz rocked back and forth. Then Marie-Claire stood up and went behind Franz. She gently pulled his swing toward her, gave it a push, and away he went. He pumped with his legs and soon he soared as high as the top of the lilac trees.

When the tea bell rang, Marie-Claire caught one of the ropes and the swing spun around, hitting her in her side. Franz jumped off. Without a word, he came over to Marie-Claire and put his little arms around her waist, as if to say he was sorry. Then he crunched away through the gravel, his head high, conscious of his status in life.

Marie-Claire wished she could have held the little boy

or at least patted him on the head, but he had walked off in such a hurry.

Too demonstrative for an English schoolyard anyway, she reminded herself. Her father had warned her about the English. "Do not kiss, do not cry, do not pat, do not sigh; be as imperturbable as the surface of a brook under a summer sky. But remember, Marie-Claire," he had added, "during a crisis, the English act promptly and calmly. They do what can be done first, without yelling or shouting at the top of their voices."

She smiled as she patted her side; her coat, fortunately, had cushioned the blow. She remembered how last summer Aunt Renée had screamed and thrown up her hands when Uncle Mo, who was undoubtedly dreaming of their dolphin pool, forgot to scrape his muddy boots before entering the kitchen . . . and then he had dared to poke a dirty finger in the lentil soup.

When her mother was annoyed, she never yelled. But then her mother was American. She would turn pale and crisp her fingers, just as she did before she placed her hands on the piano keys, and talk very slowly, in a voice almost devoid of expression.

"Come on, Claire," said Colette, sticking her head out of a classroom window, "tea time. I've been looking all over for you. If we don't hurry up, they'll be clearing the tables soon and we won't get any jelly scones."

Colette and Marie-Claire joined the group of stragglers stampeding to the refectory. They promptly slowed to a walk when they came in sight of the refectory nun and remembered to cross themselves before they sat down.

"You know," said Marie-Claire to Colette, "I have never seen Mother cry."

"Whatever brought that up?" said Colette, as she stretched an arm out for the scones, which had already been placed at the end of their table. "Grown-ups don't cry in public. Especially not ladies, and in a foreign country never. Hurry up. Sister wants to clear."

"You consider home a foreign country?" The thought outraged Marie-Claire.

"Course not, silly. I'm just looking at things from Mother's point of view. Remember she wasn't born in France."

"She's a Boston Brahmin." Marie-Claire repeated the words she had heard Grandpa Sterling use.

"It must have been very difficult for Mother at first. Think how difficult it would be for us if we visited the United States, and they speak English there. And you must admit the French are terribly demonstrative. It's not just a question of verbal expression; they speak with their eyes, their hands—"

"They . . . they?" Marie-Claire was incensed.

"Again, look at it from Mother's point of view." Colette smiled. Her unflagging admiration for their mother was something Marie-Claire could not always understand.

"I wager Mother is a cupboard expressionist," continued Colette.

"A *cupboard* expressionist?"

"Yes, that's someone who lets off steam behind closed doors."

"Is that what you do, Colette?"

"Isn't that what most people do?" Colette tossed her blonde mane.

To her dismay, Marie-Claire realized Colette had been brainwashed by the British. She had become as stodgy as suet pudding.

Before Marie-Claire packed for the Christmas holiday, she gave Franz a holy picture with the gold inscription,

"May God bless you," and on the back of it she wrote: To dear Franz, in memory of your stay at Saint Ethelred's. Your friend, Marie-Claire Lavalette, 18 December 38.

# 6

In front of the great door at Saint Ethelred's grew a monkey puzzle tree. No one seemed to remember when this evergreen sentinel had been planted, its convoluted branches with sharp, prickly leaves had guarded the school entrance for so many years.

After the Christmas holidays, weeping sores appeared on its trunk, and its leaves turned brown, then dropped.

Because of what had happened in Austria and Czechoslovakia, many persons of Celtic origin, whose Druid ancestors had worshipped the sacred oak, considered the passing of the monkey puzzle tree a bad omen. Marie-Claire counted among the guilty. Her Gallic ancestors' Druid priests cut down mistletoe with golden scythes.

"Nonsense!" cried Mother Eulalia, "your pagan ideology is just the sort of stuff that spreads panic among the less educated members of society. Didn't our prime minister assure us there would be peace in our time? I don't want to hear anymore about this monkey puzzle business."

She meant what she said. Known instigators of the rumor stayed after evening prayers and were made to recite three rosaries on their knees, without benefit of cushions. "If anyone so much as uses a scarf to kneel on," warned Mother Eulalia, "her penance will be doubled."

In March, however, when Hitler violated the Munich Agreement, and paraded through Prague with his troops, Mother Eulalia relented. Now, during Mass, after the elevation of the Host, the whole of Saint Ethelred's prayed to God for peace on earth and to Our Lady, Queen of Angels, for protection.

And she ordered air raid drills twice weekly.

To the gold medals of the Virgin and their guardian angel they already wore on chains around their necks, Marie Claire and Colette added a Saint Christopher, urgently sent from Paris before the long trek home for the Easter holiday. Easter Sunday would come the beginning of the second week in April that year, 1939. On the front of the medal a brawny Saint Christopher, with biceps and calves like a circus strong man's, ferried a pint-sized Christ, and on the reverse side were inscribed the girls' names and home addresses.

"These medals have been blessed by the archbishop," wrote Victor. "I want you to wear them at all times during the voyage, even if you should get seasick."

The very mention of seasickness caused Marie-Claire to hold her stomach. She had been plagued by "growing pains" this semester. "Growing pains" felt like the stitches she usually got in her side during walks, only these were definitely in her belly.

"You're probably about to get the curse," Joan had told her, sympathetic for once, "and there's nothing you can do about it except grin and bear it."

"Probably gas pains," Matron had said. "Cut down on the cabbage."

But when that didn't bring relief, to her delight Marie-Claire was dispatched to the infirmary for a day. She lay abed, out of sound of bells and air raid whistles, and enjoyed fresh-baked cookies and milk at tea time. The pains miraculously disappeared.

The experiment was conducted a second time, a few days later. After that, Matron, who "brooked no nonsense from simpering girls," prescribed strong doses of cod liver oil in the dispensary.

Medals jingling, Marie-Claire climbed the clothing room stairs, two at a time, to say good-bye to Mother Genevieve. Her old friend huddled near a charcoal stove. *How pinched and drawn her face looks,* Marie-Claire thought to herself but Mother Genevieve's hands moved as busily as ever, twisting thread around blue buttons, smoothing the lapels of blue blazers.

"How well you look, my child," exclaimed Mother Genevieve, "all that cod liver oil has put roses back into your cheeks."

Marie-Claire made a face. "It tastes so horrible," she said, "like pouring slime down your throat."

Mother Genevieve adjusted the glasses on her nose. "Consider it part of your lenten discipline. We usually mortify our bodies to strengthen our spiritual senses. But in your case you are strengthening both."

"I never thought of it that way," said Marie-Claire.

"Many things will happen to you in life that you never thought would happen. Remember the French proverb: Never say, 'Fountain, I shall not drink of your water.' "

"Yes," muttered Marie-Claire, "I never thought I would have 'growing pains.' "

"Don't mutter, child. You sound like an old woman. Growing pains are part of growing up, that is all there is to it."

Marie-Claire blushed. Growing up went awfully slowly and confusingly. Her monthly period still had not arrived.

And now, after vigorous exercise, she sometimes got nosebleeds.

Then her thoughts turned to the monkey puzzle tree.

"*Ma Mère*," she suddenly asked, "are we going to have another war?"

Mother Genevieve crossed herself. "Lord forbid!" she exclaimed, and she almost scratched herself on the pincushion that was tied around her wrist. "The Great War was 'the war to end all wars.' Why such morbid thoughts?"

Marie-Claire hung her head.

"Is it that pagan monkey tree business? Aha! You need more spiritual tonic. Pray the Secret from the Mass for Peace:

O God, who suffereth not the nations who
believe in Thee to be overwhelmed by any peril . . ."

Then she rattled off the rest of the prayer without losing a stitch.

"I will look it up in my missal," said a solemn Marie-Claire, "and I promise you I will include it in my evening devotionals."

"God bless you, my child," said Mother Genevieve, "until we meet again." And she gave Marie-Claire her crucifix to kiss.

# 7

But in the spring Mother Genevieve took sick and was no longer able to climb the steps to the Clothing Room. In her stead, Marie-Claire encountered two impassive younger nuns, who shooed her away.

She clung to the bannisters as she descended the well-worn stairs. One, two, three . . . eight, nine, ten steps. She had never given them any thought. She fled down the corridor and the next flight of stairs until she found herself under the stone archway of the great door, staring past the stump of the monkey puzzle tree to the vast expanse of lawn, where birds basked in pools of green sunshine. The rhodedendron bushes had never appeared more glorious. Huge blossoms, more vivid than a bishop's cassock, burst among the shining leaves. Along the country roads, on the perimeters of lush, green fields dotted with dandelions, hedges abloom with hawthorne and woodbine intoxicated the bees. Bluebells carpeted the woods; in the thickets grew yellow primroses, with leaves as soft as velvet.

To think that Mother Genevieve could be leaving this springtime world for the mysteries of the next—up there, beyond the blue ether. Mysteries, the nuns had taught her, could only be understood when you reached God's kingdom. Marie-Claire shuddered, although the sun warmed her cheeks. To her, mysteries conjured up a formless black void, and smoke, and steam, and muffled voices rising out of nowhere. But what about God's golden throne, and the angels and archangels with all their halos pouring streams of golden light? Still, there was purgatory to undergo, purgatory, between Heaven and Hell. And unlike Hell, with its leaping flames and prodding devils, no one knew what purgatory looked like.

Purgatory is only temporary, Marie-Claire chided herself. Mother Genevieve probably has a lot of indulgences saved up in her prayer bank—hundreds of days. She might have an instant passkey to Heaven.

Comforting herself with such thoughts, Marie-Claire walked back inside to prepare for the noonday meal. In the washroom she scrubbed her ink-stained fingers with pumice stone. Contemplating herself in the mirror, she smoothed her lanky hair with the small comb every Saint Ethelred's girl carried in her flannel underpants' pocket. She decided that after lunch, when she went on the school walk, she would pick a large bouquet of primroses and leave them at the infirmary for Mother Genevieve.

The postulant at the infirmary door was a large, raw-boned girl with cheeks as red as an apple. She hesitated when Marie-Claire handed her the flowers, then lifted a corner of her gray apron to wipe away a tear. "Bless her soul," she said, speaking of Mother Genevieve, "she's as shriveled as a newborn bird, but her spirit is at peace."

Struck dumb with grief, Marie-Claire could only stare at the girl. Then she turned on her heel and ran all the way back to the locker room. The place was empty by now. Marie-Claire opened the door to her closet and huddled behind it, waiting for her racing heart to slow down.

The rest of the afternoon passed as in a dream. Marie-Claire's body went through all the paces: standing at attention when the teacher entered the classroom; mechanically opening and closing books; following the girls next to her through the corridors to the refectory; and going to study hall, where she read and reread *A Day in the Life of a Roman Slave* as if it were a prayer of supplication, without paying attention to the meaning of the words.

Surely, consolation, of sorts, would come during music practice. Today, however, the notes Marie-Claire produced on her violin sounded scratchy. *It is as if I'd neglected to rub rosin on my bow,* she thought.

In chapel, before Benediction, Father Woodruff asked

everyone to pray for Mother Genevieve, who was not expected to live, and this elicited a gasp of surprise from everyone except Marie-Claire. She fixed her eyes on the golden monstrance, which contained the body of Christ. "Give me strength," she prayed.

When Sister Teresa appeared at recreation and invited Marie-Claire and other music students to listen to a concert over the radio, she knew her prayer had been answered. They were to hear the gifted young violinist Sister Teresa had spoken so highly of, Yehudi Menuhin, play Beethoven's violin concerto. Eagerly she drew up a chair in front of the large radio cabinet and waited for the balm to heal her troubled soul. And the minute she heard the soloist's joyous opening phrase her spirits soared with the music. She remained spellbound throughout the entire piece.

All the next day the memory of the sublime music continued to work its magic for Marie-Claire. In study hall she started writing a poem about it.

> Music fills one to the very height
> Of sweet emotion and delight . . .

But at Benediction, when Father Woodruff announced that Mother Genevieve had passed away and that he would say a Requiem Mass for her on Thursday, the spell broke. Focusing on the little white window in the center of the monstrance, Marie-Claire prayed and prayed for strength and felt no consolation. The gorgeous monstrance, its golden edges radiating like sunbeams, seemed but an empty case, and so she turned to the statue of the Blessed Virgin for solace.

\* \* \*

"Claire, you must not mourn so," whispered Colette to her sister after the Requiem Mass. Marie-Claire stood in the dormitory, pulling off her chapel veil. "Like all nuns, Mother Genevieve was a pious old lady, who probably won't have to wait long in purgatory before she goes to Heaven."

Marie-Claire dabbed at her eyes, then blew her nose. "Yes, I know," she said.

Colette took her sister's crumpled veil and smoothed the white netting. Marie-Claire sat down on her bed. All through the Mass she had to press her knees together to keep from shaking, and now her legs were like those of a rag doll's with the stuffing removed.

She had tried not to look at the black-draped coffin, but she couldn't help getting a speck of black in the corner of her eye, being the second girl from the aisle.

Then there was so much processing around the body. She could hear the squeaky shoes of the altar boys, the rustle of Father Woodruff's silk cope, the tinkling of the incense burner against the chain—one, two, three . . . one, two, three—every time a censing took place. The spicy incense was overpowering, nauseating. But worst of all was the *Dies Irae*.

> Day of wrath! O day of mourning!
> See fulfilled the prophet's warning.
> Heaven and earth in ashes burning . . .

In her missal Marie-Claire had followed the English translation of the Latin chant. It recalled a ghostly procession of monks, skulls draped in brown hoods, skeleton feet treading hot coals. . . . Mother Genevieve was too cheerful a person for so much music in a minor key.

Marie-Claire took a deep breath and sank against her

pillow. She tried to think back on some part of the ceremony that could be of comfort to her. Then she remembered Father Woodruff praying that the angels conduct the soul into Abraham's bosom. Abraham's bosom she could not visualize. But the soul of Mother Genevieve she saw rising into the Heavens, surrounded by clusters of angels, like the Virgin in the painting of the Assumption. Marie-Claire closed her eyes.

Colette sat down on the bed and held her hand. Marie-Claire heard the murmur of concerned voices. "Marie-Claire, let me get you a cup of tea," said one.

"Yes, tea should do her good," said another.

"Plain, with a little sugar." *That would be Joan's voice,* Marie-Claire thought.

"I'll fetch water for her washbowl, so we can put a cool cloth on her forehead," the voice continued.

The springs creaked and Colette got off the bed. Then she heard Matron walk in with that heavy, mannish tread of hers. *Oh no, not Matron right now,* she thought, *when my stomach is churning and there's a dry, rancid taste in my mouth.* She could feel Matron's penetrating gaze beaming onto her like the ray of a searchlight.

"Got a tummy ache again, Marie-Claire? Is that it? I want you to open your eyes and sit up very slowly. There. This should help a lot."

Matron held out a tiny cup of yellow fluid and Marie-Claire hesitated. If it was cod liver oil, she knew she would retch and make a fool of herself all over Matron.

"Don't worry, this is not your usual tonic," said Matron wryly.

Holding her stomach, Marie-Claire slowly reached for the cup with her other hand.

"This is what the French prescribe for many ailments—cognac. You're familiar with this, I'm sure." Matron raised her chin, like a captain commanding his troops. "Sip it slowly," she ordered.

Marie-Claire obeyed. Instantly a gentle warmth suffused her. The stuffing reappeared in her limbs.

"Now, I want you to rest for an hour," said Matron, "and then you may resume your normal schedule." She turned on her heel and marched out of the room.

Colette smiled. She was standing at the foot of the bed. "Honest, Claire, I wasn't the one to fetch Matron," she said.

*Don't perjure yourself,* thought Marie-Claire.

The dormitory emptied before the bell rang. Gym time. Marie-Claire lay back and gazed at the ceiling. High above her danced the grey shadow of a branch, its leaves a kaleidoscope of blurred forms shifting with the breeze. Birds twittered in the tree outside the window. The breeze carried with it the fragrance of woodbine.

Before she closed her eyes again, Marie-Claire crossed herself. "Lord," she prayed, "don't let me think of that monkey puzzle tree any longer, and grant Mother Genevieve remission of all her sins."

# 8

"It's Saint Petronilla tomorrow."

"No, Saint Angela."

"I like Saint Petronilla better," insisted Marie-Claire.

"What difference does it make?" asked Colette, twirling her tennis racket. "They're both listed on the same day."

"Don't you like the sound of Aurelia Petronilla? I think it's beautiful. It rhymes. Besides, she knew Saint Peter."

"Saint Angela is the most important virgin of the two. She's the patron saint of Christian education, Mother Eulalia said."

Marie-Claire dared not contradict her sister. No one could fault Mother Eulalia.

"Father Woodruff is saying early Mass for Mother Genevieve tomorrow," Marie-Claire said then.

"You don't sound happy about it," Colette replied.

"Gosh, what if my string happens to be pulled out?" Marie-Claire was referring to the string on the rest card, that little green cord over which Mother Eulalia had dominion and which meant the difference between rising at the crack of dawn and luxuriating in a warm bed for an extra hour before breakfast.

"You could ask Mother Eulalia to change your rest day," suggested Colette.

"She's never done that," Marie-Claire said.

"There is always a first time for anything."

"Hum," grunted Marie-Claire. She was torn between gratitude toward Father Woodruff for helping the soul of her friend and disappointment at the possibility of passing up an extra hour's sleep, which she needed desperately now that prize giving was coming up—prize giving with its attendant recital in which she was a soloist. Prize-giving recitals made Marie-Claire more nervous than conduct card ones, because everyone was present then: parents, nuns, and sometimes even the bishop.

"While you deliberate, let's go sit down on this bench," said Colette.

"I'm not deliberating," retorted Marie-Claire, "I've already made up my mind. I'm going to early Mass, regardless."

"I knew you would, Sis. Let's sit down anyway. I have a secret to tell."

"A secret?" Marie-Claire tingled with anticipation. "But couldn't we go inside?" Secrets to her were like hot chocolate, more delicious if imbibed in the coziness of a room.

"It's too far," said Colette. "I have to practice my backhand."

The sisters pulled out their handkerchiefs and laid them on the pollen-covered bench.

"I got a note from Jean-Paul de Joux," whispered Colette.

"Jean-Paul?" Marie-Claire responded, puzzled.

"The countess's nephew."

"The man who came charging by on his horse and scared Uncle Mo half to death?"

"Yes!" beamed Colette.

"Well!" exclaimed Marie-Claire. She'd thought the intruder very rude to upset Uncle Mo, when he was busy concentrating on where to dig next at the Roman excavations.

"It was his aunt's land," said Colette, as if she could read her sister's mind, "and one of her prize bulls had gone astray, remember?"

"No, I don't," said Marie-Claire. "I was too busy helping Uncle Mo with the mosaic."

"Yes, well, listen to this." Colette's eyes sparkled as she held up a small sheet of blue paper. "Jean-Paul informs me that he will be spending the summer at the castle and hopes we will be returning to Randonette to 'help the professor in his labors.' That's what he calls Uncle Mo, 'the professor.' " Colette chuckled. "I wonder where he got my address?"

"Gosh, I don't know," said Marie-Claire. She turned

pensive. "Oh, Col," she blurted, "will we really be seeing Uncle Mo this summer? All year I've been thinking about the excavations and—"

"The dolphin pool," interjected Colette.

"Yes."

"Don't worry, I'm sure we'll be going to Randonette," Colette replied.

"But how can you be so sure? We were sent there last year because of the war scare. What if everything turns out all right after all. I mean, what if Hitler doesn't break any more rules?"

"Listen, Sis," said Colette, with the mysterious air of a soothsayer, "I'm as certain of the fact that we'll be going to Randonette as I am that these buttercups under our feet are yellow and that the tree over there has a forked branch."

Colette jumped up and sauntered toward the tennis courts, the pleats of her blue, athletic tunic swaying gracefully over her hips. Marie-Claire watched her without envy, only marveling at her assurance and taking comfort in her prediction.

Then Marie-Claire checked the little French calendar she carried in her bloomers' pocket to keep track of the various saint's days—in France every day was a saint's day. *Not even three weeks till the end of school and prize giving!* she thought.

Marie-Claire had never won anything in the two years she had attended Saint Ethelred's; but this year she had received such good marks in Ancient History she felt confident she would be crowned with a laurel wreath and be awarded a handsome, leather-bound book inscribed with gold letters, with her name on the first page, under the Saint Ethelred's crest. How proud she would be to show it to her parents and Uncle Mo. *If only prize giving wasn't accompanied by that darn concert. . . .*

*You know what Sister Teresa says*, she reminded herself silently. *"Practice, practice, practice, so that your fingers move on the board as if they had a mind of their own, and you can draw your bow with such assurance that everyone will wonder at the beautiful sounds you create."*

During dress rehearsal, when sunshine streamed through the tall, Gothic windows of the concert hall, Marie-Claire thought only of the history prize.

The Saint Ethelred's girls were ranged in neat tiers on steps above the stage, Marie-Claire in the row behind the wiggly juniors. Choral practice came first, and today Mother Eulalia sat as a lonely spectator in the center seat, first row, across from the desolate arena.

"Smile, smile," she entreated the girls, before the choral director waved her plump hands for the Walter de la Mare:

> In Hans' old mill,
> His three black cats
> Watch the bins
> For the thieving rats.
> Whisker and claw
> They crouch in the night,
> Their five eyes
> Gleaming gre-een and BRIGHT.

The thin, shrill voices of the juniors shrieked the second verse's opening lines, and Marie-Claire cringed.

> Squeaks from the doorstep,
> Squeaks from where
> The cold wind stirs

> On the empty stair
> Squeaking and scampering ev-ery where.

When the seniors plodded up the mill stairs with Hans for the start of his day's work, Marie-Claire could read the director's lips. "Heavy, heavy shoes," she was mouthing, "wooden clogs, which threaten to fall off at every step."

The song ended with a repeat of the first verse, in stage whisper falsetto, which usually produced spasms of giggling from the juniors. But today Marie-Claire and the others in her row had been instructed to tug at the juniors' pinafore sashes.

Songs with lyrics by Francis Thompson and Gerard Manley Hopkins—both good Catholics—and Shakespeare rounded out the program. The finale in this year of international turmoil, when Europe tottered on the brink of war, was an original composition by the choral director in praise of her native land, which on the program was marked Anonymous. It concluded with a flourish:

> That shining jewel, that favored land,
> That EN-GLAND!

As the Saint Ethelred's girls reached these lines and the piano accompaniment soared to treble heights, even Marie-Claire could not help experiencing a thrill she would normally have deliberately resisted. So much for the power of poetry and music. Mother Eulalia flushed with pride. She would have dabbed her watery eyes if the girls had not been watching her.

"Bend your knees as you sit down, girls, and keep your backs as straight as possible," called Mother Eulalia. "Heads high. That's it. And smile, smile. Fold your hands in your lap. Yes . . . Now, let's all stand up and practice sitting one more time."

Obediently the waves of blue tunics crested tempest high, then subsided with a gentle thump. With hardly a rustle of her black gown, the choral director left center stage to stand quietly against the wall, her head and torso framed in the white reflection from a window above.

Then Marie-Claire disappeared backstage with the rest of the music and elocution students on the program to practice entrances and exits on cue from Mother Eulalia. After that, Mother Eulalia selected random individuals to act as prize winners. As each girl stepped down into the arena, Miss Brown played a few stunning measures of Chopin's Heroic Polonaise, the one with the martial air.

On prize-giving day the music never failed to stir Marie-Claire, and it brought tears of joy to the victors who, like ancient Greek athletes, kneeled before Mother Superior to be crowned with a laurel wreath and to receive from her august hands their books, dedicated in Gothic script. The books remained the spoils of the victors, but the laurel wreaths were returned to God at the altar rail, during Benediction. Everything at Saint Ethelred's was AMDG, *ad majorem Dei gloriam* (to the greater glory of God). This was written at the top left-hand corner of every theme and examination paper and inscribed in stone above the great door.

"We're finished, Ma-ree." Joan punched her in the ribs. "I'll race you to the door."

Marie-Claire and Joan joined the happy throng stampeding into the June sunshine and the pungent odor of new mown grass and sorrel. Both girls flopped onto the lawn and gazed at the sky, which today was the color of bluebells between fleecy clouds. They watched a black-robed figure coast down the hill on her bicycle, veil billowing in the breeze.

"Look at her go," exclaimed Marie-Claire. *Two more days and she and Colette would be sailing for France and the long-awaited summer vacation. And who knows when they might join Uncle Mo in Randonette.*

"Looks as if you should have a good crossing, if this weather keeps up," said Joan.

"Just what I was thinking," beamed Marie-Claire.

"No need to ask Matron for any of that seasickness medicine, or have you outgrown all that stuff? You know what I mean."

"No, I don't," said Marie-Claire, who knew very well what Joan was hinting at, but she was too embarassed to admit that her monthly period had not yet come.

"Never mind, Ma-ree. Let's look for a four-leaf clover."

# 9

Marching into the concert hall on prize-giving day, Marie-Claire was sorry her parents could not be in the audience to hear her perform. As usual, her mother was practicing for a concert, testing the keys of some unfamiliar grand piano.

The hall was packed. Behind the two front rows of black-garbed figures stretched acres of flowered hats and smooth, masculine heads, interspersed with small faces that were miniatures of their grown-up counterparts.

The audience applauded politely at every song. But as the last chords of the patriotic anthem resounded in the great hall, the spectators rose, as if with one accord, and their applause was thunderous. It sent shivers down Marie-Claire's spine.

Then Marie-Claire stepped down on stage, waiting in her appointed place for the other musicians and elocutionists to join her. They filed through the rectangular opening into the bowels of the auditorium.

Backstage no one spoke. As always, the minute they stepped into the dark passageway they were all infected with stage fright, each girl reserving her breath to calm her stomach, standing only inches from one another yet isolated in melancholic cocoons.

The fear was so contagious that after tuning her instrument, Marie-Claire decided to distance herself still farther from the others before her hands got too clammy. Her number, *Le Cygne*, by Saint-Saëns, was the last one on the program, and Marie-Claire had practiced it until she could play it in her sleep. Now she removed her shoes and ran down the corridor toward the air raid shelter, where chairs were lined up against the wall ready for the next drill. She usually thought of those chairs as repulsive instruments of torture, associating them with precious loss of sleep; but now she plopped down on one to put her shoes back on before tiptoeing into the storage room that contained the golden harp.

Like a king's throne, the harp sat on a dais, majestic and alone. Its strings were mute from years of disuse and Marie-Claire let her fingers glide across them, first one hand then the other, her arms ever so graceful. Now her blue tunic became a flowing, white garment; her dark hair coiled into a bun tied with golden ribbons, like a maiden on a Greek vase. She pressed the harp's pedals and fingered the golden acanthus leaves carved on the tall, fluted column. Without doubt, the harp was the most elegant of instruments.

When Marie-Claire tiptoed out of the room she was assailed by an ominous silence. No voices on stage, no tinkling of piano keys. To her horror she noted the corridor was empty. In the light at the end of the tunnel arms waved at her.

And then she was seized with panic. She ran uphill, her shoes echoing like hammer strikes, her heart pounding. Now she could hear ripples of half-contained laughter. She stopped in her tracks. They were all laughing at her, the mouse trapped in the hole. What should she do? She wanted desperately to turn around and go back to the storage room and hide until the ceremony was over.

But two years of dogged discipline and the thought of the history prize urged her to continue up the corridor, at a discreet walk. Silence mercifully reappeared. Came the grating of the piano bench across the stage floor. Pause. Then the flowing beauty of a Brahms' intermezzo, which she realized was not part of the regular program. *Miss Brown must be filling in for her. Dear Miss Brown.* Marie-Claire inhaled a giant, musty breath and expelled every ounce before she picked up her instrument and walked, head high, to center stage, her eyes fixed on the banked figures on the other shore.

While she listened to the accompanist's opening measures Marie-Claire tucked her violin under her chin, slowly raised her right arm, and the minute she drew her bow across the strings a majestic, white swan glided across quiet waters. Miss Brown and she played in perfect harmony. As Marie-Claire's little finger quivered with lyric vibrato on the last high note, and Miss Brown descended octaves in graceful arpeggios, the audience burst into applause.

The prize-giving ceremony passed as in a dream for Marie-Claire, who wished she could fly out of the Gothic windows like a celestial being and vanish into the blue sky to regain her composure before facing the audience again.

Like an automaton, at the strains of Chopin's Heroic Polonaise she stepped down into the arena to receive the history prize for her class, carefully averting her eyes when Mother Superior crowned her and placed the book between her hands. As she rose, she couldn't help noticing the icy stare of blue eyes in ruddy, matriarchal faces, the adjustment of spectacles on patrician noses—faces in a nightmare. Only the tickle of paper leaves on her forehead and the cool smoothness of leather in her hands were proof of reality as she returned to her seat.

"Congrats, old girl," whispered Joan, without moving her head, "you got what you deserved."

*I made a fool of myself,* thought Marie-Claire, fighting back tears. *What if Mother and Father had been here?*

"All hail to the victor!" shouted Joan, as Marie-Claire was carried into the dormitory on a seat of clasped hands at the head of a triumphant procession; then she was dumped unceremoniously onto her bed, in the best Saint Ethelred's tradition.

"Let's see the spoils," someone said.

"Ay yes, give it to me," said another.

"*Greek and Roman Mythology,* no less."

"Where are the nude gentlemen?"

"With illustrations from the Vatican collection of ancient art," pointed out Marie-Claire.

"That must mean they're all wearing fig leaves."

"Yes." Marie-Claire reclaimed her prize from so many

greedy fingers and polished its fine leather on a corner of her bedspread. She straightened her paper wreath, which she was about to give up at Benediction.

"Well done, Sis." Colette popped her head in the door. She was all smiles. *An inquiry into what happened during the recital will probably come later*, thought Marie-Claire.

But next morning, when Colette and she, laden with suitcases, gas masks, tennis racket, and violin case, struggled down the passage to the great door, Colette still had made no mention of it.

The taxi, which was to drive them to the station for the first of their many train trips on their journey home, awaited them. And on the front porch paced Mother Eulalia, a lonely sentinel in meditation, hands thrust into the opposite sleeves of her voluminous habit.

Mother Eulalia leaned over and kissed both girls on their forehead. "May Saint Christopher accompany you on all your journeys," was her prophetic dismissal.

Months later, during the German occupation of France, Marie-Claire would remember those words. Now, as they drove past the rhododendron bushes, she turned to catch one last glimpse of the austere black figure standing under the pointed, Gothic arch, which itself looked all the more austere since the demise of the monkey puzzle tree.

*The French Village*

# 10

City Hall clock chimed the hour seconds after the tolling of the church clock, as Victor drove into Randonette on a fine August afternoon, and Marie-Claire checked her watch. Religious time and secular time coexisted here. "The mayor versus the parish priest," Uncle Mo had told her, "each affirming his authority in an uneasy truce between church and state since the French Revolution."

"Which one?" she asked Colette.

Huddled next to her sister in the back seat of the old Peugeot, Colette stretched her legs and yawned. "Doesn't matter. In the country they really operate on sun time—up with the chickens, to bed with the cows."

"You said it!" Victor exclaimed.

Mindful of the bicycles strapped to the roof of the car, he slowed going throught the village square.

"I see the green cross, the green cross," shouted Marie-Claire.

Her mother told her to hush, saying she would alarm everyone.

The green cross signaled the pharmacy, midway on the rue Principale, which ran uphill toward the forest and the castle. A white caduceus hung in the center of the cross—two writhing serpents on Mercury's staff. This sign was the only one on a street of grey stone houses glued together in one continuous facade.

And over the pharmacy hung a balcony, decked with pots of red and purple fuchsia. Not even the mayor's house boasted such an ornament. "It's not in the mayor's political interest to set himself apart," Uncle Mo had said, "but a man like me, who is on call twenty-four hours, is entitled to some of the finer things of life." The village had no doctor. Uncle Mo treated people and animals and only in the summertime, when two pharmacal students tended the shop by day, did he indulge in his archaeological pursuits.

As soon as the car squeaked to a halt in front of the pharmacy, out popped the inhabitants of the main street: stout women, arms akimbo on their aproned hips, stood on their door sills. Their florid faces reminded Marie-Claire of plump radishes.

The bell on the pharmacy door tinkled merrily. "Come in, come in, one and all," shouted Uncle Mo. "You're just in time for rabbit stew. And today we've closed the pharmacy for two hours in your honor."

He wiped his mouth with the huge napkin that was tucked inside the collar of his white, pharmacist's coat. First, he embraced his sister-in-law, rather gingerly in consideration of her foreign background, then he smacked his brother on both cheeks. Colette and Marie-Claire he gathered to his bosom in a bear's vise that, literally, took Marie-Claire's breath away.

"Yummy, smell that sauce," said Marie-Claire when she had recovered her voice.

Uncle Mo led the way into the kitchen through the glass-paned door that separated the pharmacy from the living quarters in back, the top of his bald head crowned with a black beret. The beret was his trademark. Marie-Claire could not remember ever seeing him without it.

"Well, here they are, Renée," he announced to a stout

little woman in a white coat who was stirring the stew in a cauldron on top of the iron stove. "On time, just as I predicted. Set four more places."

"They are already set," replied Aunt Renée. She interrupted her task long enough to kiss the family on both cheeks. "Take your places in the dining room. I am coming right away."

"We'd like to wash our hands first," said Susan.

"Of course, of course. You know where the privy is."

The privy, screened by a flowering bush, was appended to the kitchen by a covered walkway. An old baptismal font stood near the door of the privy, under the handle of the water pump.

Meanwhile Uncle Mo plunked down on his appointed dining room chair near the radio, which loomed, beehive-shaped, on a table behind him.

"Such uncertain times," he muttered, when all were seated.

"That Eetlair," said Victor—he could never pronounce the H—"has something up his sleeve as always, demanding the annexation of Danzig. The British will not agree to that."

"And neither will the French," asserted Uncle Mo. "Yes, that Danzig affair stinks like you know what."

"Careful, my little Maurice." Aunt Renée intervened.

"All right, all right."

Uncle Mo poured some of his strong, Algerian wine and he and Victor drank to the glory of France, but his sister-in-law cupped her slim hand over her glass.

Colette and Marie-Claire cut their wine with water. Still it warmed the stomach more than Saint Ethelred's tea ever did. Why Uncle Mo preferred Algerian wine, though living in vineyard country, they never understood.

"If you ask me," said Victor, "the Munich Agreement

was a breach of French honor. I say no French king would have abandoned his allies as the French Republic abandoned the Czech people."

"Get off your royalist high horse, Victor." Uncle Mo pounded the table. "We're all living in a republic now. The British king never intervened, did he? What about that craggy old Chamberlain with his black umbrella, eh? Telling everybody there would be peace in our time?"

"I still say we were the first to betray the cause of the great Czech patriot, Masaryk."

"My history teacher told us that if every country in the world honored every single treaty arrangement ever made, the world would be in a perpetual state of war." Marie-Claire unwittingly came to her uncle's rescue, and Colette stared at her sister openmouthed.

"She did, did she?" Uncle Mo beamed. "Very good, my child. Fantastic! To think such a pronouncement should come out of a convent. Those little religious ladies are certainly enlightened."

Marie-Claire blushed. She knew Uncle Mo never attended church. Although not a communist like the mayor, he was a liberal and always made disparaging remarks about Catholics. She forked another mouthful of stew.

Her mother turned toward her and smiled. "Delicious, isn't it?"

"Yes," admitted Marie-Claire. She noticed the shadows on her mother's delicate face; they converged under her eyes as on the center of a lily petal. Passionate French rhetoric wore her mother out.

"Finish it then."

"Eat, eat your fill everybody," said Uncle Mo. He sopped up his gravy with a hunk of bread, his hairy hand describing a clean circle on his plate. Uncle Mo had a gargantuan appetite despite damaged lungs. He had been gassed in the Great War. "If you don't finish Renée's stew, we'll have to feed it to the pigs."

"Oh no, we won't." Aunt Renée smiled coquettishly, shaking her sausage-roll curls. She arranged them every morning with a curling iron. She was responsible for the pharmacy inventory. Claudine, the swineherd's daughter, did the heavy cleaning and helped with the food preparation. In the summertime, while Uncle Mo was off excavating, Aunt Renée supervised the young men in the pharmacy, spying on Jean and Jojo through the glass pane in the kitchen door.

Uncle Mo smiled at her and poured some more wine. He passed the salad bowl to his sister-in-law. "Have some, Susan, if you don't mind a few dandelion leaves in there, and take some cheese along with it." He impaled a piece of cheese on the end of his knife, like a peasant, and popped it into his mouth.

Under the table Colette pressed her sister's foot. Then she got up to help Aunt Renée clear the dishes. Marie-Claire heard excited whisperings in the kitchen but she could not make out what the two women were saying.

"Ah!" exclaimed Victor and Susan, when Aunt Renée reappeared with a large bowl of *oeufs à la neige*. The frothy egg whites were like icebergs in a custard sea, and everyone clapped. Aunt Renée's plump cheeks flushed a deeper pink she was so satisfied with the outcome of her dessert. Strong black coffee was poured into little cups.

"Here are your *canards*, girls," said Uncle Mo. Marie-Claire and Colette each received her lump of sugar dipped in Aunt Renée's rich brew.

"Isn't it time for the news?" asked Victor suddenly.

Uncle Mo's beret slipped to a rakish angle as he leaned back in his chair to turn on the radio. Came a low humming sound, as of bees in a hive and suddenly, so it seemed to

Marie-Claire, she heard a rustling outside the dining room window.

"Did you know, girls," said Uncle Mo, "that in the very early days of mythology Apollo was considered the navel of the world?"

"I do," responded Marie-Claire. She glanced out the window and thought she saw two little heads bob behind the open pane.

"Just the Langlos kids," said Uncle Mo, "pay them no heed."

"Oh, don't tell me," said Aunt Renée. "They've probably been at my raspberries again." She jumped up from the table and waddled into the kitchen.

"My radio," said Uncle Mo, "is my only contact with the world outside Randonette. With this marvelous instrument I not only inform myself but several of my neighbors as well . . . Oh, give them some stew, Renée," he called to his wife. "Those children only get meat once a week."

"How is Madame Langlos?" Colette asked.

"Working her pretty fingers to the bone so she can have enough money to buy cosmetics and lace petticoats like the city girls," muttered Uncle Mo.

"I can't get through right now, too much interference." He switched off the radio. "I'll be off to the excavations. Not many sick people around here these days, except for *Père* Boudet, who is a very old gentleman, pushing ninety. More sick cows. Some people yank so hard on their udders they give them mastitis."

Uncle Mo got up from the table. "Girls, have I told you the story about the 'perpetual pill' that made the laxative rounds of a three-member family?" Uncle Mo chuckled as he looked at Colette and Marie-Claire.

"Please, Maurice," said Susan Lavalette, "not at the dinner table."

Uncle Mo held his tongue and leaned over to shake his sister-in-law's hand. He was always very formal with her because she was not French. Pulling off his white coat as he walked, he went out into the kitchen.

"Just a minute, Maurice," called Aunt Renée.

Colette pushed back her chair. "May I be excused?" she asked her parents.

"Ah, let her go," said Aunt Renée, watching Susan's hesitation. "She's young and strong."

"Can't I go too?" Marie-Claire stared at her sister. *Why, she's going to the excavations without me,* she thought, in a sudden anguish of betrayal. *How can Colette do that to me? She knows how much the excavations mean to me. . . .*

"Uncle Mo is just dropping me off someplace," said Colette, and Marie-Claire believed her.

"And where would that someplace be?" Victor raised quizzical eyebrows.

"I'm just going to the post office to make a phone call," said Colette.

"Aha! Very well then, run along." Victor waved his hand.

# *11*

Uncle Mo and Aunt Renée's bedroom window opened onto the balcony overlooking the rue Principale, whereas the guest bedroom enjoyed a view of the garden and the museum, against a backdrop of green hills dotted with white cows and bristling trees.

The museum, a bungalow set on a patch of grass and wildflowers, contained the artifacts of Uncle Mo's numerous excavations. Its key, Marie-Claire knew, remained in the pocket of his trousers by day and was tied inside the tip of his bonnet at night. The museum was fronted by a small, rectangular pool, separated from the privy by a row of clipped boxwoods that Aunt Renée deplored. Boxwoods, she said, reminded her of death and vigils.

A gnarled old apple tree shaded the rest of the garden, which extended straight back to a dirt lane. The whole yard was enclosed by a picket fence, as was the village custom. A few straggly rose bushes grew against the fence, but mostly thickets of raspberry canes cultivated by Aunt Renée, who made a thick syrup out of the berries. The Langlos children were forever climbing the fence to pick her fruit, and Aunt Renée was forever shooing them away good naturedly; she would never have used a stick on the children.

"Some day I am going to put netting over my vines," she told Marie-Claire, as she closed the shutters of the guest room, "to discourage children and birds. Birds leave red droppings all over.

"Let me see, did Claudine put lavender next to the chamber pot?" Aunt Renée got down on her knees and opened the night-table door. "Claudine is a good worker but she's not used to the niceties. I have to keep reminding her."

She struggled to her feet, satisfied that the sprig of dried blossoms lay on the shelf next to the bulbous china pot. "If you should pee-pee during the night, don't forget to place the pot outside the door in the mornings."

"No problem," said Marie-Claire. She had been given the same instructions last summer.

"Rest well, little one," said Aunt Renée. "I'll be in the pharmacy if you need me." She closed the door as she left the room.

Marie-Claire lay down on the matrimonial size bed. She didn't want to close her eyes before Colette returned, and in order to stay awake, she listened for the strident buzzing of the saw mill, the only sound disturbing the afternoon quiet. Even the cowbells had stopped tinkling.

Her mother had gone to the hotel to rest, while her father roamed the village in search of the picturesque. The hotel on the village square boasted a flushing toilet down the hall.

"I can't understand why Maurice's museum is more important to him than modern plumbing," she had heard her mother say to her father once.

"*La culture*, culture," he boastingly replied. "My dear, you as a musician should know that France places culture above every thing else."

"It's the same with all Europeans." She sighed.

The museum. Marie-Claire tingled with delightful anticipation at the thought that perhaps this year Uncle Mo would show her his inner sanctum. He'd collected all kinds of precious things and was the envy of public museum curators. To think that tomorrow, after her parents had left, she would have the privilege of helping him in his excavations, of being present, perhaps, during some important discovery. Oh, if only Colette were here right now.

Marie-Claire sat up on one elbow and listened for Colette's light footsteps on the stair. She had a good idea what that telephone call was all about, but it had never occured to her before that the castle had a telephone. Castles belonged to another era, one of candlelit sconces and footmen in gorgeous livery and horseback messengers in the night. . . .

When at last she heard Colette's measured tread, Marie-Claire jumped off the bed and opened the door.

"Are you still awake?" was all Colette's greeting. She was flushed and out of breath.

"Weren't you expecting me to be?"

"Of course." Colette flung herself down on the bed and stared at the ceiling. "Jean-Paul wonders why Mother and Father are going back to the city tomorrow," she said at last.

"Why?"

"Think, Claire. Why do you suppose they took the trouble to drive us all the way out here? Because you hounded them about the excavations?"

"No."

"You heard Father talk about Hitler demanding the annexation of Danzig?"

"Yes."

"Well, Jean-Paul says the Poles are up in arms about the prospect of losing their outlet to the sea." Colette yawned. "Gosh, that wine of Uncle Mo's is so powerful. The Nazis are committing acts of sabotage and terrorism against the Poles. . . . " Her voice trailed off. Incredibly, she was beginning to fall asleep; but then Colette could sleep under any circumstance.

"Is that all you talked about?" asked Marie-Claire, clinging to the expectation of some happy announcement from her sister, something that would not totally mar her own joyous mood.

But Colette was now sound asleep, and Marie-Claire abandoned her vigil and succumbed to her own fatigue.

Claudine came barging into the bedroom with suitcases in both hands. She dumped them next to the wardrobe, then opened the shutters. "*Voilà*! The bikes Madame Renée says you should not leave out on the sidewalk. She says put them against the storage shed." Claudine rubbed her hands over her apron before leaving the room.

Colette and Marie-Claire arranged their clothes in the old armoire riddled with wormholes as small as pinpricks. The wardrobe had belonged to Aunt Renée's grandmother and had been part of her dowry. It had two doors concealing a row of narrow, cotton-lined shelves on one side, a high horizontal rod for hanging clothes on the other side. The rod was so high Marie-Claire had to step inside the cabinet to reach it. Fortunately, the armoire stood on solid, clawed feet.

"What else did Jean-Paul tell you?" asked Marie-Claire, carrying a pile of socks and underwear as high as her chin.

"The castle has a tennis court—just a plot of grass. He's been weeding and rolling it and trying to keep the animals out. We can use it when we want."

"But I don't play."

"Oh, I'll teach you, Claire. It isn't that hard when you set your mind to it. I brought along two rackets."

*And all I brought was my mythology book and my poetry book*, thought Marie-Claire. "I don't know about you, but tomorrow I am going to the excavations," she announced with a skip and a whoop.

Under a sky as blue as a porter's trousers, Uncle Mo warmed up the old Renault, and Marie-Claire and Colette waited patiently on the sidewalk, as did the women of Randonette, while the young village men smoked in the back of the open truck.

When at last they got the signal to board, everyone

sighed with relief and off they drove, the truck leading the triumphant procession. The men chattered and waved at the girls, as if this were their first expedition. *But then, thought Marie-Claire, you never know what Uncle Mo will find, and every trip is fraught with adventure.*

They coasted downhill and through the square, where old men snoozed on benches under the plane trees, then along the narrow street past Church Square and the stolid Romanesque sanctuary with three brick portals, symbolic of the Trinity. At the village limits they bounced and rattled across the old wooden bridge.

Uphill they droned past the cemetery, where the dead in their stone mausoleums, adorned with china flowers, almost touched each other. Then they descended into open country, scattering dust on the roadside cornflowers, passing through a patchwork of hedged, emerald fields studded with cows—udders low and full to bursting—and yellow sheaves of wheat splashed with poppies. In the distance, vineyards striated the bases of mountain slopes.

They stopped alongside an empty pasture. "Destination Randonette Digs, everybody out," shouted Uncle Mo, as he pulled the squeaky emergency brake. The men leaped down. A tall, brawny fellow rushed to open the door for Colette.

By now the excavation trenches, which crossed the field at right angles to a little brook, were long enough to show the configuration of the Roman pool. Round tiles were stacked inside each trench—the heating system of the pool.

The men placed their canteens in the shade of hazel bushes that grew by the brook. (The Romans used hazel twigs as divining rods, Uncle Mo had told them.) Then, with picks and shovels, they gathered around the pharmacist.

"Back up, please. Everybody back up. I must have absolute quiet." Uncle Mo adjusted his beret, then he stuffed one hand in his pocket and stood perfectly still, his eyes scanning the ground as if searching for stray *sous*.

With a sweep of his arm he motioned away a last imaginary spectator. The men leaned on their shovels and picks and held their breath, and when he removed his watch and chain from the pocket of his vest you could almost hear the watch ticking.

Dangling the chain in his right hand, he slowly paced back and forth. *The magic moment*, thought Marie-Claire, who—like the men—also held her breath.

Back and forth Uncle Mo went, until the chain began to jerk, like a golden worm. "This is where we dig," he said.

Marie-Claire clapped her hands.

"*Ça alors*, listen to that," said the men.

"He's a magician, our pharmacist."

"*Formidable!*"

The men murmured and shook their heads. They shook their heads whenever they took a notion to it, whether it be yea or nay or wonderment at the powers of the pharmacist. With his watch chain, Uncle Mo accomplished what the Romans had done with hazel twigs over a thousand years before in their search for water. For the pharmacist and the glory of the village, the men gladly contributed a couple of muscle hours on a fine, summer afternoon.

Marie-Claire watched them at work, assiduously hacking at the ground. The sweet odor of trampled grass mingled with the sweat of their bodies. Jean, the tile-maker; Jacques, the baker; Pierre, the cowherd; Joseph, the butcher; and Jean-Marie, the blacksmith's apprentice, whose wife was heavy with child.

Colette and Marie-Claire lay back in the cool grass and squinted at the sky through outstretched fingers.

"Come along, little one," said Uncle Mo. He grabbed Marie-Claire's hand and pulled her up, the effort making him cough. "Stop dreaming about all those little angels up there. There's plenty of glory down here. To work, the two of you."

The sisters combed the freshly turned dirt for small squares of mosaic—grey and black, white and blue—which had once formed the flooring of the pool. *Colors of the fish and sea,* thought Marie-Claire.

Uncle Mo searched for more earthenware tiles. "The tiles were originally under the pool floor," he said to the girls, as if they didn't already know this by now; but Uncle Mo never tired of explaining the intricacies of ancient civilizations. "Fires were built in the trenches to heat the pool."

"A heated pool, gosh, how modern!" Colette exclaimed. She leaned back and stretched her shapely legs.

"The Romans also had hot and cold running water in their houses and public baths. Gymnasiums, art galleries, libraries, et cetera, et cetera, were attached to those baths." All these tidbits of information Uncle Mo proclaimed in a loud voice for the village men to overhear.

"Et cetera, et cetera." Jean, the tile-maker, winked at Uncle Mo, and they both laughed. Colette blushed.

"Is this a private swimming pool?" asked Marie-Claire. *Perhaps dolphins would be too sacred a subject for public pools,* she thought. *After all, dolphins have long been associated with the gods.*

Uncle Mo's reply reassured her. "This pool, I think, belonged to some wealthy Roman official. We shall uncover his villa next, God willing," he added.

When he removed his beret to wipe his glistening bald

pate, Marie-Claire saw the reincarnation of a Roman elder standing before her. Wisps of gray hair fringed his forehead, touching the tips of his ears. His eyebrows curved in bushy arcs over dark, penetrating eyes. A prominent lower lip showed his strength and determination. And his nose—the high-bridged, long-tipped full nose—was a Lavalette trademark.

"*Holà!*" shouted one of the men, as he leaned over and picked an object out of a shovelful of dirt. Immediately the crew stopped digging, and all heads turned in his direction. He held up a moldy key. "The key to Caesar's palace," proclaimed Joseph.

Uncle Mo beamed. "Bravo, Joseph, my boy, bravo!" He walked over to the young butcher and clapped him on the back. "It may not be the key to Caesar's palace, but there is a villa somewhere, a nice little statue of Bacchus in the peristylium, a wine cellar . . . " He rubbed his hands together. "Dig on, lads. The day of glory has arrived."

In a neighboring field a cow mooed. Other cows turned their heads and stared, vacant-eyed, at the people, large mouths slowly chewing the cud.

Marie-Claire jumped up and ran to her uncle's side. She was radiant, sharing his happiness. Despite the bucolic atmosphere, this discovery was far more exciting and important than any prize-giving ceremony at Saint Ethelred's. This was rolling back the years and walking into history itself.

"May I see your magic watch again, Uncle?" she asked.

"You may, Marie-Claire, but there is no magic in the watch itself. The magic comes from my powers of divination."

She turned the gold watch over in her hands. The laurel wreath on the back of the case was so finely incised you could see every leaf. At Saint Ethelred's she had given up her paper wreath at the altar rail during Benediction, and it was gone forever. Father Woodruff hung the wreaths over his arm in crushed succession. She wondered what Uncle Mo meant by glory, because he never attended church on Sundays. Sundays he sat in the neat little parlor with Monsieur Potin, the hotel keeper, reading the latest bulletin of *The Serious Archaeologist*.

"Come on, everybody," said Uncle Mo, waving the men in with both arms, like a windmill. "Time to go home. The girls must have their bread and chocolate, and I must put the key in the museum."

"Ah yes, the museum!" chorused the men.

"Soon it will be the annex of the Louvre," shouted Joseph. He rubbed a grimy hand over his sweaty forehead.

After the men had placed their picks and shovels in the back of the truck, Uncle Mo shook hands with each of them, walking down the line like a general inspecting his troops. Then the men climbed into the truck, which hiccuped in a shifting of gears and jerked down the road.

"Ah, my little ones, what a day, what a day!" exclaimed Uncle Mo, as he embraced his nieces. "It is worth every bit of the rental I pay the countess for disturbing her land. *Ouf.*" He wiped his forehead. "Thank goodness the Fair isn't till next week. I can't stand much more of this excitement."

# 12

Uncle Mo's excavations involved the village men only. Life for the women of Randonette, behind their stone facades, followed a routine as predictable as the saints' days on their calendars. They lit their cooking fires; opened their shutters; served meals on flowered oilcloths; aired bedclothes on back windowsills, weather permitting; ventured to the bakery to buy bread warm from the oven, long loaves stacked upright on the baker's red-tiled floor; tended their vegetable plots in season; and, like Aunt Renée, those who had shopkeeper husbands helped with the business—day in, day out—not counting Sundays. Except for the baker's wife, Sunday was pastry day.

But on Fair days, which occurred in the summer months, life offered new possibilities. From neighboring farms came carts loaded with livestock or produce; from the city, hawkers with their wares. The village square became an open marketplace; a place to chat, too, and exchange gossip with the purchase of a new colander or a nice fat hen.

Fairs were busy times for Aunt Renée. "Not that much sickness around here on a regular weekday," she would say, "but on Fair Day people flock to the pharmacy like homing pigeons; for their cows, mostly. By the end of the day I have that spicy odor of pulvaromat under my tongue."

And the August 1939 Fair was no exception, despite the troubled times. When Aunt Renée slowly opened the door to Colette and Marie-Claire's room early that Tuesday morning, she wore her white smock, her hair was freshly curled, and she was rouged and powdered. "No excavations today, girls," she said. "It's the Fair, you know."

She stood at the foot of their bed, hands in her pockets, waiting for them to open their eyes. "The weather is fine. Thank God my floors won't take too much of a beating with all those people who come trampling into the pharmacy."

Marie-Claire rubbed her finger over the blanket, following a yellow band until it jumped off the bed and ran across the floor—a slice of sun from the shutter slats. When Aunt Renée opened the shutters, the band became a golden rectangle that slid under the door and disappeared.

"What a glorious sight," exclaimed Aunt Renée, standing by the open window. "The dew on the grass sparkles like a thousand diamonds. Won't stay long, though. Reminds me of my childhood, when I used to lead my pet cow to pasture." She stood quietly, lost in memories Marie-Claire could not relate to, never having lived in the country for very long.

"Get dressed, children," said Aunt Renée, when at last she turned around. "This morning I'll bring you your *café-au-lait* on your uncle's balcony."

Colette and Marie-Claire pulled on their clothes and ran into Uncle Mo's bedroom, where they stood shyly by the window until Aunt Renée reappeared with a tray of hard, crisp rolls, honey, and bowls of pale yet fragrant coffee.

Up and down the street, shutters clattered open. The smoke of wood fires curled up into the blue sky. They watched *Père* Louchard, a drummer boy in the infantry in '14, station himself uphill, near the pinewood. A smart drum roll. Then came his announcement. His powerful voice carried to where they sat on the balcony. "Monsieur Du-los has for sale three pigs at sixty francs a pig. Monsieur Rou-lard has four pairs of young ducks," a pause, a clearing of the throat, then "at for-ty francs a pair."

When *Père* Louchard had finished his recitation, he shuffled a few meters downhill and started all over again. "He will keep this up until he reaches the café," said Aunt Renée, "then he will sit with his cronies and for the rest of the morning they will sip coffee and brandy as they recount their wartime adventures in the poppy fields of Flanders."

Carts and carriages soon lined the street. Horses neighed and pawed and shook their harness bells, while others munched their feed, noses encased in gunny sacks.

Baskets on their arms, the village women now stepped out of their stone houses. Like a ritual, each one glanced at the weather vane on the church steeple etched against a cloudless sky. *The center of their universe,* thought Marie-Claire. They ambled toward the stone cross on the clay diamond, which was part of the village square, where calves bellowed and pigs grunted. Under the sycamore trees in front of City Hall, hawkers cried their wares and in that din Marie-Claire could still make out the cackling of chickens.

"Here comes Julot," said Aunt Renée. "Look at him, if you please."

Down the middle of the street, a red-faced man with tousled hair under a crooked cap led a string of mules. He smiled and greeted an imaginary audience with the air of a man leading a pack of prize Arabian horses. When a black cat darted between his legs, he crossed himself, muttering prayers and oaths.

The barber's wife across the way came out onto her stoop. "Aren't you ashamed of yourself, Julot," she shouted in her cracked, old voice. "Already one glass too many and you have not yet made a sale."

His cap balanced precariously over one ear, the man stopped in his tracks. He shielded his eyes with one hand and stared at the old woman as if he were scanning a point on the distant horizon. He rocked on his heels.

"Someone had better be ready to catch him when he falls is all I can say." *Mère* Brunot turned in disgust and disappeared into her house.

Aunt Renée shook her head. "Down to the pharmacy I go," she said. "I'll be needed for poultices and bandages." She leaned over the balcony railing for one last look at the "parade," as she called it, marching by her door—the butcher's wife; the baker's mother-in-law; the pregnant wife of Jean-Marie the cowherd, whose protruding belly caused her to waddle like a duck; and behind them, at a respectable distance, Madame Langlos, who took in wash, with her two children firmly in tow.

Carrying the breakfast tray, Marie-Claire followed her aunt downstairs into the kitchen where Claudine busied herself with the ironing, her square peasant hands smoothing the skirts of long white coats.

"Don't forget to scrape the carrots, Claudine," said Aunt Renée before she went into the pharmacy. Claudine made a face behind Aunt Renée's back.

The bell on the pharmacy door tinkled continuously, until someone propped it open. Through the glass pane in the kitchen door, concealed behind a gingham curtain, Marie-Claire watched Uncle Mo and Aunt Renée. Uncle Mo mixed potions from powders in yellow glass bottles, which were ranged on shelves behind him. Those were human medicaments. Across from him Jean and Jojo worked the veterinary shelves with Aunt Renée. Jojo gave her a huge pill in a glass jar—the pill was big enough for a hippopotamus—and a large metal ring with some paste, which she mixed in a tin.

A young man doffed his cap as he entered the pharmacy. Marie-Claire cracked the door, the better to watch him.

"*Salut*, Monsieur Maurice, Madame Renée," he said, affecting a villager's speech, but Marie-Claire knew at once by his stance and the cut of his jacket that he was no common villager.

Aunt Renée beamed at him and tilted her head coquettishly.

"Greetings to you, Monsieur le Comte," said Uncle Mo, barely looking up from his work.

"For my aunt." The young man handed Uncle Mo a crumpled piece of paper that he removed from his pocket.

"A little minute," said Uncle Mo.

Marie-Claire gazed at the dark-haired boy with a face as smooth as one of those painted statues in church; but the glint in his gray eyes and the suggestion of a dimple in his square chin (an indication the devil had kissed you), showed he was no plaster saint. He was a good head taller than the rumpled, baggy villagers surrounding him, and he leaned his elbow on the counter with an ease that was definitely aristocratic.

While Uncle Mo deciphered the prescription, Marie-Claire fingered the pleats of her navy skirt, which hung about her hips like the drooping petals of an inverted daisy. "Oh Lord," she sighed as she looked down at her blouse, "I'm still so flat. Cover my head and anyone looking at me sideways would wonder whether I was coming or going."

"The prescription for madame your aunt," said Uncle Mo, adjusting the glasses on his nose, "should be ready in about thirty minutes."

The young man drummed his fingers on the counter. "I would like permission to escort your nieces, the Demoiselles Lavalettes, to the fair," he said.

"But of course, Monsieur le Comte," said Aunt Renée, "They would be only too happy to accompany you."

"Permission granted," grunted Uncle Mo. He pestled medicaments in a white mortar.

Marie-Claire quickly pulled the door too. Her heart beat violently.

Uncle Mo rapped smartly on the kitchen door. "Marie-Claire, the nephew of madame la comtesse would like to take you and Colette to the Fair. Run upstairs and tell your sister. And don't forget," he raised an index finger at his invisible audience, "the juicy hen you promised me.

"Let's see now," he muttered as he returned to the counter, "zero point twelve milligrams of belladonna for Madame Giroux three times a day; that old biddy mustn't take a laxative with that."

Colette was brushing her hair, ever the fairy tale princess. Marie-Claire could imagine her sister hanging her golden locks out the window for Prince Charming to make his ascent and then his conquest.

"Jean-Paul is here," Marie-Claire announced breathlessly. "He would like to take us to the Fair."

"Get changed," said Colette in a matter-of-fact way. The news was no surprise to her, and Marie-Claire realized the two of them had planned this outing.

"What shall I wear?" she asked.

"Anything but that somber uniform. You're not going to church, you know."

"I know. I think I'll wear my pinafore." Marie-Claire opened the armoire doors, jumped to grasp the corner of a plaid skirt, and on the second try was smothered in pink and grey. After she had pulled the garment down over her body, she removed her skirt and flung it onto the bed. She ran her fingers through her hair.

Colette sat at the dressing table smoothing her eyebrows, but she jumped up instantly when Marie-Claire had changed into sandals. The sisters left the room arm in arm.

In the kitchen Aunt Renée greeted Marie-Claire with the oilskin shopping bag. "You put the chicken, legs tied, all the way down into the bag and hold the handles together tightly."

Marie-Claire nodded, but the prospect of carrying a live chicken did not delight her. Out of the corner of her eye, she watched Colette disappear through the door into the pharmacy.

"Here is the money, little one, and three pieces of candy," said Aunt Renée, stuffing everything into Marie-Claire's pocket. "Run along. You mustn't keep them waiting."

*Now it's "them,"* thought Marie-Claire, with sudden bitterness. *Colette and I were arm in arm just a minute ago, and now it's "them"—a separate identity—not the two of us anymore.*

Her frown turned to smiles, however, when she shook Jean-Paul's hand. He seemed genuinely pleased to meet her and gallantly offered her his arm; the three of them were off to the fair.

"I understand your mother is American," said Jean-Paul. "Have you visited the United States?"

"No, not yet," answered Colette and Marie-Claire both.

"One of my ancestors fought in the American Revolution. He was one of Lafayette's adjutants."

"Oh, that should interest Claire; she's a history buff." Colette spoke up magnanimously.

"Americans are a vital, energetic people, infused with new blood. In France we are withering on the vine, don't you think?" He turned his attention toward Marie-Claire. "We are oppressed by too long a history."

Marie-Claire could not believe her ears: a man of the nobility talking that way. "I am proud of my French heritage," she said, "from the ancient Druids through the last Bourbon kings."

"Spoken like a true French girl." Jean-Paul smiled at her and all was forgiven.

By now they had reached the clay diamond, where farmers contained their milling livestock.

"Anyone for mules?" asked Jean-Paul. "If not, we'll meet in front of City Hall in half an hour."

Without so much as a backward glance, Colette followed him into the street and Marie-Claire was stuck with the purchase of the chicken.

She elbowed her way through the bustling crowd on the square, grateful for the shade of the plane trees. The hawkers' cries were deafening. On their wooden tables they offered everything from womens' brassieres to bottle corks, jumbles of picked-over material in open piles.

Enticed by a familiar aroma, Marie-Claire found the waffle man and watched him ladle batter onto iron grills. Instantly it bubbled as it rose, and when he turned the cakes, on the other side were perfect, golden diamonds—just like the waffles in the park in Paris on a Sunday afternoon. Marie-Claire missed those outings with her parents.

Dutifully she continued toward the poultry vendors and listened to a litany of praises from a woman dressed in black, from head scarf to hose and shoes. So many chickens to chose from—white, black, brown, and speckled. Their legs were tied, thank goodness. Marie-Claire wished Colette were here to help.

The woman in black offered two speckled chickens for the price of one. "This may be our last fair," she said, "considering the uncertain times."

"One is all I need, thank you," said Marie-Claire, eyeing the birds' scrawny necks. When she turned away, the woman muttered about the ingratitude of the human race and little girls in particular, and Marie-Claire wanted to hide behind the nearest tree trunk.

"I suggest you take this one," said a man's familiar voice, "and she's just five francs." Jean-Paul barred her passage. He was holding a plump white hen, which he stuffed into the oilskin bag.

Without a word, Marie-Claire handed him the money. She peered around anxiously for Colette, thrilled at Jean-Paul's intercession on her behalf, yet at the same time intimidated by his presence; he was so handsome.

Colette was sitting on a bench, looking on with a satisfied smile. It was she, after all, who probably had sent Jean-Paul to the rescue.

All three took the dirt lane home, back of the village houses, Marie-Claire trotting to keep up with Jean-Paul and Colette. The chicken's head poked out of the bag, red crest jerking, little beady black eyes blinking.

Jean-Paul sang softly, in a bass voice,

*I pushed that first valve down.*
*I pushed that first valve down.*

He snapped his fingers to the beat and shuffled along the red clay road, kicking occasional stones. Colette hummed the tune. Soon all three were singing.

*And the music goes round and round*
*Oh oh, oh oh, oh oh,*
*And it comes out here.*

The chicken squawked. "Give me that bird," said Jean-Paul. "I'll carry him by the feet, that should shut him up."

When Marie-Claire hesitated, he plunged his hand into the bag and grabbed the fowl, swinging it upside down so violently she thought the poor creature would die of fright. "Squaw, squawk, SQUAWK," it went.

*And the music goes round and round*
*Oh oh, oh oh, oh oh,*
*And it comes out here. SQUAWK.*

When they reached Uncle Mo's gate, Jean-Paul pulled a penknife out of his pocket, cut the strings binding the chicken's legs, and it fluttered over the fence, squawking and clucking so that Claudine came screaming into the yard, her apron over her ears.

The chicken zigzagged across the yard, stopped momentarily in front of the pool, squatted on its yellow legs, and was about to dive in when Jean-Paul lunged and grabbed it by the neck. Without a word he handed it to Claudine. She tucked the fowl under her arm and went off in the direction of the storage area.

Jean-Paul grinned as he clicked his heels and bowed to the girls. "See you for tennis," he said, before he left them.

Colette laughed so the tears ran down her cheeks. "Did you see the way he bowed to us, Claire? If we had been married ladies, he would have kissed our hand. That's the custom among aristocrats."

"I know. Mother Genevieve once lived in a fine castle, and I'm sure she had her hand kissed anyway."

"What else did she tell you?" asked Colette. "Many nuns take the veil to atone for the greatest scandals."

"The story of Heloise and Abelard. It happened during the Middle Ages. They had an affair; she had a child; and because he was a famous churchman, he had to become a monk and she a Mother Superior."

Colette's blue eyes widened with astonishment and

Marie-Claire smiled. When would her sister stop thinking of her as an unsophisticated child?

"I heard you girls got me a fine chicken," said Uncle Mo, as he came into the kitchen. His white pockets overflowed with empty packets, pieces of gauze, and who knows what other objects, which caused strange bulges in his white coat; his beret barely clung to the back of his head. He leaned over the sink and splashed water on his face, shook his wet hands, and wiggled his hairy fingers, which curled under like giant spider legs. "*Ouf!*" he exclaimed.

The exclamation extended to an exhalation through puckered lips, and it was followed by a paroxysm of coughing. "People today like I've never seen," he said, "and no one came for *Père* Boudet's medicine. I'll have to send you girls to the farm." He chuckled and winked at Colette; the farm belonged to the castle. "Not this afternoon. The old guy still has a few centilitres of his medication left. Go on a quieter day, when you can combine business and play."

# 13

"Lollipops! lollipops!" screamed the farm children, jumping on the stoop.

"Hush, children," snapped Madame Boudet. She slipped into her wooden shoes and ran out to greet Colette and Marie-Claire as they dismounted from their bicycles.

"One must excuse them, *Mesdemoiselles*, Madame

Renée spoils them. Every time you come with medicine they expect candy. *La mère* is waiting for you inside."

*How did the grandmother know when we would arrive at the farm?* wondered Marie-Claire. The childrens' cries, of course. Those little pinafored rascals were like scout dogs. Not as bad as the geese, though.

"Beware of the geese," Aunt Renée had told her, "never dismount before you get to the farmhouse door. They might follow you and try to pinch your derrière."

Colette and Marie-Claire followed the farmwife into the common room and submitted to *Mère* Boudet's bitter coffee, topped with thick cream. The old woman never spoke, just sat back at a respectful distance and smiled at them. It was the same ritual every time they brought medicine for the old man, who lay on his bed behind a curtain, whimpering. They never saw the old man.

"I'm going ahead to the tennis court," said Colette to Marie-Claire, after they had paid their respects to *Mère* Boudet, "Jean-Paul is expecting me. Meet me there."

*Later,* thought Marie-Claire, *I don't want to spoil your fun* (despite her sister's coaching, she was still a poor tennis player). *Today I'm going to see what farm life is all about.*

One after the other the sheep scurried into the pen, bleating piteously.

"Poor babies don't want to come down in August," said Madame Boudet to Marie-Claire. "It's juicier up there." Her finger aimed pistol-like at the distant mountains. "Grass soft like velvet . . . But in these uncertain times I want all my animals home at night. Now, let's go milk la Céleste and la Marie."

Marie-Claire followed the woman along the beaten path, thinking, *"Uncertain times,"* that was all anybody talked about since the Fair.

She watched the farmwife plunk her stool down in the straw under the cow's udder and set to milking. Fine streams of liquid hit the wooden bucket in rhythmic squirts, a barnyard metronome squishing time. Knee-deep in litter, which scratched her bare legs, Marie-Claire recalled the voice of Mother Genevieve, now in the Lord's green pastures:

O God, who suffereth not the nations who
believe in Thee to be overwhelmed by any peril . . .

She remained in the byre after the farmer's wife had carried out the buckets of foaming milk, warm and sweet; she had tasted it. The pungency of the stable was like a heady wine. Warm fur, milk, and a pervasive ammonia odor mingled with the scent of straw; the fumes rose to the rafters in a bluish haze where gnats twirled. She leaned forward to pat la Céleste's flank, feeling her warm breath on her neck. La Marie snuffled in the neighboring stall. The sheep scratched in their pen.

Suddenly la Céleste lifted her tail and Marie-Claire backed away to avoid being splashed by a golden stream. She stepped out into the fresh air of the farmyard. A rangy boy in blue overalls filled a drinking trough. His yellow hair bristled like straw.

"M'selle Colette went that way." He pointed past the farmhouse door, where chickens pecked jerkily in the dirt. A fine rooster strutted around the chickens. The fowl drank out of a black saucer; raising their beaks after each gulp, they seemed to peck at the sky.

"I know," said Marie-Claire.

She jumped on her bicycle and pedaled up the rutted lane to the castle. What a day for tennis. A breeze so gentle it scarcely rustled the leaves in the beechwood. There had been no rain for over a week, and on that grass court the ball would bounce a little higher today.

Poor Colette. More field mice than humans frequented the court on the other side of the building that the countess had converted into a barn for horsefeed. The court could not compare in the slightest with the athletic facilities at Saint Ethelred's. (Not that Marie-Claire cared a whit.) Madame la Comtesse was more interested in horses than anything else. Horses were a family passion. According to legend, a Philippe de Joux had had the temerity to acquire a hundred horses, when only the king of France could own such a prize. He had to relinquish the hundredth stallion, but not before he had immortalized himself and his beast.

Peeking through the closed gates of the castle into the immense courtyard spotted with weeds, Marie-Claire glimpsed the bas-relief of the stone horseman. In solitary grandeur he rode between the two great balustrades, like a fragment from the Parthenon frieze she had seen in the British Museum. But the red roof tiles above him were mossy with age. The roof was in danger of caving in, and no one inhabited that portion of the castle.

Marie-Claire rode on down the lane. At the barn she dismounted, placed her bicycle next to her sister's, and taking out her pocket comb she fluffed her hair. Strange. Where was the dull thump of the tennis ball? It was so quiet all you could hear were the crickets singing.

A sound of muffled giggles came from inside the barn. *Could it be?* Marie-Claire leaned against the weathered pine wall and told her rapidly beating heart to please abate. Through a plank fissure she spied her sister descending the ladder from the hayloft, her hair sprinkled with little dry twigs and flowers. She was so close Marie-Claire could have reached in and plucked the twigs out of her hair, and the sight of her sister in that condition took her breath away. Then two strong arms grabbed Colette by her waist and she disappeared from Marie-Claire's gaze, her legs alone kicking the air. A man laughed softly, then all was quiet again, except for the crackling of the straw, like a log burning in a fireplace.

Marie-Claire turned her head away, but her feet remained glued to the ground. So many conflicting emotions paralyzed her. Hadn't Colette told her to meet at the court? How was she to know Colette had arranged this romantic tryst in the meanwhile? The audacity of it. And Jean-Paul's attentions to the younger sister had all been out of pity, pity for the ugly duckling. Oh yes, now it was all too clear. Just part of an aristocrat's manners. Though mischievous, he was also debonair. He polished his boots and combed his hair, black hair as lustrous as the cavalier's in the brilliantine advertisement poster that was pasted on the side of the first village house.

When she heard Colette's startled whimpers, Marie-Claire was frightened. She glanced nervously around her. The grounds were deserted. Only a butterfly darted over the wall separating the lane from the castle. In the far meadow, horses grazed. Marie-Claire chided herself, a convent-bred girl who had read the great myths, seen grandiose representations of love in stone and on painted canvases in the Louvre, without understanding their basic, earthy truths . . .

"*Canaille*," shouted Colette all of a sudden. The invective ripped the air like a two-fisted punch. Marie-Claire heaved a sigh of relief.

"But *chérie*."

"Scheming, deceitful beast."

"My little tiger." The man laughed softly.

"Take this . . . and this."

The straw crackled. Angry flames leapt to the ceiling, the conflagration of Colette's rage; for the first time, Marie-Claire feared for the life of the man inside the barn.

A startled mouse darted out the door. If Colette could scare the mice, the rat might soon follow. Marie-Claire gripped the handlebars of her bicycle, ready to take off at any time.

The man spoke now in low, reassuring tones, probably pleading his case. But Colette climbed down the ladder and bolted out the door.

"How long have you been standing here, little spy?" hissed Colette, running her fingers through her tousled hair. "Never mind, follow me."

"What about Jean-Paul?"

"Follow me, I said."

Colette grabbed her bicycle and the sisters ran through the roadside grasses, guiding their bikes around sticks and stones until they reached the beechwood. Then they jumped into the saddles and sped downhill all the way into the farmyard, scattering chickens and geese, which set up such a cackling and a honking that the farmer's wife exclaimed, "Whatever happened to the village girls? The devil is on their tail." The girls did not slow down until they reached the main road.

That evening, unable to sleep, Marie-Claire lay on her back counting sheep. Curly, plump, little animals trotted into the pen, but always the sound of crackling straw intruded before they were safely inside.

"Col," she whispered, "did he . . . did he, uh . . ." She caught herself before the words tumbled out the wrong way. She sighed. What did she know about sex anyway? Bits and pieces picked up during Gargoyle Club meetings. The Saint Ethelred's girls always giggled, so she had trouble separating fact from fiction. In Paris, whenever she and Colette visited their aunt and uncle, Cousin François was never around . . . and Franz had been so young, a well-surrounded oddity in a convent school.

"Did he what?" asked Colette.

"You know what I mean."

"No." Colette's sharp denial was her best defence.

"Thank God!" exclaimed Marie-Claire.

"Thank God for what? Although he's only seventeen, the poor boy might be going off to war to get himself killed."

"Poor boy!" exclaimed Marie-Claire.

Colette continued her train of thought. "You know what Jean-Paul told me?" she asked. "The French do not have the will to fight; they lack the proper military equipment; their armaments should be in a museum. But aristocrats are always the first to come to the aid of their country. Jean-Paul would join his father's cavalry regiment."

"War, war," muttered Marie-Claire, "uncertain times."

"Claire, you're not only digging into the ancient past with Uncle Mo, you're living there, too."

Marie-Claire sighed. She could not bear to think that some terrible catastrophe might disturb the excavations now that Uncle Mo was about to uncover the villa and she had assembled, like pieces in a jigsaw puzzle, grey and black mosaics in a curved pattern—the dolphins' backs.

Colette stretched out a comforting hand. "Claire," she whispered, "I'm sorry you were there, truly I am. You won't tell anybody, will you?"

"Well," sputtered Marie-Claire. Her thoughts went around in circles, chasing each other by the tail. *Weren't we all supposed to play tennis today? Colette gave me absolutely no warning she and Jean-Paul were contemplating a romantic tryst—if that's what they call the riproaring, crackling fight that scared the living daylights out of me.*

"You won't, will you?" pleaded Colette.

"I'm not a tattletale." *Lord, help me. These are not just uncertain times, they're crazy times. If only Mother and Father were here. What should I do? Is Colette going to get into trouble? Mother of Heaven, help me . . .*

"Night, Claire." Colette's voice was that of her own calm self again.

"Night, Col."

*Have faith,* Marie-Claire told herself silently. *Colette has been the reasonable, logical one in the family.* Marie-Claire turned on her stomach and plumped her pillow. Before she fell asleep, she promised herself she would beg Uncle Mo to show her the museum while Jean and Jojo still worked at the pharmacy.

# 14

"*Audaces fortuna juvat,* Fate favors the audacious." In a stentorian voice Uncle Mo read the Latin inscription over the museum entrance. "Do you kow those three words cost me over a month of human prescriptions?" he told Marie-Claire. "The engraver came from town, had to be wined and dined, et cetera. Never mind, glory must be most carefully considered; more so than the suit you choose to be laid out in—a suit will rot in no time—else future generations will laugh at you and say, 'That man may have dug up some interesting old stuff, but he didn't know how to cross his *Ts*.' Stone lasts forever, you know." He chuckled as he pushed open the creaky door.

Marie-Claire followed him into the hut.

"There's the key to the villa," said Uncle Mo. "Doesn't look like much, does it?" He turned the corroded, blue object over in his hands.

"I want to hold it." In her eagerness Marie-Claire almost knocked it down. "I've never held anything that old before."

"Don't let it shock you."

She glanced at the old man to see if he was serious. *After all, a person who could divine where one should dig for Roman ruins with a mere pocket watch must have some kind of magical power,* she thought. "Aren't you going to put it into a glass case?" she asked.

"What for? This isn't the Louvre."

It certainly was not. Shell-encrusted Roman amphorae stood directly on the rough, cement floor. Most of the exhibits were crowded onto a wooden shelf that ran the length of one wall. And high above this shelf the sun lit small, dust-spattered windowpanes. Cobwebs gathered in damp corners. The room smelled musty, like the dank interior of her uncle's family vault near Paris.

She spotted a row of grinning skulls on top of a closed, wooden cabinet and shivered with fright. "Wh-hoose heads are those?" she asked.

"Roman ladies."

"Honestly?"

"Of course."

Uncle Mo leaned toward her and whispered, "Don't tell anybody about them, little one. It's against the law to keep human remains at home." His brown eyes were serious. "Don't worry, I shall give them to the people at

Cluny some day. Now, let me show you something really interesting.

"You could stab your boyfriend with one of these." He fingered a long, bronze hairpin. "Roman ladies also sprinkled gold dust in their hair, did you know that? Some even wore blonde hairpieces cut from the heads of their Germanic slaves."

Marie-Claire listened, fascinated. Uncle Mo knew so much more than her Ancient History teacher at Saint Ethelred's. She followed him around the room. On the wooden shelf were coins, irregular in shape, black with age and corrosion. Nearby stood a large, stone head with huge eye cavities and features so disfigured they seemed to have been eaten by leprosy.

Uncle Mo picked up a squat, oval-shaped bronze vessel with a spout like a sauceboat's. "Aladdin's lamp," he said.

"Ah, yes."

"And look at this charming little glass bowl with one handle still attached. . . . But my favorites and my prizes are these." He stroked the small, delicate form of a bronze Jupiter, portrayed as a young Roman dandy, with shoulder-length hair and toga rolled up to expose a magnificent chest; only an elaborate crown revealed his divinity.

Then Uncle Mo showed Marie-Claire a miniature draped Venus, playfully balancing a young Cupid on her shoulder, her tiny lips stretched in a smile that was unmistakably carefree.

"Ah, how lovely!" exclaimed Marie-Claire.

They heard a knocking at the museum door.

"Maurice, come quickly," called a breathless Aunt Renée. "It's time for the newscast at seventeen hours. I just heard there will be a special announcement."

Uncle Mo paled and Marie-Claire wondered whether

he was sick. He grabbed her arm and propelled her out of the hut.

As they went alongside the pool, Marie-Claire thought how starkly formal it was, how out of character with the rest of the garden. Today it reflected cottony clouds.

Back of the picket fence near the dining room window stood the Langloses. Madame Langlos leaned her pretty head against her husband's chest; he had one arm around her waist. They both looked so sad Marie-Claire thought they were in mourning. The children were nowhere in sight.

Behind the Langloses congregated women in checkered aprons, hands resting on their stomachs, heads turned toward the open window, listening to the crackle of the radio. No one spoke and Marie-Claire became acutely aware something terrible would soon be announced, and she and all those people—like spectators at a funeral—would be powerless against it; they would all be merely witnesses after the fact.

When she and Uncle Mo entered the dining room, Colette was already sitting at the table, head bowed, golden hair spilling over her hands. Aunt Renée pattered about.

Through the static they heard the garble of foreign prattle, as from a great distance, then the weak voice of a French language translator.

"Sit down, Renée, for the love of God," thundered Uncle Mo.

"Men and women of Danzig," said the translator, "for twenty years you have been waiting for this hour. Today, September first, Danzig has entered the great German Reich. Our *Führer*, Adolph Hitler, has liberated us."

Uncle Mo increased the volume and the voice boomed through the room, rattling the mirror behind the sideboard. "For the first time, the swastika, the flag of the German Reich, flutters over the public buildings of Danzig . . ."

Marie-Claire thought she heard a collective sigh from the people outside.

"Maurice, please," begged Aunt Renée, fluttering her plump little hands.

"Do you think for one moment I make this racket on purpose?" snapped Uncle Mo, as he adjusted the volume. "I'm not the maker of these infernal machines. Good God, I'm a discoverer and preserver of past and present civilizations." His head shook so the beret quivered.

Over the radio the impassive translator's voice described the "mood of rejoicing" in the "liberated city."

"Hum, those Huns just march in and take over a town, then have the nerve to call themselves 'liberators'." He pulled off his beret and slapped it on the table. If it had been a piece of crockery, he would have smashed it.

When the announcement came of a speech by the *Führer* himself, Uncle Mo yelled, "*Ta gueule.*" The radio clicked into silence, and Aunt Renée hurriedly closed the windows for fear more vulgarity would follow. She waved to the spectators outside. Then she tiptoed over to the sideboard. Doors opened. Bottles clinked. She held up a decanter of ruby fluid so thick the sun could not shine through. *A bottle of blood*, thought Marie-Claire.

"Raspberry syrup," Aunt Renée said, smiling at Uncle Mo and the girls, "from my very own canes. We'll all have a glass. Come to the kitchen with me, my little Colette. I have fresh water from the well."

"The Comforter," muttered Colette to Marie-Claire as she rose.

Dear childless Aunt Renée, always thinking of sweets.

Uncle Mo patted Colette's arm. "This time France will

honor her treaty commitment. You can tell that to your father when he arrives."

"Oh, when will they be here, *tonton*?" gushed Marie-Claire, using the affectionate term all French children use for their favorite uncle.

"The Lord only knows!" exclaimed Uncle Mo. "Those two artists continue living in their ivory tower up till the very last moment. . . . " He gesticulated toward the ceiling. "Here the men have already received the call to arms, despite that fat sausage of a Mussolini's attempt at mediation. Ha! ha! How can you trust *les spaghetti* when he takes over Ethiopia and carves himself a piece of one of his neighbors. I refer to poor little Albania last March—"

A paroxysm of coughing overtook him and he muffled the sound in his handkerchief. His face turned red, his eyes bulged. "Renée, bring me some brandy, my love."

Marie-Claire rushed to pat him on the back.

"No use, my child . . . the gas. Slow poison." Uncle Mo wiped his eyes with his handkerchief before he gulped his brandy. "In twenty years it hasn't got the best of me yet, though."

Marie-Claire looked puzzled.

"Twenty years since the Great War, since I was in the infantry and the medical corps. . . . You don't know what it is like to come upon fields littered with bodies after a battle and see the vultures circling in the sky above."

"Will Father have to serve?"

"No, little one. They would never call up an old man of forty-seven."

Marie-Claire smiled with relief, but Colette sat as in a trance, cradling her glass in her hands, gazing at its pink contents as if it were a crystal ball in which she desperately wanted to conjure a vision of the future.

\* \* \*

Next day *Père* Louchard, the drummer boy, announced what the villagers would soon learn from posters on public buildings: "From the Ministry of War of the French Republic, order of general mobilization."

When Colette and Marie-Claire came downstars for their *café-au-lait*, Uncle Mo beckoned to them from the dining room. The Chamber of Deputies had just voted on the war budget: 69 billion francs. Daladier was still hoping for a "peaceful solution to the agression of Poland."

"Ineffectual, that Daladier," muttered Uncle Mo. He turned off the radio and hurriedly wiped his mouth. "Here I must agree with your father." He kissed the girls on their foreheads as he left the room. "The boys are coming to bid their adieus." He waved to the girls from the kitchen.

"Does that mean he wants us there, too?" asked a weary Colette.

"We could watch them from the kitchen," suggested Marie-Claire.

"You can. I'm going upstairs to write Mother and Father an urgent letter. I can't understand why we haven't heard from them yet. At least, they could have sent us a telegram."

Side by side the sisters left the dining room and when they parted at the stairs, Marie-Claire squeezed Colette's hand. Then she took up her post by the door to the pharmacy.

Through the glass pane she watched the men trudge over the stoop, one by one, in their long boots, and the little bell on the pharmacy door kept tinkling.

Jean, Jacques, Pierre the cowherd, Joseph, Jean-Marie, and Langlos, the neighbor, came in; the little bell tinkled merrily each time. Uncle Mo shook hands with each one, just as he had done that day at the excavations after the discovery of the key. But they were all solemn now. *Little boys with stony faces waiting for conduct cards,* Marie-Claire thought. *No, how stupid and insensitive I am. They're going off to war, like Colette said, to be killed.*

The men's faces lit up momentarily with forced smiles of conventional politeness, as they listened to Uncle Mo. All she could see of him was a white rectangle and the black beret above, popping up and down as he spoke.

In a semicircle now, caps in their hands, they stood facing the orator, and Marie-Claire imagined the monologue: he spoke to them of the glory of the village and of the honor of the Motherland and of his pride in them, too. At this they blushed and shook their heads. They were hot in those uniforms, which probably smelled of mothballs and had been retrieved from old wicker trunks that had never traveled anywhere. They pulled at their tight collars and rolled their khaki shoulders as though they were encased in hair shirts, like those worn by saints and hermits.

Uncle Mo placed his hands on the shoulders of each man and kissed him on both cheeks. Then he raised his hands, like the priest at the end of the Mass; *"Ite missa est,"* he said, "Go, you are dismissed." They filed out the door, their thick soles scraping the door step. And the little bell tinkled merrily.

When on the following day Aunt Renée sent Marie-Claire to the pharmacy storeroom for Ovaltine—to mix with warm milk as a soothing drink for Colette's nerves—Émile Potin came in, cloppety, cloppety, dragging his clubfoot. Marie-Claire buried her nose in the tins on the storeroom shelves until Uncle Mo arrived.

*"C'est la guerre,"* said Potin, hands dropping to his sides

"At least you don't have anything to worry about," said Uncle Mo. "You won't be going off to fight."

The young hotel keeper looked at Uncle Mo with watery green eyes. *You coward,* thought Marie-Claire. *You're not to be trusted.* Sundays when she returned from church and saw him limping out the kitchen door after discussing archaeology with Uncle Mo—he never left by the pharmacy door then—he gave her the impression he had something to conceal.

"I won't have many guests at the hotel," Potin lamented. "It will be the end of the *Hôtel du Cerf*, just as we were getting started."

"Nonsense," said Uncle Mo, "soon you'll have a houseful of refugees from the city."

Marie-Claire felt a surge of happiness. Her parents were bound to be among those refugees, for Uncle Mo only had one guest room.

Potin snickered, then laughed a hollow laugh—he was a skinny man without much belly—and Marie-Claire wanted to slap him in the face. *The men who worked so hard for Uncle Mo at the digs have gone off to war and so has Langlos, and here is this complaining coward,* she thought.

"Rose is pregnant again," said Potin, "Another mouth to feed. I almost forgot, I came for her tonic."

"Poor little thing!" exclaimed Uncle Mo. "When all your clients arrive, you should ask the Langlos woman to help out at the hotel. The girl needs the money and Rose will need help, believe you me."

Potin winked at Uncle Mo. "Not such a bad idea," he said.

Uncle Mo pulled out his watch and Marie-Claire decided to make a run for the kitchen door, clutching her can of Ovaltine.

"Is that the girl who won the history prize?" asked Potin.

"That's the one," beamed Uncle Mo, "my little English convent school niece," he said, and Marie-Claire was compelled to smile at the interloper—through gritted teeth. "It's time for the news, *petite*. I am charging you with the task of turning on that infernal machine. Warm up the hive."

"Willingly," Marie-Claire replied and barged through the door, dropping the can of Ovaltine on the kitchen table before passing into the dining room. She turned the radio knob and the dial lit up green, while the needle quivered then settled down. She opened wide the dining room window.

When Colette, Aunt Renée and Uncle Mo appeared, everyone sat at his appointed place at the dining room table.

The announcer's voice sounded more rapid than usual. Came a long pause, then the voice of the French Premier. With eloquence he said, "War has been imposed on us, on this land of liberty, where the respect of human dignity has found one of its last remaining havens. . . . *Vive la France!*"

"*Vive la France!*" Uncle Mo declaimed, in like fashion.

"*Vive la France*," they repeated after him.

The broadcast ended with the playing of the *Marseillaise*. The martial music of the national anthem never failed to stir Marie-Claire, although her father had instilled in her a strong dislike of its bloodthirsty, revolutionary words. Today she sat straight up, stiff with pride, her French blood coursing through her veins at such a rapid rate she thought she would burst with emotion.

When came the lines,

> Citizens, take up arms,
> Form your battalions.
> March on, march on . . .

She envisioned the village men, who only yesterday had left the pharmacy, marching across the plains toward a crimson horizon, and she closed her eyes to shut away the tears.

# 15

Soon after the declaration of war, Uncle Mo received a telegram from Victor, which he read to his nieces: "Return English school canceled / Must impose your hospitality little longer / Reassure girls parents well and busy."

"You see, Colette," he said, "your parents are abandoning you and your sister to my care. Renée will be delighted." Uncle Mo chuckled.

"Hum," said Colette, and Marie-Claire knew what her sister was thinking.

"You don't sound very grateful, little one. Are you pining after big city life?"

"Oh no, *tonton*," Colette replied. "I just wondered—"

"She wonders why Mother and Father have not written her," Marie-Claire interposed.

Colette blushed.

"Is something wrong, my child?" Uncle Mo asked.

This time Marie-Claire held her tongue.

"Nothing." Colette forced a smile.

"Now that the men have gone off to war and the excavations have ceased, life at Randonette does not offer much in the way of distractions."

Colette shook her head.

"You must not worry about the war. You have heard the communiqués from the Maginot Line. The French and British troops are well ensconced behind their fortifications."

"I know," said Colette.

One morning at breakfast, when Uncle Mo had puffed through the pharmacy door, Colette announced she was going to the harvest. Marie-Claire felt a pang of jealousy.

"Ah, the harvest," Aunt Renée moaned softly. "Harvesttime used to be so merry at the farm. When work was finished, everyone sat at a long table, groaning with food. And then came the toasts. Oh, the toasts! Each man tried to outdo the other, until we collapsed on our chairs from laughter. And then came the singing, the clapping, the dancing. . . . This year there will be no dancing, of course, no singing, and we shall only toast our gallant absentees. Not your uncle and I. Your uncle will not leave the pharmacy for unnecessary reasons as long as the men are at the front." She stood up and tugged at the skirt of her white smock, which clung to her formidable underpinnings.

"The nephew of madame la comtesse is still here?" she asked, addressing Colette. "I'm astonished he has not left for the university."

"He's helping his aunt around the castle until the harvest is over," said Colette.

"Of course . . . Taste some of this clover honey, girls. It's from the farm. *Mère* Boudet sent it to us." Aunt Renée took the lid off the jar. "*Voilà*. To work now, I'll see you at noon." She blew them a kiss before going into the pharmacy.

Colette and Marie-Claire stared into their bowls, both so quiet all you could hear was the clock ticking on the crockery shelf. With her index finger Marie-Claire sucked crumbs off the pink nasturtiums in the oilcloth design. Here they were, Colette and she, sitting by the warmth of the wood stove, eating breakfast like French village girls, dipping their bread in the rich *café-au-lait* instead of sipping dishwater tea at Saint Ethelred's. Marie-Claire had dreamed of this time, but now they were both so absorbed in their separate thoughts they could not speak. This Marie-Claire had not foreseen.

With the appearance of Jean-Paul, Colette had passed through a strange door into another room—had fallen, as in *Alice in Wonderland*, through the rabbit hole. Falling in love, they say. Lovers existed in a fantasy world of their own and they had left her behind . . . left her with her shattered illusions, now that the excavations had been interrupted by the village men going off to war.

Reaching for consolation, Marie-Claire dabbed honey on her bread and spilled more crumbs as she bit through the hard crust. The village men had gone off to war and the Roman villa might never come to life. The key would remain in the museum as mute testimony to that one wonderful afternoon, when everyone had thrilled to the excitement of an important new discovery.

"A *centime* for your thoughts," said Colette.

"I was thinking of the excavations."

"Of course, the ex-ca-va-tions."

"Why not?"

"Because the excavations are ancient history, that's why. I suppose you're happy we shan't be returning to Saint Ethelred's?" Colette's tone was gruff, but her mouth trembled. She lowered her eyes and a tear crept down her cheeks.

"Happy? Course not, Col."

Marie-Claire realized how much her sister missed her friends and the rarified atmosphere of the old palace school, where she was part of the team. Oh, if only Mother and Father were here. If only she had thought to bring her violin.

"Do you realize, too, that when Mother and Father do come, we won't be able to stay here much longer. Uncle Mo is too busy; his house is too little to accommodate the whole family. Mother and Father would have to stay at the hotel." Colette sniffed.

"I hadn't thought of that," admitted Marie-Claire. She shuddered at the memory of Uncle Mo's prediction about a houseful of refugees and Émile Potin's gloating laugh. So far, the hotel had received a family from near the German border—Alsatian Jews on their way to Marseille and emigration to South Africa. Their patriarch had fallen ill and was recuperating in Randonette.

"Where would we go?" Marie-Claire asked.

"Who knows? But we can't go on being separated like this." Colette took out her handkerchief and blew her nose. "Jean-Paul told me not to be fooled by the lull at the front."

*Why is he always so scary?* Marie-Claire wondered. *"Another calm night at the front, there is nothing to report" had been the latest communiqué. Last night they had listened to English comedienne Gracie Field's funny, high-pitched voice and dapper Maurice Chevalier's witty repartee in a special performance for the Allied troops right there at the Maginot Line.*

"Wars," Colette said, "do not usually progress in the autumn and winter, Jean-Paul told me. The Nazis did their thing in Poland when the weather was right. They shall wait until spring to invade us."

"Is that what he told you?" Marie-Claire tried to keep her voice steady, despite a sinking feeling in her stomach. She flicked crumbs off the table. But Colette leaned on her elbows and sipped her coffee.

"Don't act so horrified, Claire. You're supposed to be a history student. You should know all that."

Marie-Claire thought of Hannibal crossing the Pyrenees from Spain into southern France and surprising the Romans there. The Romans, under Julius Caesar, had subdued all of Gaul, despite the bravery of the first French hero Vercingetorix (but it had taken Caesar nine years to do so). *Winter invasions, let's see.* All she could think of was Napoleon's Russian campaign and the fateful retreat from Moscow, when a dejected Bonaparte, chin resting on his chest, rode his horse through a vast, snowy landscape. *Yes, winter invasions were usually a failure.*

The Great War she had not studied yet. But there existed constant reminders of it: men like Uncle Mo who had been gassed and coughed a lot of the time; large words printed in chalk on boxcars, like TWENTY-FOUR MEN AND SIX HORSES; bus and train seats reserved for handicapped veterans; and in every little town square a statue inscribed: TO THE GLORIOUS MEMORY OF THE CHILDREN OF——WHO DIED FOR FRANCE, 1914–1918. In Randonette they were inscribed on a tablet inside the church.

Just then Claudine bustled in from the garden, banging the door after her. *"Bonjour, les Demoiselles.* Still at your coffee? Leave your bowls on the table and go upstairs and get ready for school."

Marie-Claire smiled. Her parents had not thought to tell Uncle Mo to put them in school yet, and Colette hadn't even mentioned it.

"We're still on vacation, as far as our parents are concerned," said Colette. "And I am going to the harvest."

"Tut, tut," scolded Claudine, shaking her head, "*Mesdemoiselles,* the lazy ones."

# 16

After the harvest Colette came home pale and withdrawn and immediately took to bed.

"Tut, tut," said Claudine.

"Well, you can't say she drank too much," said Aunt Renée, "her cheeks would be flushed."

"Jean-Paul is leaving for the university, but he plans to enlist," Colette told Marie-Claire before she lay down with her face to the wall. "The nobility are always the first to defend their country. This duty, he says, is like a brand burned into their consciousness at an early age, and there's no escaping it." Colette twisted her handkerchief. "Remember what Father said about seventeenth-century France? 'One son for the church, one for the king, and one for the army.' "

Marie-Claire nodded. *What an amazing turn of events,* she thought. *No nonsense, athletic Colette, who kept her chin up like the best of her British classmates at Saint Ethelred's, now making herself actually sick over history.*

"Affairs of the heart," diagnosed Uncle Mo, when on the third day Colette was wracked by a fever. "I cannot do much for her. She will have to heal herself."

Marie-Claire carried upstairs steaming bowls of Aunt

Renée's chicken soup and countless cups of lime blossom tea. Her sister had never been so ill. Not even when the whole dormitory at Saint Ethelred's came down with chicken pox. And when the fever broke, she turned pale and listless again. She looked like one of those marble effigies on a royal tomb, her features set amid sunken cheekbones even more exquisitely chiseled than in the bloom of health.

*Like the Lady of Shalott* . . . Sitting next to the prone, white-gowned figure of her sister, Marie-Claire opened her poetry book and read the last two stanzas of Tennyson's sad poem about the enchanted lady.

> And at the closing of the day
> She loosed the chain, and down she lay;
> The broad stream bore her far away . . .
>
> Lying, robed in snowy white
> That loosely flew to left and right . . .

Suddenly ashamed of the images she was conjuring up, Marie-Claire closed the book and touched her sister's warm hand. *Oh Lord,* she prayed silently, *please make Colette well again, please. I'll drag myself on my knees on flagstones and say ten rosaries. When Jean-Paul enters the army I'll make perpetual novenas to Saint Barbara to protect him from sudden death. I'll even go to early Mass every morning.*

"Colette, little one, what can I do to put the roses back in your cheeks?" lamented Uncle Mo. "Perhaps a cup of oxblood every morning—warm, with a twist of lemon." He sterilized a milk can and sent Claudine off to the butcher's, with strict instructions to insist on the first bleeding.

"Culinary enticements, perhaps." He took his gun

down from the parlor rack and got permission from the blacksmith to shoot some of the squab he raised in pens in his backyard. They would be served on toast, in wine sauce.

"Mushrooms," decided Aunt Renée. Aunt Renée and Marie-Claire scrunched through the woods, scanning every log and tree stump, every mossy patch, for the spongy, flower-shaped, yellow *chanterelles* that Aunt Renée later transformed into mouth-watering delicacies in her frying pan.

Marie Langlos dropped in after work with a small basket of brown eggs; eggs collected from under a setting hen, she said, which had twice the power of regular eggs and would restore a person's appetite.

Then, to Marie-Claire's tremendous relief, Aunt Renée announced one day that Susan was coming. Marie-Claire felt sure her mother's presence would accomplish what folk remedies and culinary enticements would not.

On the day her mother was due, Colette got out of bed, washed her hair, and sat by the bedroom window in the pleasant September sunshine, toweling the long, fine strands of spun gold. She craved an apple and Marie-Claire obliged. She even came downstairs for lunch and surprised them all by requesting a second portion of cabbage and sausage.

In the old Renault, Uncle Mo set out for town to meet his sister-in-law at the railway station. "Be back in time for tea," he shouted over the loud putput of the motor. "Don't forget the *madeleines*." The *madeleines* he requested were not available, of course, since the pastry shop was only open on Sunday, as everybody knew.

Aunt Renée insisted Colette sit in the kitchen where she could "watch the birds and butterflies," while she and Marie-Claire took up their post at the pharmacy door. But by aperitif time there was still no dark green sedan visible on the crest of the hill, so she sent Marie-Claire to the post office to inquire about telegrams and telephone messages.

"Nothing. No child, nothing, nothing," said the postmistress. She slammed the window's iron grate.

Marie-Claire returned to the pharmacy with tears in her eyes and resumed her vigil with Aunt Renée. When a black hearse pulled up in front of the shop, they were both speechless with horror. Aunt Renée shook her head. She crossed her hands over her heaving bosom. "Jesus, Mary," she sighed before she collapsed in a large heap on the cane chair.

Marie-Claire ran into the kitchen, screaming for Colette. Quietly Colette went for the smelling salts, patted her aunt's wrists, and placed a pillow under her head.

"Auntie," said Marie-Claire as Aunt Renée's eyes fluttered open, "look, the curtains of the hearse are tied back. Definitely no coffin in there. Why, I see two people moving with cases in their hands."

"Oh, my God," exclaimed Colette, "it must be Mother and Uncle Mo. Can you imagine that? Yes, it's Mother carrying your violin, Claire."

"Mother, Mother" was all Marie-Claire could say.

Aunt Renée's cheeks flushed a deep pink, up to her tiny, gold-studded earlobes. "Name of God," she muttered, "what a dirty joke to play on me."

The driver of the hearse jumped out and stood at the curb, ready to assist the distinguished blonde lady in the gray tweed suit and gray felt hat with the snappy brim, who carried a violin case in her gloved hand and carefully tilted it upright in front of her as she stepped onto the uneven pavement. Uncle Mo, in mufti, but still crowned with black beret, trailed his sister-in-law. Like punctuation marks, round heads dotted the open windows up and down the street. Uncle Mo waved at the heads, not heeding Aunt Renée's barrage of demands for a quick explanation.

Susan pecked her sister-in-law on the cheek. "We are all right, Renée, I assure you," she said, with a trace of her native accent. "The car broke down in Chalon, and clever Maurice commandeered the hearse to tow it back to Randonette. We thought it would be more comfortable to ride in the hearse, that is all."

She handed Marie-Claire her violin and leaned forward so her daughter could kiss her on the cheek.

Marie-Claire clung to her mother's sleeve and rubbed her cheek against the soft wool while Susan embraced Colette.

"How pale you look, Colette," she remarked, as she cupped her eldest daughter's face in her strong hands.

"Mother, you gave us such a scare. I don't know how we shall ever get over it." Colette laughed.

"See that space in there." Uncle Mo pointed at the hearse's dark interior. "It is just long enough and broad enough to accommodate a coffin—"

"Oh, come on, Maurice."

"It is also very handy for transporting bath tubs and such. You can also squeeze four people on the *banquettes* on either side. We could rent it for an expedition to the digs, don't you think so, little one?" He winked at Marie-Claire.

The girls laughed until their ribs hurt. Long after the driver of the hearse had left his empty coffee cup and brandy glass on the kitchen table, they giggled and held their breath to calm their hiccups.

When Susan went up to the guest room to unpack, Marie-Claire uttered a silent prayer to Saint Christopher for her mother's safe arrival and for Colette's recovery, which she thought was like one of those miracles in a fairy tale.

Not until she curled up on the parlor sofa that evening—she had insisted Colette share the guest bed with Susan—did she think of the vows she had made: saying rosaries on her knees on a rough floor could be accomplished in the village church, where the stones of the nave were uneven with age; as for the novena, when Jean-Paul enlisted she would pray for his safety every night of the war, not just for nine days at a time; but going to early Mass, that presented a problem. People would wonder why she had become so devout all of a sudden. And it would be cold and dark; she would not be allowed to walk the streets alone. It would be almost as dark as it was now in this little room known as the parlor, which, in reality, was Uncle Mo's retreat.

Her mother and Colette thought she was brave to sleep downstairs alone. Yet the room was so filled with books and records of Uncle Mo's excavations, pictures of his army days, framed diplomas, old abandoned pipes that still exuded a tobacco aroma, that the aura of the man was more telling than his absence. The darkness itself was alive, vibrating specks of shades of gray—a field of energy before her eyes.

Marie-Claire reached up and ran her fingers over the spines of the books, as if all the wisdom they contained would inspire a solution to her problem. The fat ones she knew were bound volumes of the *Journals of the Serious Archaeologist,* which Uncle Mo and that hotelkeeper, Potin, consulted Sunday mornings; the slimmer ones were probably genealogy books. Uncle Mo was fond of relating how the Lavalettes had inherited their long, Bourbon nose from a mistress of Louis XIV. The cracked and torn leather bindings belonged to old history books Uncle Mo had acquired at flea markets.

"Enough of that," complained her heavy arm. Marie-Claire let it drop. When she lay back down she closed her eyes and prayed to Saint Angela, the patron of Christian education. "Consult the priest the next time you go to confession," came the answer, "he can loose you from your vow."

# 17

"Your mother and I agree it's time you girls went back to school," said Uncle Mo.

Marie-Claire pulled a long face.

"What's the matter? Don't you like Latin?" Uncle Mo cleared his throat before declaiming, "*Gallia est omnis divisa in partes tres*; Gaul is a whole divided into three parts."

When Marie-Claire did not respond, Susan looked up from the sheets of music spread before her on the dining room table. Her eyes were blue glass. Although she had no piano, she still "practiced" every day, the fingers of her strong, square hands moving over the wood as if they touched a keyboard.

"I thought you would welcome going to a French school again, Marie-Claire." She sighed.

"The village school is very small," said Aunt Renée, "the schoolmaster is a fiery redhead, just like his sister."

"Ah, Renée, my love, stop acting like a hen with newly hatched chicks. We have no secondary school, but the girls could still profit from composition and arithmetic—and history, of course." Uncle Mo winked at Marie-Claire.

"True, idleness never did anyone any good," admitted Aunt Renée.

"The teacher must be quite old not to be at the front with the other men," ventured Marie-Claire.

"Oh ho, oh ho," chuckled Uncle Mo. "So, you don't like old men, hey? After all those pale English nuns you were hoping for a change?"

"Oh, *tonton*," said Colette, who had been listening with a frown on her pretty face.

"Teachers have not yet been mobilized, thank goodness. The leaves have not yet fallen."

"But they have," said Marie-Claire, staring out the window at the gnarled, bare branches of the apple tree.

"That was not what I was referring to," Uncle Mo replied. "I was thinking of what is going on at the front. The war games. How much longer can they last? These little skirmishes where the mice come out of their hole and taunt the cat, calling out, '*Sale Boche* (dirty head of a Fritz), shit on you.' Then the cat reaches out a paw and pretends to scratch one of them, and all the mice scurry back into their hole again. If we only knew what the cat had on his furry mind! If we could just march right on over there like full-blooded Frenchmen and really bop him one!"

Frost had burned the chrysanthemums when Victor drove into Randonette, loaded down with canvases, palettes, portable easels, et cetera. Women and old men, bundled to their noses, passed under Uncle Mo's bare balcony, like ships leaning into the wind. At night there were no streetlights. Black curtains hung behind closed shutters and only a sliver of light coming from under the door indicated the pharmacy.

Victor and Susan settled into the "bridal suite" of the hotel, decorated with faded Fragonard prints, in which lords and ladies picnicked and cavorted in the royal gardens. But at Uncle Mo and Aunt Renée's insistence, the girls remained in the guest room above the garden. After school, however, Colette and Marie-Claire went directly to the hotel. Marie-Claire practiced her violin, while her mother sat in the easy chair, humming corrections in her clear, high voice, and Colette posed for her father on the window seat.

"Aren't the winds fierce this year?" asked Uncle Mo, when the whole family was seated at Sunday dinner in the room behind the pharmacy. "They blow cold and despair, such cold as we have not experienced since the French Revolution, I am told." He dragged bite-size pieces of cheese across his plate on the point of his knife.

"The pool is not frozen," said Marie-Claire.

"Actually, not since the War of 1870," mused Uncle Mo, who had paid no attention to his niece's remark.

"Oh ho," chuckled Victor, "mustn't blame the Revolution, must we?"

Uncle Mo stopped tracing the map of France and popped a morsel of cheese into his mouth. "If it wasn't for the Revolution, we'd all be obliged to go to church on Sunday holding a little *fleur de lys* in one hand . . . and lords would still be claiming their manorial rights. Since you are the father of two young women, Victor, I don't have to remind you what those rights were all about, do I?"

"No need." Victor raised a cautionary hand.

*Manorial rights. What are they talking about?* wondered Marie-Claire. She knew that before the Revolution peasants did not own their land and gave a portion of their harvest to the lord of the castle . . . She looked to Colette for an explanation. Colette was staring out the window. Then Marie-Claire noticed the blush on her mother's cheeks. *Better not ask,* she thought to herself. *It must have something to do with sex.*

"How about some dessert?" asked Aunt Renée. She waddled to the sideboard to reach for a platter of *éclairs* and *choux à la crème,* which she had purchased that morning after Mass. *"Voilà,"* she beamed as she placed the pastry in front of her husband. But the men still had their minds on politics and war.

"To what do you attribute this general despair you were talking about, Maurice?" asked Victor.

*Surely he knows the answer,* thought Marie-Claire; *he's just playing the role of polite guest.* Without hesitation, she answered, "Blackouts."

"Very true, my little girl," said Uncle Mo. "Blackouts and long nights when there's no one to warm your bed don't help morale, that's certain."

"Blackouts lead to accidents," Colette added.

Marie-Claire winced. On her way back to the pharmacy from the hotel one night she had stumbled on the uneven sidewalk and fallen against the curb, splitting her lip. Her fault for running in the dark. Although the hotel lobby was dimly lighted, she wasn't prepared for the blackness outside, like a giant inkblot over the street and houses. The yellow sliver of light from the bottom of the pharmacy door hung somewhere in this void. It certainly wasn't a beacon of reassurance.

"Don't forget, too," said Uncle Mo, "that many of the older folk have vivid memories of '14. Remembrance of past horrors leads to anticipation of worse ones to come. That's human nature." He stirred his coffee. "And fear of the unknown is the worst fear of all. Don't you agree, Susan?" He turned toward his sister-in-law, who stared at the pastry on her plate. Susan nodded without saying a word.

"We have no hero to reassure us, no one in government, I mean," said Victor.

Uncle Mo paid no attention to his brother's remark. He drained his coffee cup. "Did you know that *Père* Dunet hung himself last night—in his long johns?"

"Careful, Maurice," said Aunt Renée.

"Maurice, I wish you would confine your coroner's report to to the pharmacy." Susan rapped the table with her fist.

Marie-Claire gasped. Such an outburst was so unlike her calm, dignified mother.

Uncle Mo blushed and lowered his head. "All my apologies, Susan," he muttered. "We country people forget we are offending city people's sensibilities."

Marie-Claire glanced at Colette, who was already staring at her with a look of recognition. Letters from America must be upsetting their mother. But she would not discuss their contents with them other than to say, "Grandfather and Grandmother Sterling send their love," and "When the war is over, they shall visit us again."

Only yesterday, when Marie-Claire had entered the hotel, bringing with her a blast of cold air, she had noticed a familiar red- and blue-bordered envelope on the dingy desk in the lobby. Madame Langlos, gliding by with feather duster, had placed her hand on it, as if she were swearing a solemn oath on the Bible. Cloppety, cloppety, Émil Potin had limped through the kitchen door and scowled at her, or perhaps he was scowling at the person who had let in the cold air. When she had taken the letter upstairs to her mother, she had found her gazing out the window. Her mind must have been a thousand miles away.

"Renée," said Uncle Mo, as the company rose slowly from the table, "I'm closeting myself in the parlor with Victor. Don't disturb us unless the shop bell rings."

Next morning Marie-Claire woke up before dawn and heard muffled voices under the window. She slipped out of bed without disturbing her sister, tiptoed downstairs to the dining room, where Aunt Renée never bothered to close the shutters, and concealed herself behind a curtain.

In the misty backyard next to the pool, stood Uncle Mo—still in night bonnet, shirt, and robe—and two uniformed *gendarmes*, all engaged in animated conversation around a bundle of—clothes? She rubbed her eyes and pressed her nose against the windowpane. Puffs of fog floated off the pool. *Good Lord*, she thought, *there are feet sticking out of the bundle.*

The sun broke through the clouds, and Marie-Claire saw to her horror that the feet on the edge of the pool belonged to the body of a half-submerged woman. Petticoats ruffled around ballooning, lace-trimmed buttocks. The grotesque white shape glowed in the dim light. When the sun broke through again, burning off the fog, she saw dark hair floating in the pool like seaweed.

Fascinated, she watched Uncle Mo and one of the *gendarmes* bend over and slowly lift the body out of the pool. Water dripped, no, flowed out of the body, as though from a bundle of wash; arms dangled in front of it like a puppet's. Gingerly, a *gendarme* and Uncle Mo placed the body on the grass, turning it on its back. The bloated face was pink. A white foam, like soapsuds, erupted from the mouth and nostrils.

The *gendarmes* removed pads and pencils from their

pockets and took notes, while Uncle Mo walked slowly around the body. He pressed his palms together and lowered his head, as if he were praying. He squatted and carefully examined the fingertips, then the hollow of the woman's right hand. He struggled with her left hand, which was so firmly clasped no amount of prying could open it.

Holding her stomach, Marie-Claire ran upstairs to her room and reached the basin in time to retch. Her stomach stuck in her throat. She leaned over the basin with her mouth open, gripping its cold sides, her throat stretched as far as it would go. She was so nauseated her nose tingled. The basin rocked.

"What's the mattter?" murmured Colette, still half asleep.

Marie-Claire retched again and a bitter taste filled her mouth.

"Don' open the shut-tesh."

Colette sat bolt upright. "Good Lord, Claire, what happened?"

But Marie-Claire could not talk right then. A trickle of yellow fluid ran down her chin. She rinsed her mouth and wiped it.

Colette jumped out of bed and ran to help her sister. She dampened a towel and wiped Marie-Claire's glistening face. Marie-Claire leaned on her sister as she tottered to her bed, which loomed high above her. When she climbed in and lay down, her legs trembled so she had no control over them.

"I . . . I went down-stairs . . . " She could not keep her teeth from chattering. "There was a body . . . in the pool."

"A body!" Colette was so horrified she never closed her mouth.

Marie-Claire arched her toes to control the trembling in her legs. "A bo-dy, a woman's."

"Let's wake Uncle Mo."

"He already knows. The *gendarmes* are there, too."

"Take a couple of deep breaths, Claire," said Colette. "That's it." Then Colette put her arms around her sister and rocked her. "Oh, Claire, Claire, always in the thick of things. I'm sure you never expected our stay at Randonette to turn out like this. Don't you wish, sometimes, we were back at Saint Ethelred's and our only concerns were conduct cards and whether we had enough money to buy all the sweets we craved on Saturdays? Who could that woman be? Uncle Mo said the older people were killing themselves, but this must be murder."

Marie-Claire closed her eyes and pretended to fall asleep. She did not feel like answering any questions right now—Very gently Colette laid her head down on the pillow—Her sister's ministrations were, indeed, soothing, as her limbs relaxed now, a pleasant warmth creeping over her body. Soon she was fast asleep.

# 18

When Marie-Claire woke up the second time, school had started long before. But she was in no hurry to get out of bed. After what had happened at dawn, she couldn't face the complexities of arithmetic, nor Caesar's *Commentaries on the Gallic War*, although the subject of the Latin text interested her. Naturally, as it was ancient history and also the history of her country. What would she and Colette look like walking across the old wooden planks of the schoolroom floor past a sea of inquiring faces to confront the frowning, redheaded schoolmaster, the heels of their shoes echoing like peasant clogs?

*I told you so, you're the one who wanted to go to school in Randonette.* Colette's scolding echoed in her mind when she drifted out of a shallow sleep. Exhaustion had pulled her under, like a giant wave. But Colette's cries were all part of her dreams, she realized, when she saw her sister standing mutely at the foot of the bed.

"What shall we tell Aunt Renée when we go downstairs?" asked Marie-Claire. She had missed her bread and *café-au-lait*, and now her stomach rumbled from hunger.

"We'll tell her the truth," said Colette.

"She wouldn't understand," Marie-Claire replied.

"I don't know what else to tell her. Sorry, Claire."

The oilcloth on the kitchen table gleamed clean and empty. Coffee bowls and saucers had already been placed in their racks on the varnished pinewood shelf. Stew simmered in an iron cauldron on the stove. The girls had to content themselves with cold, stale bread and milk stolen from the pitcher that contained the day's cooking supply.

They glimpsed Aunt Renée in the dining room, sitting alone dabbing her eyes, oblivious to all other sounds except the music of the radio. Colette and Marie-Claire tiptoed a little closer and listened incredulously while Tino Torand crooned,

> I have come to see
> All of Andalusee-e
> Cradle of poese-e-e
> And o-of love . . .

Aunt Renée's head swayed to the accompaniment of guitar and castanets. A Spanish love song!

"The comforter is comforting herself for a change," whispered Colette.

"Cradle of poesy and love," hissed Marie-Claire. "How ridiculous." The Spanish Civil War had ended only last spring. She remembered accounts of priests and nuns being set afire, of children eating rats.

"Let her be, Claire," retorted Colette, "It's the music she's listening to, not the words."

Over the radio, Torand's passionate tenor voice recalled Carmens and Figaros dancing under leafy boughs on a town square, dark eyes glinting in the moonlight.

Marie-Claire countered with the opening lines of a Shakespearan sonnet, whispering it like a chapel prayer:

Like as the waves make towards the pebbled shore,
So do our minutes hasten to their end;
Each changing place with that which goes before . . .

"What are you muttering?" whispered Colette.

"Wait." Marie-Claire searched her memory for the lines she was looking for.

> Nativity, once in the main of light,
> Crawls to maturity; wherewith being crown'd
> Crooked eclipses 'gainst his glory fight.

Crooked, such a wicked sound. "And the crooked shall be made straight" welled up from her religious upbringing. Crooked suited a world turned so wicked that old men hung themselves at night and women drowned in shallow pools.

Colette nudged her again. "Wake up, Claire. You'd

better prepare yourself. This song has only one more stanza."

"I think I am beginning to feel sick again."

Aunt Renée, now transported into Spanish heaven, closed her eyes, her fingers drummed the table, her lips moved in perfect synchronization to Torand's quivering voice.

> And, despite the mountains, at this hour
> I conserve, like a flower
> All the fragrance and the power
> Of that Spanish land.

"Mmm . . . " sighed Aunt Renée as she opened her eyes. When the radio clicked into silence, Marie-Claire smoothed down her hair and tightened her bathrobe sash.

Leaning her whole weight on the table, Aunt Renée rose slowly. "Poor soul, she can't be buried in hallowed ground," she muttered as she walked toward the kitchen, rocking her white bulk from side to side. "Her spirit will wander throughout eternity, like the mist through the poplars." Aunt Renée appeared to be coming through the mist herself, unaware as she still was of the girls' presence. "To think that I yelled at her children every time they climbed the fence to get my raspberries. Lord forgive me." Her fingers scrambled over her bosom, in a gesture reminiscent of the sign of the cross.

"Madame Langlos!" exclaimed Marie-Claire and immediately placed a hand over her mouth.

"What are you children doing home at this hour?" Aunt Renée stared at the girls as if they were apparitions.

"Do you mean to say Madame Langlos cannot be buried in the village cemetery?" asked Marie-Claire.

"Don't act so astonished. You are a convent girl and

should know the church doctrine on suicide. It was suicide, indeed. Your uncle found a note. He had to break her hand, it was so tightly clenched around it. And the the paper was so sodden he couldn't make out the writing. . . . Poor thing."

Marie-Claire turned her head away. She could hear the bones snap in Madame Langlos's fingers, and to fight incipient nausea she deliberately concentrated on the arabesques in the kitchen cloth, following a green stem with her eye until it got lost in a maze of orange petals and curlicues.

"Marie-Claire woke up sick," said Colette. "Then she went back to sleep and I didn't want to disturb her."

"So, today you decided to play hookey?" Aunt Renée's eyes narrowed. "If you only just came downstairs," she said, placing her hands on her hips, "how did you happen to know about Madame Langlos? Please, *Mesdemoiselles?*"

Marie-Claire and Colette looked at each other. "Auntie," said Marie-Claire, "when I woke up I heard voices underneath the window. I went down to the dining room and saw the body in the pool."

Aunt Renée sighed. "Sit," she ordered. She plunked herself down at the kitchen table and crossed her arms under the shelf of her bosom. "Let me get this straight. The shutters are closed, the sun just rising, and a thirteen-year-old, who usually sleeps on both ears, hears whispering under her window—"

"I'll be fourteen next month," said Marie-Claire.

"Thirteen, fourteen, what's the difference? You're still like a newborn calf, barely licked by her mother. I say, Lord protect us, we must have another clairvoyant in the family."

She glared at Marie-Claire. "Child, do you know that

when your uncle was your age he dreamed his little fox terrier would die a violent death and next day, *voilà*, the little dog was shot accidentally by a hunter as he chased a rabbit through the underbrush."

Under the table Colette's slipper kicked at the hem of Marie-Claire's robe.

Marie-Claire felt like a Christian who had been thrown to the lions, and she appealed to a whole category of saints, including the newly canonized ancestor of Sister Teresa, Saint Manfred.

"Why did she kill herself? She was not an old person." Colette was indignant.

"Despair, my child, part of the general despair. Don't ask me why." Aunt Renée shook her head and closed her eyes, which had misted over.

"Uncle Mo found a note, you said."

"Yes, but he couldn't make it out, it was so sodden." Aunt Renée sniffed. "Stop concerning yourself, child, about adult problems."

"In times such as these, one does not have a right to be a child anymore," Colette proclaimed.

"Well!" Aunt Renée exclaimed.

"Father told me that was what Grandmother said twenty years ago during the Great War."

A tomcat meowed and hissed outside the kitchen door, startling Aunt Renée. "Scram, Minou," she yelled, then she calmly faced the girls again. "It's Potin's fault, I say, gossipping about her giving favors to the hotel guests, just because she was pretty and cleanly dressed, which is more than I can say for Potin's wife. Poor woman, he runs her ragged, in more ways than one. . . . " Aunt Renée pursed her lips. She had said too much already.

"Oh, please continue," said Colette. She was as white as a ghost.

"Just tales, I'm sure that's all it is, tales spread by Potin. She probably resisted his advances. You know the Langloses were devoted to each other. Such a handsome couple they were." She dabbed her eyes and the girls respectfully lowered theirs.

Aunt Renée smote her forehead. "How could she have had the courage to keep her head under three fingers of water. She must have drunk more than one bottle of wine, that is certain, and it must have been red wine. Red wine goes to the head."

Marie-Claire shivered as she thought of the bloated body lying on the grass, and she squeezed her eyes shut to block out the vision of it.

"I sent Claudine over there with candles and boxwood," said Aunt Renée. "The priest is coming with Holy Water—she won't be denied that. The neighbors and I shall take turns at the vigil until Langlos gets here. Your uncle sent his commanding officer a telegram."

"Why didn't she confide in anyone?" asked Colette.

"She could not. She had her pride, you know."

"But if she was innocent, why did the rumors upset her?"

"*Ma petite Colette*," said Aunt Renée, patting her niece's hand, "you still have much to learn about life. Ah yes, you haven't lived in a small village long enough to learn about rumors, how every time you walk down the street you sense people staring at you behind their curtains, and in church you hear them whispering behind your back. I know . . ."

Marie-Claire and Colette stared at each other. What could neat, proper, plump little Aunt Renée possibly have to hide?

"I lost the only two children I ever gave birth to many years ago, and an old biddy who dabbled in witchcraft told everyone I had the curse of Saint Jules. One of my brothers, who was a sailor, had contracted an unspeakable disease, you know...." Aunt Renée blushed. "Well, that was years, years ago."

"What's this? What's this?" asked Uncle Mo, as he burst through the pharmacy door with a beaker of purple fluid. "Chitchatting on a weekday when you should be in school."

"Today is not like every day," said Aunt Renée.

"Ah, you can say that again. If we have many more like these, it will definitely be the end of me." He took a large handkerchief out of his pocket and mopped his brow, as when he was out in the field directing the excavations. Only then it was summertime. "Watch the pharmacy, Renée," he said. "I'm going down to the cellar to fetch another bottle of wine. Langlos will be lunching with us tomorrow. And watch those girls. I won't have them gallivanting around the countryside when it is not Saint Charlemagne's Day."

Colette took her sister's hand and hurried up the narrow staircase to their room.

"What's the matter?" Marie-Claire asked.

"The rumors," whimpered Colette. She sat down in the little straight chair and held her head.

"But Aunt Renée said they were probably not true."

"She didn't put it in those words."

"She said they were tales spread by Potin."

"I still can't believe a person would kill himself over a tale." Colette shook her head. "You realize Father is a guest at the hotel, don't you?"

"Oh no!" The allegation stung Marie-Claire like a swarm of wasps.

"Yes, Claire, think about it."

"Father would never *do* such a thing!"

"He's only human and—"

"*Col*, how can you talk that way about our father?"

Colette leaned forward in her chair and whispered, "Marie Langlos was very pretty, too pretty for her own good."

Marie-Claire shook her head. She wanted to put her hands over her ears, to block out all the awful things Colette was saying, but she was compelled to come to Madame Langlos's rescue. "The last time I saw Madame Langlos," she said, "she looked so tired and sad. There was a letter from America on the counter and she placed her hand on it, as if it were something sacred, you know."

"Bosh!" Colette exclaimed, as she jumped up and opened the armoire door and pulled out coats and mufflers. "Come on, Claire, you and I are going to the hotel."

# 19

"We're closed," said the servant girl to Colette and Marie-Claire. Although it was near midday, the girl was down on her hands and knees scrubbing the tile of the hotel café floor. "Closed because of a death in the establishment. And Monsieur Potin has turned off the heat." She ran her fingers under her dripping nose; her knuckles were a web of red fissures. "If you're going upstairs, watch the corridor. Monsieur Potin made me wash everything today as if it were Friday. Don't know what's taken a hold of him."

They clomped up the narrow, bare, wooden staircase

and tiptoed down the hall, over linoleum dazzling wet under the glare of naked bulbs—one over the staircase, one near the WC at the end of the hall. The odor of disinfectant emanating from the WC wrinkled their noses. It was enough to raise the unconscious.

When they knocked on the door to their parents' room, Victor shouted "Enter" in his deep, everyday, matter-of-fact voice. He stood before his easel, sketching with short, easy strokes, totally absorbed in his task. He wore a long, fringed muffler wrapped twice around his neck, one end dangling over his shoulder.

"Children!" he exclaimed, when at last he turned around, "Is it Saint Charlemagne's Day?"

"No, Father," they chorused. Marie-Claire hung her head. Colette and she had disobeyed Uncle Mo's strict orders not to leave the pharmacy. What if the servant girl downstairs were to tell Claudine of their escapade?

"Something terrible happened today," said Marie-Claire. She closed the door and Colette and she remained near the threshhold, diminished to the size of kindergarten children by the awe of their project: confronting an adult, a much-loved parent at that, on suspicion of immorality. Marie-Claire stared at her unsuspecting father. His wavy hair, parted in the middle, revealed a high, noble forehead; between his brows, concentration lines left permanent creases; his eyes were dark, but kindness shone in their depths; and his high-bridged, long-tipped nose was definitely aristocratic. But she realized, with a twinge of pain, that aristocrats were not always to be trusted; the barn scene still crackled in her mind.

"Come on in, my darlings, don't just stand there. Your mother went to the post office. She should be back soon. Such weather we are having, isn't it?"

"We've only got a minute," said Colette.

*Haven't even got that,* thought Marie-Claire.

Victor placed his charcoal on the easel ledge and sat down and crossed his legs. "All right, daughters," he said, "tell me what is bothering you so." His expression was one of genuine concern, there was no denying it.

"Something terrible happened today," said Marie-Claire again, and her legs started to tremble.

"Sit down, child. You look as if you've seen a ghost."

Marie-Claire sank onto the red velvet loveseat, shiny with age, and Colette joined her. *Why doesn't Colette speak up?* she wondered. *This confrontation was her idea.*

"Drink some of this hot coffee. Yes, drink it. I need some myself, my fingers are stiff from the cold. Drink first and then tell your father what happened."

"Madame Langlos drowned in Uncle Mo's pool," blurted out Marie-Claire, golden droplets of coffee spilling over her chin.

"I know, I know." Victor nodded. He was very grave. "Such a tragedy. A beautiful young woman who had everything to live for—a fine husband and two children. After one's country, what else is there to live for except family?" He was talking to himself. "What happened is part of the general despair in France today. When a fickle Republican government shows no fortitude in its international dealings and at home, how can one expect to find it in individuals?" Again, he was questioning himself. "If only I were ten years younger and could ride with the others." He sighed.

"Father," said Colette, "there are rumors surrounding Marie Langlos's suicide." Colette's voice was cold and accusing.

*Please, please, dear God,* prayed Marie-Claire, *don't let it be true.* She wanted desperately to run to her father, to sit on his lap and be comforted, as she used to do when she was a small child.

Victor's dark eyes flashed and his lower jaw protruded menacingly. "How, pray, did such rumors reach two innocent young girls? I demand to know."

"Aunt Renée says that in a small village gossip gets around. The story goes that Madame Langlos gave favors to hotel guests, although Aunt Renée thinks Potin might have invented such tales because she resisted his advances." Colette was firm.

"*Sacré village!*" Victor exclaimed. "Why doesn't everybody mind his own business?"

"There was a note," Colette added, "but it was so soggy Uncle Mo couldn't read it."

"Perhaps when it dries, your uncle will have the answer and everyone will be satisfied." Victor's voice was sarcastic.

"Come on, Claire," said Colette, "Aunt Renée will be looking for us." She spoke in a deadpan voice. Tears welled in Marie-Claire's eyes. After she opened the door she hesitated before stepping into the corridor; through her blurred vision the floor seemed so wet it flowed like a river.

"Are you leaving without even kissing me good-bye?" asked Victor. "Ah, *ma petite*, I didn't mean to upset you." He pulled out his large handkerchief and dabbed Marie-Claire's eyes. Marie-Claire hugged her father. *I love him anyway; I always will*, she thought.

"You and Colette run along, now, you'll be late for lunch. And when you return this afternoon, after school hours, your mother and I will have something important to tell you."

Colette and Marie-Claire swung their mufflers over

their noses. The wind brought fresh tears to their eyes and burned their lungs. They huddled together as they crossed the bare expanse of red clay where, on Fair days, farmers used to exhibit their livestock. The stone shrine in the center of the diamond pointed skyward like a solitary grave marker. The wind had swept the square clean of rubbish and living beings. Next to City Hall, where the letters HÔTEL DE VILLE needed another coat of black paint, a platoon of bare sycamores stretched their stumpy branches. Last summer their leaves provided a thick canopy. Marie-Claire wished she could conceal herself from the glares of Aunt Renée's neighbors, who would surely be in the kitchen by now discussing the morning's tragedy.

"Come on, Claire." Colette grasped her hand and they marched briskly into the country lane, past empty pastures and withered vegetable plots. Marie-Claire followed her sister through the garden gate.

A murmur of voices greeted them when they entered the kitchen. The women were there, talking among themselves in low monotones, as if they were in church. Dark shawls were draped over the back of the kitchen chairs, filling the room with gloom.

"Don't just stand there, Claire, take off your coat and muffler and hang it on the peg before Aunt Renée sees us." Colette never lost her bearings.

The women surrounded them, uttering little clucking noises of concern. All except a snub-nosed, freckled redhead, noticed Marie-Claire, thinking, *She must be the schoolteacher's sister.*

"*Pauvres petites!*" exclaimed the shoemaker's wife as she held their faces in her calloused palms. "Their noses are as blue as a rooster's tail feathers. I said to old Monsieur Ragaud the other day, I said to him, this weather's not fit for man nor beast."

"Before Saint Felix's Day we always hang our hams in the alleyway beside the shop," said the butcher's wife, "but now I'm afraid if the freeze doesn't get them, the wolves will. They're smart, the wolves. I could tell you some stories about them."

Marie-Claire was astonished. Colette and she stood next to the stove thawing their bones and no one questioned why they weren't in school.

"Just think of the cattle," said the baker's wife, a farmer's daughter who had married in town, "standing around in the hay till their hooves rot."

"Tut, tut, Lucille," said the tall widow lady from the drygoods shop. She wore a cardigan over her black dress. "Think, rather, of our poor absentees behind the lines and knit them woolen socks. I still have skeins of merino." She sighed. "Who knows when I'll get more . . . now," she said, encircling Colette and Marie-Claire with her long, skinny arms. "We'd better give these girls a sip of something hot. Coffee, perhaps?"

"Coffee at this hour?" asked the barber's wife. "It will cut their appetite." Her old voice quivered. "Better to give them a glass of Dubonnet."

"Did someone want Dubonnet?" said Aunt Renée. Mindful of the company in the kitchen, she propelled herself sideways through a half-opened door. "I have a bottle in the sideboard."

"Not for me." The women shook their heads and Marie-Claire held her breath. But *Mère* Brunot said nothing more, nor would she have dared to make another suggestion, now that the owner of the house was present.

"Well . . . " Aunt Renée was puzzled. She shrugged her shoulders. "As you wish." Then she pecked each woman on the cheek and glanced at Colette and Marie-Claire. "You had better go upstairs to your room, girls," she whispered, "but first, help me add more wood to the stove."

They pried off the burner tops with long, iron hooks and shoved kindling into the holes, while sparks flew. Click click went the heavy lids. The stew in the cauldron simmered on. Then the girls excused themselves and withdrew—to the top of the staircase, where Marie-Claire insisted they keep in touch with what was going on in the kitchen below.

"Before we discuss this tragedy," Aunt Renée warned the assembled women, "I must tell you what Maurice said: that we must accept Marie Langlos's death with dignity. 'Like Roman matrons,' he said." The women looked puzzled.

"But I tell you," said Aunt Renée, "let each one burn several candles for the repose of her soul. Poor woman . . . Can't have a decent, Christian burial."

"Why shouldn't she?" The redheaded woman spoke up for the first time.

"Ma'm'selle Dupond, I beg your pardon, but you know the church's doctrine in these matters." Aunt Renée squared her majestic chest.

The *rouquine*'s eyes were cold, blue flames, but her hair flamed redder than burnished copper. "Why shouldn't she have a Christian burial?" She crossed her arms over her shriveled breast. "Did she not attend church every Sunday and Holy Day of Obligation?"

The women nodded.

"Did she not perform her Easter duties?"

The women murmured among themselves.

"The mayor is having it out with that priest. His niece's body will not be thrown to the dogs."

"*Oh là, oh . . .*" The women covered their mouths with their hands. *Mère* Brunot crossed herself.

"Don't you doubt what I am about to say. If Marie Langlos had been a wealthy member of Parisian society, she would have had a funeral at Notre Dame, with organ sounding, bells tolling, et cetera."

"Ma'm'selle Dupond," said Aunt Renée, "I'll thank you not to utter blasphemies in my house."

"Just tell her to shut up," shouted the baker's wife. She grabbed her shawl. "Dirty communist," she muttered under her breath, as she passed the infidel.

"What did you say?" Mademoiselle Dupond asked.

"I say you're nothing but a dirty communist, who does not even believe in God." The baker's wife spat those words under the *rouquine*'s very nose, as she flung her shawl over her shoulders.

"Well! You're nothing but a hypocrite."

"Communist!"

"Hypocrite!"

"Enough!" shouted Aunt Renée, and she squeezed her white bulk between the two women just as the baker's wife screwed up her lips and showered her opponent with spittle. Aunt Renée mopped her forehead. "Saints in Heaven!" she exclaimed. "Marie's body is still lying on the bed, and here we are fighting among ourselves."

"I'll leave you to it," said the schoolmaster's sister. She picked up her shawl and, head high, trotted out the pharmacy door.

The baker's wife dropped her shawl and sat down at the kitchen table with her head in her hands.

"I can't stand anymore of this," whispered Colette. "Let's get in there quickly."

"Agreed," said Marie-Claire. She pulled the bedroom door gently to. Then she flung herself onto the bed. "The day is only half over and I feel as if I've lived a hundred years. I can't believe all this is happening right now." She rolled onto her back and hung her head over the edge of the bed. The warm rush of blood nourished her brain. Downstairs they were discussing the problems of Madame Langlos's funeral, and no one wondered why she had killed herself. And how was it, if the weather was so cold, that Uncle Mo's pool had not frozen over?

Colette yanked her up. "I know the world is topsy turvy right now, Claire, but don't add to it. You're as red as a beet."

When Marie-Claire and Colette returned to the hotel, most of the shutters were closed. Their footsteps echoed on the wooden staircase it was so quiet inside.

In their parents' room they sat across from Susan and Victor on the shiny velvet loveseat, while Susan poured hot chocolate from a thermos, chocolate heated on a small camp stove. *What a cheerless place a hotel is when the café is closed and you can't hear the low-pitched roll of men's voices, interrupted by an occasional loud guffaw, or the clinking of crockery and glasses, or the scraping of chairs and the clomping of boots on the tile floor. It's like a haunted house*, thought Marie-Claire.

"I'm sure you realize, children" said Victor, when the chocolate had warmed their stomachs, "that we cannot stay in Randonette much longer, for a number of reasons that I need not go into." He looked them in the eye and kept one arm protectively over the back of his wife's chair. "I have decided to accept a position as art teacher in a boy's school for the duration of the war. In Caldaquès. No great cultural center, but the dear friend who summons me tells me there are no blackouts down there in the southwest. 'You would hardly know the country is at war,' he says."

Victor looked away then and Marie-Claire understood

her father's embarrassment. After this morning's patriotic outburst, when he was talking of fighting for his country, he was now planning to get away from it all.

"We shall rent a house," said Victor; "your mother will have a piano."

"We shall live like a family again," said Susan, "not that we don't appreciate all the loving care your aunt and uncle have given you girls."

"When are we leaving?" Colette asked.

"As soon as it's decently possible," Victor replied.

"I wish we could leave tomorrow," blurted out Marie-Claire.

Colette turned on her with a look of disdain. "Some people's loyalty," snorted Colette, "is like thin ice, it cracks—"

"I know how shocking this dreadful experience is for you girls," Susan put in quickly, "but we must do our duty and stand by Uncle Mo and Aunt Renée. We cannot leave until the funeral is over and Monsieur Langlos has returned to his regiment." She spoke so calmly she might have been Mother Eulalia making an announcement at convocation, and Marie-Claire looked for any indication of what her mother's true feelings were. But Susan kept her hands folded in her lap and her eyes properly downcast, as the solemnness of the occasion dictated.

*If only I could look into the depths of those light blue eyes that are so pale they shine like glass—clear, but unbreakable, of course,* Marie-Claire thought to herself. *A person's soul is in their eyes, they say. Perhaps Mother does not want to betray herself by showing her dismay. She is the "cupboard expressionist" Colette talked about that afternoon at Saint Ethelred's—a hundred years ago.*

Next day, Colette and Marie-Claire sat at dinner in

Uncle Mo's dining room, while he poured the last dose of his Algerian wine out for Private Langlos and talked in quiet tones, without his beret, for once.

The Langlos children sat in the kitchen with Claudine, who plied them with carrots and potatoes and wiped their sad little faces.

Marie Langlos was buried on a bright, still morning, when the air was alpine crisp and the leafless vineyards were like fishermen's nets cast over the mountain slopes, with her head against the cemetery wall and her feet on the side of the road.

And on the eve of the departure from Randonette, Colette learned from her father that Uncle Mo had revealed to him the contents of Marie Langlos's note—as best he could decipher it. "I love my husband too much," it said, "to bring shame on him."

"I don't know what to make of it," Colette reported to Marie-Claire.

"I'm sure it means she killed herself because she loved her husband and was very lonely," said Marie-Claire. "So you don't have to worry about Father anymore."

*Caldaquès*

# 20

"Please, no tearful sidewalk scenes." Uncle Mo insisted they embrace in the kitchen before their early morning departure. His white smock still hung on the wall peg, but his beret was perched on the back of his head and his gold watch chain gleamed against his dark-vested paunch. Marie-Claire would always remember him thus. Aunt Renée stuffed Colette's and Marie-Claire's pockets with sweets.

After dinner the night before, Uncle Mo had pressed tiny packets into their hands. "A coin for each of you," he'd said, "to ensure safe passage to the land of Dis. I wouldn't want you girls to be left stranded by Charon and then not to be able to join me in Elysium. I have already reserved my place there."

"Lord, no!" exclaimed Marie-Claire.

"Oh yes, my child. I shall be waiting for you."

Marie-Claire clung to him, feeling his pagan warmth through the stiff, starched smock, and she silently invoked a power stronger than that of the gods of Orpheus, who had been unable to prevent his beloved Eurydice from returning to the land of the dead. *Surely,* she thought, *a person as good and kind as Uncle Mo will go to the Christian Heaven, despite his pagan beliefs.*

Uncle Mo gently pushed her away. "Now, upstairs the two of you. Up, up, you need your beauty sleep."

As they lay abed that evening, excited at the prospect of an unfamiliar journey and their minds playing over the events of the past week, Colette said to Marie-Claire, "Uncle Mo was only referring to the natural sequence of things. He is bound to go first, after all; his lungs are bad and he is older than Father."

"You don't suppose he is thinking of taking his own life, do you?" Marie-Claire asked. "I mean, talking about reserving his place down there."

"Don't be silly, Claire, he knows how important he is to the people of his village. More important than the mayor, even the priest, in some ways. Why do you suppose Marie Langlos chose to end her life in his backyard? She trusted him to make the neccessary arrangements after she was gone."

"Don't talk about it. I can't get rid of that awful picture in my mind, and to think that pool is outside our window." Marie-Claire shuddered.

After a while she said, "I suppose by giving us the coins Uncle Mo was taking care of our immortality."

"Oh, come now," scoffed Colette, "you sound as pagan as he does."

Marie-Claire sat up, pulling the sheet with her. "Col, don't you realize that parting with two of his precious, hard-found Roman coins must not have been easy for him?"

"Lie down, Claire." Colette yawned and turned on her side, signifying the issue was closed.

Marie-Claire lay on her back and stared at the pale strips patterning the ceiling—moonlight through shutter slats. Uncle Mo had given her the coin as a tangible reminder of his excavations, as a legacy, and perhaps a silent imperative to carry on his work. She vowed to herself she would return to Randonette, to find the rest of the dolphin pool and the villa, some day . . .some day . . .

The shafts of moonlight had compressed into dancing waves. Then she was going to sea in a horrible, ink black boat, ferried by a hirsute Émile Potin, while an owl, emissary of the goddess Minerva, hooted mournfully. . . .

As she clung to Uncle Mo's dark vest, listening to the ticking of that magic watch, Marie-Claire thought again of last night's promise. "I'll be back after the war is over and look for some more mosaics. I will."

"I'll hold you to it, little girl," he said; "meanwhile, be sure and study your Latin."

He walked with her and Colette to the car waiting at the curbside. The old Peugeot was packed to the roof and sagging so the trunk seemed to sit on the rear axles. "It's a good thing you girls are light, or I wouldn't guarantee your getting through the first mountain pass," he chuckled.

"Mountain passes?" the girls chorused.

"I was only joking. The Massif Central is not that steep."

But when they had left the outskirts of Randonette and cut cross-country they started to climb; the farther they climbed the icier the roads became. Colette and Marie-Claire huddled in the back seat, bundled against the cold, and on the steam of her breath Marie-Claire sent up many a prayer to Saint Christopher, whose effigy bobbed merrily under the rearview mirror. Once they reached the high plateaus, white meadows arched against the clouds. Windbreakers pierced those clouds like grey comb's teeth. Gray, too, were the walls of desolate farmhouses, with boundaries of lava stone; and of the inns where they stopped for food and lodging, where guests assembled at one long wooden table and slept between coarse sheets and in the mornings looked down at limitless valleys, at towns so distant they resembled lonely flocks of sheep.

When at last they had corkscrewed down the mountain—the descent more perilous than the ascent—they reached the banks of a broad river and saw cliffs dotted with pines and russet oaks. They had traveled back into autumn. Windows were cracked open, mufflers and wool caps shed. *Seasons may be reversed, but not emotions,* thought Marie-Claire. When her father mentioned cave shrines in those cliffs, where prehistoric ancestors painted the liveliest buffalo and reindeer, all she could see in her mind's eye were gray, blue, and black mosaic dolphins cavorting on the floor of the excavated pool.

Victor honked when they arrived at a guarded railroad crossing.

"Be right down," yelled the guardian of the crossing, as she stuck her head out of the cottage window. A blue-smocked peasant leaned his elbows on the sill. "*Eh là, les voyageurs,*" drawled the old man. "You emigrants?"

"You might call us that, *grand-père,*" shouted Victor.

"Victor, hush," said Susan.

In the back seat Marie-Claire nudged Colette. Her mother had remonstrated with her father without bothering to look at him. Sometimes she wondered whether her mother had any sense of humor at all. Were all serious musicians that way with their mind so full of notes all the time?

"How is the road to Manternau and Caldaquès?" asked Victor.

"The road to Manternau, it is as flat as the bricks here." The old man patted the ledge. "But the road to Caldaquès, I don't know about. That's not my country."

"Thank you, *grand-père*."

"*Salut*."

The woman raised the red and white barrier and the car rumbled over the tracks; Marie-Claire held onto her trembling violin case. Then it hummed along the smooth road to Manternau, traversing a pine forest carpeted with ferns and yellow broom. Forest sometimes yielded to barren marshlands, on the edges of which were long, low farmhouses with thatched roofs. So comfortable was the ride that it lulled the passengers to sleep.

"Ah, *sacrebleu!*" exclaimed Victor as the front wheel struck a hard surface and there was a shrill sound of dragging metal. He stopped abruptly.

Marie-Claire opened her eyes and saw they had left the pine forests behind and were traveling a narrow road, bordered by tall trees, pruned like candelabra.

"Must be stone in the shoulder of the road," muttered Victor.

"Girls, wait in the car," said Susan. "Let your father examine the damage first."

Victor stood on the running board and leaned over the hood. "Wheel's done for. You will all have to get out and help me unload so I can change it. Look's like the remains of a stone barrier over there."

"I hear geese." Marie-Claire ran up the road. In a pen were the fattest waddlers she had ever seen. How they cackled and strutted.

"Wait until you see the covered market in Caldaquès," her father called. "Now come back here and pitch in."

She dutifully helped unload boxes and suitcases from the trunk of the car. Then Victor went to work with jack and wrenches, grunting all the while, and the women sat on the dry grass behind the trees. When the last bolt had been tightened on the new wheel, Victor joined the women folk and mopped his brow.

"Jean Dreyfuss tells me they sell fresh geese and duck livers once a month at the covered market, and every sales person has a recipe to go with them."

"Ugh!" said Marie-Claire, thinking of slimy, pink objects sliding all over the tables.

"Jean, who is from Alsace and a marvelous cook himself, promised to make his own foie gras for New Year's in port jelly. We are all invited."

"With truffles, I suppose," said Susan.

"Of course."

Such news did not impress Colette. She had her back turned on the road and was staring over the fields.

*Into the vineyards near Randonette?* wondered Marie-Claire, *or perhaps the courts of the Sorbonne, where a tweedy young man had perched on a windowsill with other students, before trading in his books for a sword and gun.*

"Back to it, ladies," shouted Victor.

Silently Colette helped Marie-Claire replace luggage and boxes. Marie-Claire could sense her sister's pain, Colette's muteness more eloquent than words. Side by side they worked, yet the memory of Jean-Paul always came between them now, so that Marie-Claire could not divine her sister's innermost thoughts.

"Ouch!" Marie-Claire stubbed her toe on the running board before stepping into the car. She withdrew to her corner and nursed her smarting foot and stared at the white kilometer markers on the side of the road.

Twenty . . . fifteen . . . five . . . They were approaching Caldaquès now. Soon the first old houses appeared on the outskirts, advertisements painted on peeling walls. A yellow dog ran into the street and barked at the car. When they crossed a stone bridge over a gently flowing river, they had arrived in town.

# 21

CALDAQUÈS—HOME OF CURATIVE SRINGS FROM THE ROMAN ERA proclaimed the sign in the riverside park. The sign abutted the scalloped railing at the foot of the monument to the glorious dead. As they drove by, Marie-Claire glimpsed a bandstand in the center of the park, and through the bare tree branches beyond it curved the white walls of an arena. Bullfighting must be a local sport.

"Look quickly, girls," said Susan. She pointed to a woman in a flowered apron who was filling a saucepan with water from a hydrant at the curb. She took two eggs out of her pocket and lowered them into the pan and covered it.

"By the time she gets back to her kitchen," said Victor, "she will have soft-boiled eggs for lunch. Yes, the water is hot. Now, do you get the significance of the town's name? *Calda* means 'hot water' in Latin. They tacked on *aqua* for good measure."

"Oh, I should have realized," said Marie-Claire. But Caesar's *Commentaries on the Gallic War* were giving her a hard time.

"Caldaquès, hum . . . " muttered Colette.

"And over here is the Majestic Hotel, typical of modern French architecture." Victor snickered. "Those arches curving into the sky, what are they supporting? And those crenellated turrets on the upper corners, are they medieval, or Moorish? The architect could not make up his mind. I tell you, we need to return to the glorious seventeenth century. They really knew how to build then—for style and endurance."

"Where are the curative springs?" asked Colette. "Surely not just in hydrants."

"Wait and see," said Victor. "I'll tell you this much. The mud from the river is what rich people come to the Majestic for. They coat themselves with it and sit in hot tubs. Cures their rheumatism, they say. And then they go across the way to the park to watch the *Courses Caldaquaises*—spectacle, not bull fight. These, Jean says, are reminiscent of the ancient Cretan games, with acrobats and tumblers."

The car slowed to a crawl as they drove along a narrow street, where men and women on bicycles threaded their way through pedestrian traffic. The street opened onto the town square.

"The source of your curative springs, there you are, Colette." Victor parked the car so everyone could admire the grandest edifice they had seen since they left Paris last August. In the center of the square was a magnificent arcade supported by tall, tapering columns of small, perfectly fitted bricks built around a large rectangular pool. A frieze of horizontal bands of bricks topped the arcade so that it resembled a Roman temple, minus the pediment.

Water gushed out of lion-headed spigots, lower than street level, and they realized the pool was in reality a bubbling fountain. They descended a flight of steps and timidly stretched their hands under the gushing water; Marie-Claire was surprised by its warmth.

"History tells us a Roman emperor brought his daughter to Caldaquès to treat her rheumatism in the hot springs and the miraculous mud from the river," said Victor, his voice rising above the din of the rushing water, "and this is his *ex-voto*. A grand thanksgiving, isn't it? Now, people from all over Europe come to the Majestic Spa. It is the main source of the town's livelihood, or was before the war broke out, and only emigrants like us are foolhardy enough to travel. I doubt there are any more bullfights either. It takes young men with muscles and nerves of steel to handle bulls." He leaned against the fence that enclosed the fountain, breathing the gentle fumes.

Across the street old, beret-clad men sat playing dominoes at café tables. The specialty shop next door displayed cans of *foie gras,* artfully stacked to resemble the Majestic. Outside a stationery store stood carousels of postcards with impossibly blue skies.

"Back into the car, all of you. We must stop by Jean's house to get the key to the villa." Victor briskly wiped his forehead and bounded up the steps, rejuvenated by curative fumes.

*"The key to the villa"* . . . *Now we're going back in time,* thought Marie-Claire, *to the excavations at Randonette and Joseph's shout of triumph. How uncanny it is standing here next to this Roman temple right in the center of town.*

"Come on, Claire." Colette grabbed her hand and pulled her up the steps—back to reality—while a kaleidoscope of images wove in and out of Marie-Claire's mind, the past and the present fusing occasionally, then separating into distinctive shapes.

She hardly noticed they had crossed the square of the covered market and were on the outskirts of the old town when the Peugeot broke down on a hilly, tree-lined avenue. Steam hissed from the radiator.

"Just like the hot fountain," said Victor, "but the old steed made it. We're right outside Villa Hortense."

A tall, bald gentleman came running to greet them with a watering can. He leaned into the front window, taking Susan's hand and kissing it. Colette and Marie-Claire he acknowledged with a gracious nod. Marie-Claire was astonished to hear him introduced as plain Jean Dreyfuss, he seemed so aristocratic.

The hood was raised, then water gingerly inserted. After much discussion and shaking of heads, Victor decided to chance it to their final destination, and Jean handed him the key to the villa. The car coasted downhill and swung into a narrow street, where every little house, separated by a walled garden, exhibited its own distinctive architecture.

"*Mon Repos*, here we are," said Victor as he pulled on the brake, "the plaque is on the gate."

Before them was a huge wooden gate with crossbeams. *Just what one would find in a farmyard*, thought Marie-Claire. And the house was white stucco, crisscrossed with more beams, hung with red balconies, red slabs of shutters concealing the windows. *Mon Repos* (My Rest) belied its name. Its exterior was more rustic than reposeful. She glanced across the street and saw a woman idly sweeping her front porch. She wore a red hat and was squinting at them from under its brim. Looking them over, of course. *I hope the people in this neighborhood are not big gossips like the villagers of Randonette*, she thought.

The Lavalettes stood on the sidewalk while Victor unlatched the gate, which swung easily on its hinges. He peered inside the courtyard. "Ah, Susan, *ma chérie*, roses, roses everywhere. How fragrant our little cottage will be in the spring," he exclaimed. He bounded up the porch steps.

Marie-Claire hesitated. She didn't like the looks of the

front door. It had a black, barred peephole, like prison doors in the films.

"Don't turn around," said Colette, "the woman across the way is squinting at us. She's sweeping her porch with her hat on, would you believe it?"

"She runs a boardinghouse for retired *pensionnaires,* Jean told me," said Victor, "and is just looking us over to make sure we are not the disruptive type."

*Oh,* thought Marie-Claire with a sinking heart, *I hope boardinghouse managers are not like hotel keepers, and I pray this house we are about to enter will have a piano for Mother and that she will be happy at last.*

The interior of *Mon Repos* was a revelation. First, a smoking room with game table and overstuffed chairs you could really sink into and a leather sofa. The parlor—God be praised—contained a baby grand draped in a fringed, Spanish shawl, whose tassels hung over the edges of the wood like a window awning. Susan played octaves, then ran her fingers over the keys, and declared that all the piano needed was a good tuning.

"We'll call the man tomorrow," Victor said.

The parlor was connected by an archway to the dining room, where a bright, stained-glass lampshade hung over the table; the radio sat in an alcove. There was a telephone next to the kitchen door and a large storage closet under the staircase.

"What does this door lead to?" asked Colette, pointing to an enormous crystal knob.

"Oh, probably the cellar," said Victor. But when he turned the handle it revealed a narrow, white-tiled cubicle, containing a huge bathtub on lion's feet. They all sighed with satisfaction.

Upstairs only the master bedroom was furnished with any attempt at rococo elegance—satin bedspread and matching valances at the windows, which dipped exaggeratedly low. "Like the puffs on Marie Antoinette's skirts," laughed Victor, "delusions of grandeur these owners have. They're probably Bordeaux wine merchants." Marie-Claire and Colette had to content themselves with faded cotton bedspreads and a caneback chair whose tattered pillow had seen better days; an old papered screen concealed their washbasin. But the room had a balcony, and what more could one ask at a time like this?

"Don't make yourselves too comfortable, girls." Victor grinned. "As soon as I unload the bicycles, I want you to go to the post office and send Maurice a telegram. I promised I would let him know when we arrived in Caldaquès. Marie-Claire, you can also tell your uncle that I have found you a Latin tutor."

"Tutor?"

"After New Year's, of course."

"Yes, Father." Colette and she exchanged relieved glances.

"A strict taskmaster," Victor continued, "the finest of Latin scholars. But don't worry," he added, noting the frightened look on Marie-Claire's face, "he won't beat you; Jean is a gentle man."

Colette consulted her watch. "Father," she asked, "could we listen to the newscast before we unload our bicycles?"

# 22

"Who is it?"

"Piano tuner," answered the voice on the other side of the peephole.

"He's here," called out Marie-Claire.

Victor raced downstairs. "Well, open the door, child."

A wizened little man, his neck wrapped in a long scarf, confronted Marie-Claire. He was carrying a black satchel. Simultaneously Susan appeared from the kitchen. She led him into the parlor and before anyone could say *"Voilà,"* Colette had flicked the Spanish shawl off the top of the baby grand, raising a cloud of dust. The little man dropped his satchel and blew his nose ostentatiously.

"Put that dirty cloth on the floor of the closet," Susan told Colette. "I want to keep the piano lid raised most of the time, anyway."

Instantly the piano tuner stopped blowing his nose. His eyes brightened. "Madame must be a professional," he said.

"How can you tell?" Susan asked, laughing.

"Madame, only amateurs keep their pianos covered with shawls, and usually a lot of bric-a-brac, too. I just came from a house where they had a bust of Beethoven, a bust of Mozart, five photographs, and two ashtrays on top of their shawl, besides the mister's collection of old meerschaum pipes. You cannot appreciate the full tonal quality of a piece with the top down."

"True," said Victor. "My wife happens to be a concert pianist. She studied with Marguerite Long."

"Is that so?" Now the little man folded his arms and gazed at Susan. *As if she were a national monument,* thought Marie-Claire.

"I don't want to keep you from doing your job," said Susan, as she motioned to the family to leave the room.

"My pleasure."

Marie-Claire lounged in the smoking room and twiddled her thumbs during the long, tedious tuning process.

Twang, twang, twang . . . The little felt hammers kept pounding the strings until the right pitch was reached.

She stepped outside. A neighborhood dog ran by, ears plastered back, tail between his legs. The poor thing could not stand the high pitches, and neither could she. She hoped the boardinghouse manager would not call to complain.

"Aren't you cold, little one?" Her father put a protective arm around her shoulders. "This tuning will last a good hour, I should say. Mother has gone upstairs; tuning always gets on her nerves."

Victor led his daughter back into the house and into the smoking room where Colette sat playing Patience. "When our little man leaves, we'll get her to try out the piano, eh?" He gave Marie-Claire a conspiratorial wink before sinking into a leather chair.

"But I haven't touched the keys in such a long time," Susan protested.

"A little Chopin," begged Victor.

"An étude," Colette suggested.

"Yes, yes." Marie-Claire could not sit still.

"We shall see," Susan said.

When she had adjusted the piano stool, Susan removed her rings with that slow, graceful gesture of her right hand that was so familiar to Marie-Claire. Eyes veiled now, she gently massaged her fingers. When at last she lowered her hands into position over the keyboard, Marie-Claire shivered with delightful anticipation. There was a moment of deep, meaningful silence. Her mother was collecting herself, assuming complete control of all her faculties.

The minute Susan launched into the fast étude, Marie-

Claire was overjoyed—overcome by the sheer beauty of the music. The notes flowed effortlessly from her mother's fingertips. Her hands were white doves that flew up and down the keyboard. Susan kept her head high, lips curled in a smile. *She's been transported to another world,* thought Marie-Claire.

When the piece was over Susan simply dropped her hands into her lap, and her face regained its usual, expressionless composure.

"More, more," insisted Victor.

"The Barcarolle."

"The Lullaby."

Susan frowned and shook her blonde head. "I don't know if I can remember all of it," she said.

"*Chérie*, we implore you. The Lullaby." Victor strode over to the piano and kissed his wife on the forehead—such a chaste kiss as one would give an angel.

Susan sighed. Hands poised over the keyboard again, she seemed to consult her memory. At last her left hand played the five familiar bass notes—the gentle, rocking motif that would continue throughout Chopin's composition. When the lyrical right hand joined in, Marie-Claire closed her eyes, soothed as always by the magic of Chopin's tenderness. Her mother sang softly along with the melody. It always amazed Marie-Claire that music so transformed her mother when she was in the act of interpreting it. Yet in her daily life she seemed incapable of communicating her own true feelings.

Marie-Claire remembered the time her father had sent her mother a gorgeous bouquet of peach-colored roses before a concert at the *Salle Gaveau*. Peach was Susan's favorite color and there was no mistaking the large, heavy script on the accompanying note. Yet when they had all come to her dressing room afterward to congratulate her, Victor beaming with pride, Colette and she expecting great exclamations of joy and surprise over the beautiful flowers, Susan had simply pecked him on the cheek, then gazed into the mirror to rearrange a lock of hair. Marie-Claire would never forget the look of dismay on her father's face, the hurt look in those deep, brown eyes.

The lullaby ended on two soft chords. Susan's hands dropped automatically into her lap, where they remained while performer and spectators, no longer burdened by their own secret problems and the concerns of war and displacement, basked in the music's magic afterglow.

Susan was the first to break the spell. "I've simply got to find a maid," she said, sweeping her eyes around the room, taking in the cobwebs nestling in ceiling corners, the motes of dust dancing in the sunlight before the windows.

"Why don't I consult a shopkeeper, *chérie?* There is a small grocery right around the corner."

"I'll go with you, Father," Colette said.

"Me, too," said Marie-Claire.

"Marie-Claire, when are you going to practice your violin?" Susan asked suddenly.

"I need another A string."

"Well, you had better ask the grocer whether there is a music store in town." Susan carefully lowered the lid over the keyboard. "I suggest you buy several strings while you are about it."

On the recommendation of the groceryman's wife, Victor hired a lusty country girl who arrived on her bicycle every morning, carrying a fresh loaf of bread, in time to heat the *café-au-lait*.

Marie-Claire had obtained her violin strings in a tiny

shop under the Majestic Arcade, and now the house echoed with music. The *pensionnaires* across the way could often be perceived behind their open windows, bundled to their ears, if the day was not too windy.

While in the parlor, Susan sat at the piano meticulously running through scales, arpeggios, and Scarlatti sonatas before tackling the more intricate passages of a Liszt étude, Marie-Claire shut herself in her bedroom and practiced her violin before the mirrored armoire door. Father poured over his art books in preparation for his term as high school art professor, and Colette attended to her own secret rites.

In the afternoons Marie-Claire and Colette were free to explore the town. They sped down the avenue on their bikes, past the convalescent home and its immaculate lawn, centered by a white Our Lady, who showered her china blessings on the plants clustered around her feet. On the side fronting the river the shutters of the home remained perpetually closed, but the road was not heavily traveled and the sisters could sit under the sycamore trees at the water's edge.

They traveled Indian file through narrow streets to the park, where a blind fiddler stood next to the closed doors of the arena, sawing away at the same folk tune. The Tricolor hung limply from the balcony above the portal between two onion domes. Cane-toting patriarchs sat on the park benches.

But the square of the covered market buzzed with activity, the farm women gladly dispensing free recipes with the sales of their geese livers and on the town square in the evenings the café lights turned steam from the hot fountain into a pinkish haze.

New Year's Eve Jean Dreyfuss invited the Lavalettes

to share a sumptuous feast of whole *foie gras* and roast duckling in orange sauce.

# 23

Marie-Claire jumped off her bicycle and dropped it against the hillside grass. "No need to worry about ants this time of year," she told herself, "they're mostly in hibernation, even here in the southwest where the climate is supposed to be warmer than in Randonette. Worry about being late for Latin tutoring."

Every afternoon when Victor returned from Le Collège de Saint Vincent, where he taught art to recalcitrant boys, the Lavalettes huddled next to the oil stove in the dining room, turned on the radio, and listened for Big Ben's deep chimes, precursor to the British Broadcasting Company's daily news bulletin. This passed for current events in Caldaquès, with postbroadcast commentary by Victor. "We must keep up our English," was his pretext when in truth everybody knew he was indulging his Anglomania, "the sisters downtown can take care of arithmetic, French composition, and the rest." This afternoon the commentary had lasted longer than usual.

Two at a time Marie-Claire now ran up the flight of steps to Villa Hortense, memories of New Year's succulent *foie gras*, spined with truffles, and nestling in ruby cubes of port jelly, still on her palate. Jean Dreyfuss could not replace Uncle Mo in her heart—nobody ever could—but what a cook he was. And he spoke several languages and translated monumental art books. And on top of this hill, among stately elms, he lived in a house with turrets and gray slate roofs, castlelike in its elegance.

She swung the great brass knocker. "I apologize for being late," she gasped, when the door swung open.

"Apology accepted. Come in, Marie-Claire," Dreyfuss said.

His radio was still playing, but at such low volume she could not distinguish words above the shortwave static, only the clipped rhythm of British speech. "BBC?" she asked.

"Yes. And I wager you have been listening to it, too."

"Yes, how did you know?"

Dreyfuss smiled in answer, then ushered her into the dimly lit, deep-carpeted living room. Logs crackled in the fireplace, and Marie-Claire had the impression of a Nordic elegance foreign to this little town near the Spanish border.

"During Queen Hortense's day, they did not go in for overhead lights and bright illuminations. But they certainly loved red, didn't they?" Dreyfuss said.

Once again she marveled at the red damasked wallpaper and tasseled red velvet curtains. The little round lamp shades glowed like pink mushrooms.

"I am only teasing about the décor, Marie-Claire. Villa Hortense is pure *fin de siècle*. Look at these *Pleasures of the Four Seasons*, if you please."

She smiled at the prints on the wall: languid groupings of wide-skirted ladies, stiff and pale as wax, who—spring, summer, autumn, winter—were never idle. Quaint pictures for a Latin scholar.

"Did you study for the priesthood?" she asked him.

"Hardly, I'm Jewish."

"Oh, I'm so sorry."

"No need to be. Do you mind if I smoke?"

Marie-Claire shook her head.

Dreyfuss filled his pipe with tobacco from a black leather pouch, and when he lit it and puffed on it the room was filled with an aroma of honey-coated, burned leaves. *Bent over the lighted pipe bowl, he is all aquiline nose and pale, bony forehead, as vulnerable as one of Uncle Mo's exhibits,* Marie-Claire thought, *those forbidden skulls he would declare some day.*

He motioned her toward a card table near the bay window and pulled out her chair—a gentility that smacked of Saint Ethelred's, and Marie-Claire remembered Mother Eulalia's admonitions to bend your knees as you sit and keep your back as straight as possible.

"Now that we all know Gaul is divided into three parts—" he started to say.

"I knew that in Randonette." Marie-Claire clapped a hand over her mouth. "Sorry," she said, "I didn't mean to be so rude."

"Yes, well . . . " He was thrown off balance. He wasn't used to young people, she could see. But puffing on his pipe, he regained his composure. "I must deliver my lecture on Caesar the commander-in-chief. Very apropos, don't you think, in view of the current political situation?"

Politics again. The grown-ups were always at it. Marie-Claire's stomach tightened, but she didn't move a facial muscle. She was in awe of this man, and she merely allowed the question to be rhetorical.

"It is interesting to analyze Caesar's tactics and compare them to what the Nazis are using now. *Celeritas*, swiftness, that was the keynote of Caesar's campaigns. Although you might think that nine good years of one's life spent in conquering a country such as Gaul, which was never totally under control, seems like a very long time. Especially when you consider what Hitler did in forty-eight hours in Poland. . . . "

Marie-Claire grunted. Bogged down in ablative absolutes and indirect discourse, she had never really considered the overall time frame of the *Commentaries*. Just getting through the morass of marches, tribal plottings on the part of the Gauls, negotiations, retaliations on the part of the Romans, et cetera, et cetera, was difficult enough.

Dreyfuss appeared not to notice her discomfort. Now that he had warmed to his subject, there was no stopping him. "By *celeritas* I mean that Caesar was swift to calculate his military moves, to implement them; and once he moved, to keep the initiative, surprise the enemy, get a wedge in there and divide his strength, then pursue him." He paused, sucked on his dead pipe, which whistled eerily, then lit it again.

Marie-Claire chewed her tongue to keep from yawning.

Dreyfuss leaned back in his chair. "And yet this man was also quick to recognize bravery wherever he saw it: on both sides of the battlefield."

"In history class we learned about Vercingetorix, the Gaul—"

"Caesar exemplified the basic Roman virtues of justice, as it was practiced in those days." He paused once again. "You know, the Geneva Convention, which regulates the treatment of prisoners in our century, did not exist then, of course. And the giving of prisoners as booty to Roman soldiers was common practice." He took a deep puff, then stared at the ceiling. "Justice, courage, moderation, an inordinate sense of organization . . . and uncommon fidelity. Fidelity, something that is missing nowadays in this country's foreign alliances."

*Gosh,* thought Marie-Claire, *this man must have studied*

*at one of the military academies like Saint Cyr or Sandhurst on top of his other accomplishments.* She stared at the orator's long, bony fingers. *No, those are not soldier's hands.*

"After Caesar's campaigns, the Gauls became loyal Roman subjects—most of them." Dreyfuss leaned forward and stared at Marie-Claire with icy blue eyes, gems of color in that pale face, and she was spellbound. "You have learned from your archaeologist uncle, I'm sure, how Roman culture civilized most of us barbarians."

All along she had kept one ear on the radio and suddenly she sat up very straight and cried, "Oh, that's Chopin's Polonaise."

"You have a fine ear. I thought I had turned the radio down to practically nothing," he said.

"Those were the same measures Miss Brown used to play at prize giving at Saint Ethelred's."

"Thrilling, aren't they?" He smiled at her.

"Yes." She pumdepummed under her breath, clacking her lips.

"Those measures of the Heroic Polonaise are now the signal of Radio Free Poland," he said. He tapped his pipe on the ashtray and felt for a fuzzy white stick in his pocket with which to clean the bowl. "I know all this ancient history must be very boring to you." He was intent on cleaning his pipe and did not look at her.

Nevertheless, Marie-Claire blushed. "I . . . I just cannot forget the Polonaise. Miss Brown played it when your name was announced, and you stepped down into the arena to get your laurel wreath and book."

"Don't ever forget that moment," Dreyfuss said, his voice rising as he turned toward her, his pale face suffused with unearthly radiance.

*If he were a Christian and had on an animal skin instead*

*of a gray, tweed jacket he would have been one of those saintly hermits in the holy pictures,* Marie-Claire thought.

"Hold onto every proud moment you can," he said passionately. Then, with half-closed lids, Dreyfuss puffed on his pipe. "History is supposed to be a record of past events. In simple terms, that is exactly what it is. In our time, however, so much tragedy has occurred in such a short span: nations overtaken; nations wiped out; nations, like us, in suspended animation. The records are blowing about like papers in a whirlwind. I moved here from Alsace, so I could work in peace. Peace—such a relative term." He was speaking to himself now. "And where shall we all go when the Phony War becomes a reality?" His voice trailed off as he walked over to the radio and turned up the volume.

"Do you miss your English school?" he asked, when he returned.

"I don't think so." Marie-Claire was still clinging to the old myths.

"Hush!" he said abruptly.

They both sat very still.

"Here is the voice of the Polish announcer. . . . 'For God, for honor, and for country,' " Jean Dreyfuss translated, " 'let us continue the fight.' "

"Where?"

"Everywhere!" He waved his pipe. "Wherever survivors of last September's blitz may be—military and civilian. The Polish diaspora and the population at home . . . Brave people those Poles," he muttered. "You know their cavalry was wiped out practically to a man. Caesar would have approved of their bravery."

He sighed. "We must continue our lesson." He got up once more and turned off the radio and Marie-Claire gazed at the wide-skirted ladies in winter posing daintily by a hearth. They all smiled at her. And one held her embroidery needle way up high, at the end of the longest thread. Such showoffs they were. . . .

Then Dreyfuss and she opened their Latin texts to book three of the *Commentaries* and tackled the problems of Publius Crassus and the Seventh Legion, which had been wintering by the ocean in the country of the Andes.

"Tack on an *L*," said Dreyfuss, "and you have the French Department we happen to be in at the moment. Isn't that interesting, Marie-Claire?"

*Eerie*, she thought. *"Plus ça change, plus c'est la même chose." I'll have to remind Colette of this passage, she probably doesn't remember it.*

# 24

"A drop of *rhum* in the tea will help the cramps, *Mademoiselle*."

Arms akimbo, Rosine stood guard behind Marie-Claire until Marie-Claire had sipped the concoction Rosine had brewed especially for the "little one," for this rite of puberty on Ash Wednesday, February 7, 1940. (Marie-Claire had scrupulously noted it in her locked diary.) But Rosine did not know what a momentous occasion this was in Marie-Claire's life. Lord, no. If she had, she would have told the whole neighborhood.

"Come on, drink some more."

Marie-Claire did not dare disobey.

She had to admit the tea warmed her considerably.

It brought blessed relief to the constricting pain in her stomach and legs and gave her a feeling of well-being to boot. She sighed a sigh of relief, which, unfortunately, Rosine interpreted for a moan.

"Ah, belly of woman!" Rosine decried. "How nature makes us suffer; how—"

"That will be all, Rosine." Return to your quarters was what Susan implied.

But Rosine would not take the hint. "One does what one can for others," she said huffily.

"Yes. Thank you very much."

"Poor little one. I remember when I was that age—"

"If only the house were warmer," said Susan. "Why didn't they put in radiators and pipe in some of that natural hot water?"

"This is the suburbs, Madame." Rosine straightened to her full, stolid height, "no free hot water here. Besides, it is never this cold in Caldaquès. The devil must have opened his ice chest."

"The truth is," said Susan, "this villa was never intended for winter living, and the owners probably only came here in the early spring, to care for their roses."

Rosine raised her hands in acknowledgement of defeat before she shuffled to the kitchen.

"I can't drink much more of this, my head feels funny," admitted Marie-Claire.

"What Rosine calls a drop of *rhum* is probably strong enough to drowse a calf," said Colette, laughing.

"Probably so." Susan shook her head. "These peasants mean well but they can be very heavy-handed. Marie-Claire, why don't you go upstairs and lie down, and Colette will fetch you a hot water bottle."

"It isn't that bad, really."

Susan looked perplexed.

"I feel much, much better," Marie-Claire declared.

Now that she had joined the club, her spirits soared. She was one of them now—a wo-man, what a rich-sounding word. Woman—the subject of man's adoration, who had inspired poets to write sonnets . . .

Colette stared at her, too.

When Susan announced she was going outside to check on the roses in the garden and Marie-Claire wanted to follow her mother, Colette muttered, "Claire, you must be out of your mind. The *rhum* obviously has gone to your head." But she resigned herself to getting their jackets off the hooks in the vestibule and insisting her sister wrap her head in a scarf before they trailed their mother down the porch steps.

The sky was leaden. A penetrating cold had settled over Caldaquès, just when Marie-Claire thought they had escaped the cold in the east. She hunched her shoulders and jammed her hands into the pockets of her jacket. She couldn't understand why her mother had elected this afternoon to tour the garden. Today was Wednesday. No school today. And Victor was painting at Villa Hortense, because there wasn't room for a studio at *Mon Repos*. . . .

"Have you ever seen so many vines!" exclaimed Susan. Tenderly she tucked a slender cane into the trellis that cloaked the stucco wall. "How beautiful our little farmhouse could be in the spring."

*Could*—Marie-Claire noted a touch of sadness in her mother's voice. *Coulds* and *woulds* were commonly used now when speaking of the future during this Phony War, when Germans and French were still glaring at each other from behind their fortifications; the War of Nerves it was called, the French waiting for the Nazis to make the first move.

"Will this weather hurt them?" asked Colette.

"Oh no, you should have seen the red roses on the clapboard houses in the area where I grew up. In June, that is. And every winter we had ice and snow."

"Really?" This rose passion of her mother's was something Marie-Claire had been unaware of. Now it inspired her to summon up appropriate English verse. But English verse always mixed roses with other flowers, so she resorted to the courtly French poetry of Ronsard: the round, velvety, deep crimson tones in his *Ode to Cassandra:*

> *Mignonne, allons voir si la rose*
> *Qui ce matin avait déclose*
> *Sa robe de pourpre au soleil . . .*

The mellifluous sounds rolled off her tongue.

"Lovely, dear. French is such a musical language when properly recited. . . . Watch your clothes."

They were passing thick, green canes of carefully spaced bushes. More rose beds skirted the wall enclosing the backyard. By the kitchen door was an herb garden where Rosine plucked parsley for their salad dressings and *blanquette* of veal. In the center of the lawn was a large cherry tree, so Rosine had told them. The tree was bare, so much barer than the stalks of roses that retained their green color, the thinner branches still stippled with brown.

"Welcome to Caldaquès," uttered a cracked, little voice from above, and the cackle of laughter that followed sounded like a broken record.

They looked up over the wall and saw two black sleeves folded onto a balcony railing, and above the sleeves an enormous grey cap.

"Jules Peyot, at your service, *Mesdames,*" said the voice, now serious. "Did you know it was going to snow?"

"Snow?" They questioned, in unison. "In Caldaquès?"

The cap now lifted sufficiently to reveal crooked nostrils and cheeks as sunken and brown as the top of a walnut shell. "I witnessed the same sky twenty-two years ago," said Mr. Peyot, "before my son left for the trenches. It was a bad omen then." The cap dropped forward; there was a moment of silence. "Don't worry about your cherry tree," said the little man, suddenly recovering his composure, "the fruit will be that much sweeter and juicier."

"Jules, get back in here," a woman's voice scolded.

One of the black sleeves shot up to touch the cap, in smart salute, before it disappeared from view again.

Susan shivered and hugged herself. She shepherded the girls back to the house.

Rosine awaited them by the kitchen door. "No more bread, Madame, sorry. I should buy two loaves every day, there is only a crust left for dinner. What shall we put in the soup?"

It was common knowledge that Rosine was the largest consumer of bread, but all Susan did was ask Colette to get on her bicycle and hurry to the bakery before the snowstorm.

"Snowstorm!" Rosine chuckled with disbelief.

"Yes, snowstorm," replied Marie-Claire, "Mr. Peyot warned us."

"Well, if Mr. Peyot says so, it's bound to happen." Rosine shrugged her shoulders. "The old ones are usually the first to know; they have a sixth sense, like barnyard animals."

*I wonder how old Mr. Peyot is?* thought Marie-Claire, as she trudged upstairs to her room. Certainly older than *Père* Boudet. But then she had never seen the old farmer; he was always concealed behind a bed curtain. She lay down on top of her bed and closed her eyes and dozed.

The minute Colette returned from the bakery it started to snow—light, starry flakes that evaporated when they met the pavement. The boardinghouse manager poked her red-hatted head out the front door, as if the windowpanes had lied to her.

Marie-Claire jumped off her bed. She dragged her heavy, navy blue Saint Ethelred's coat out of the armoire, tied a scarf around her neck, and tucked her brown hair inside a bright yellow beret. "I've got to see the hot fountain like this," she told Colette. "Come on, let's go."

"You'd better take extra precautions if you're going to bicycle," warned Colette. "Exercise sometimes increases the flow."

"I'll put one in my purse," said Marie-Claire.

When they reached the square, steam—neon pink through café lights—billowed above the fountain. Snowflakes plummeted like cotton balls, polka dotting the pink haze, and Marie-Claire thought never in her life had she seen anything more spectacular. The Roman arcade, with its elegant columns, imperiously braved the elements. It resembled a stage set in a classical drama. Fountain waters, however, still gushed out of lion-headed spigots. Icicles would have been more appropriate to the weather.

Shopkeepers and locals, standing on their stoops, wagged their heads. The men, in their awe of nature's marvelous display, crushed their lighted cigarettes under their shoes, just as they always did before entering church on Sunday.

Colette and Marie-Claire left their bicycles on the sidewalk and strolled into a café, toward an empty table.

"People here act as if they were witnessing the Apocalypse," said Colette.

"Stop speaking English." Marie-Claire looked around her. "We're being stared at as if we were spies."

A pink-cheeked café boy, whose white apron skimmed the ground, wiped off their table with one grand swipe of his cloth.

"Two hot chocolates, please," ordered Marie-Claire, whose stomach was again sending out distress signals.

"Yes, Miss," said the boy, and his grin, directed to her only, was unnecessarily large.

She removed the yellow beret—perhaps it was too bright—and loosened her coat as the boy sped into the kitchen. Before you could count to ten, he returned with a tray balanced high on the palm of his hand. "You are wintering in Caldaquès, *Mademoiselle?*" He addressed Marie-Claire as he bent over the table, and brown eyes looked into brown eyes.

Marie-Claire blushed. She had never met this boy before in her life. She lowered her eyes and stared into her cup.

"You might put it that way," answered Colette.

"This weather is not as usual. I heard my grandmother say the angels must be shaking out their feather pillows."

At this Marie-Claire could not suppress a smile. She picked up her spoon and stirred and stirred the chocolate. He meant well, that country boy, just being friendly. . . . When she looked up, he was pressing his nose against the windowpane, staring at the frosted moldings above the arcade columns. They were icings on an elaborate wedding cake.

"Claire, listen to me," said Colette. "I wish I could have seen Jean-Paul before he enlisted, before we moved to the other ends of the earth." She leaned forward toward her sister, and Marie-Claire could not stand the unhappiness in her eyes.

In Randonette Marie-Claire had been jealous of the handsome young man's attentions to her sister. Nobly she had tucked that feeling into the recesses of her heart, although it had a way of creeping out occasionally. But now she was angry with him for making Colette suffer so. "He was too young to enlist," she retorted now. "He should have completed his studies first."

"Is this the consolation you offer me?" asked a wounded Colette. Her voice was low and tired, like an old woman's.

"Oh, blast it. I didn't mean to sound so callous." Marie-Claire draped her silk scarf over her shoulders.

"Have you forgotten what he said about the nobility being the first to come to the aid of their country?" Colette retorted. "Father admires him all the more for it."

Marie-Claire decided to change the subject. "Want to know a secret, Col? Mr. Dreyfuss is Jewish. He moved here at the time of the Munich Agreement."

"Jewish? And a Latin scholar?"

"He rattles off Latin like any priest on Sunday, and he translates famous art books. He might teach me some German poetry, too."

"German might come in useful someday, but poetry?"

"Don't turn up your nose at it, Col."

"Claire, the age of romanticism is past. This is the twentieth century, remember?"

"I don't understand you sometimes. I thought all people in love usually turned to poetry to express their feelings."

"Poetry expresses another person's feelings, and Jean-Paul and I have not had the time to indulge in that luxury," said Colette. She snapped her fingers and the café boy came running. "Check, please."

Marie-Claire dropped an extra twenty-five centimes

into the saucer after Colette had paid him. The boy bobbed his curly head. He opened the door for them on their way out and wiped off their damp bicycle seats.

They pedaled through empty streets, their tires defiling the powdery snow. In front of the cathedral, however, were several women clustered under umbrellas. *Are the women going to church because they consider the weather some kind of omen?* Marie-Claire wondered. *Come on,* she chided herself, *they are simply devout Christians going to Benediction, and I had better remember the prayer about the devout nations not being overwhelmed by any peril.* The Lord was not helping matters, though, by imposing such inclemency. Besides, her stomach ached.

The square of the covered market now loomed before her, wooden stalls appearing like objects in an obstacle race. She gritted her teeth. *Cross that field and you will be home free,* she told herself. *Mon Repos is just around the corner.*

Marie-Claire shoved her bicycle under the porch steps and fled upstairs to the bedroom. At the open door she paused. The white-washed walls and bare windowpanes were blocks of ice pressing in on her, and she longed for the coziness of her own bedroom in Paris—all pink and beige and frilly curtains. When would this exodus be over?

She filled the wash basin with hot water and soaked her hands and arms. When she happened to glance out the window she noticed the snow had ceased and over the roof tops the sky streaked lemony yellow. Not warmth enough to repair her spirits, which today were seesawing madly between elation and despair; she had never experienced the like of this before.

When she had dried her hands and arms, she dragged Colette's comforter off her bed, cocooned herself in it, then flicked back the corner of her own quilt and tumbled onto her bed. She dragged the quilt up over her.

Now she could commiserate with her stomach's upheaval. "Belly of woman," Rosine had said. That sounded like something out of the Bible. Like "Fruit of your entrails" . . . or "The paps that gave thee suck." She was now part of the long-suffering sisterhood that stretched from Eve and the stain of original sin. . . . Original sin—well, thank goodness it made Eve cover herself. How chilly it would have been running around in one's birthday suit all the time.

Colette had assured her she would get used to this monthly discomfort: all part of growing up, like brassieres, silk stockings for special occasions, and later on girdles, perhaps.

She yawned, then stretched her legs, luxuriating in the comforters' downy warmth. She was about to close her eyes when, through the floorboards, she detected radio vibrations.

Father must have turned on the evening news.

# 25

"Well," said Victor, as he folded the newspaper, "it's just what they announced yesterday on the news: we're getting food cards. Starting April 1, we'll have to cut coupons for sugar, noodles, rice, margarine, even laundry soap, with separate tickets for gasoline. I say it's not too early for the government to be taking austerity measures. Daladier and his cronies have been acting like the cricket in the La Fontaine fable: singing in times of plenty, with no regard for the morrow."

Rosine shuffled into the dining room, as if on cue. "Drink up that good *café-au-lait, Mesdemoiselles*, you heard what your father said. My aunt told me we'll probably get roast barley from now on. That's what she drank in '14. Madame will be glad to know I have already taken my precautions. Yesterday I went from Laperousse to Echeverria and bought eight packages of coffee, sugar, flour, rice, and noodles." She ticked them off on her fingers. "We could store all this in the closet under the stairs. There are no mice."

"I should hope not," said Susan.

"Since butcher shops will be closing down three times a week, my cousin is bringing us hams. We could hang them in the basement. Oh yes, also ducks. I shall make *confits de canard*."

"How about duck liver pâté?" asked Victor.

"Monsieur, that is the food of archangels." Rosine patted her stomach, "so delicate, and I have not the recipe. *Confits* I can store in crockery pots in the kitchen. They should last, if the weather remains cool, till Corpus Christi."

Susan lowered her eyes, but not before Marie-Claire caught the look of dismay on her mother's face.

Rosine puffed out her chest, like a strutting turkey. "I think of everything, Madame, *n'est-ce pas?* Coffee, sugar, flour, rice, noodles." She ticked off the items again on her thick, spread fingers. "And soap for the wash, of course."

"Before spending money right and left, Rosine, you should consult madame," scolded Victor.

"Yes, Monsieur."

"Not that we don't appreciate what you are doing for

us." Then his brows contracted and he wagged a finger at her. "Everything except the way you polish the crystal. Don't you ever let madame catch you gathering horse dung again. In the city we have commercial ammonia."

Rosine giggled. "No, Monsieur, word of honor . . . But it did put rainbows in those little glass prisms."

"Disgusting!" exclaimed Susan in English.

"Rest assured, Madame, I shall follow monsieur's instructions," said Rosine with great dignity.

She shuffled back to the kitchen, the heels of her felt slippers slapping the tile. Bang, bang, bang went the kitchen cabinet doors, and Colette kept her hand cupped over her mouth to keep from giggling.

"I don't know how much more of this I can take," Susan admitted.

"Oh, she's just a peasant—a simple soul." Victor waved his hand. "She means well and she admires you, I know that. She has been bragging to all the other maids about her pretty, *English* lady piano player." He chuckled at the various misnomers. "And now she is upset you showed no appreciation about the provisions."

"You know why." Susan bit her tongue.

Marie-Claire stared into her coffee cup and kicked her sister under the table, which was a way of signaling her mystification.

"What shall we do with all that food, Victor?" her mother was saying, and her voice was low and sad. "What about tentative plans?"

"Don't worry, *chérie*." Then in a loud voice, for Rosine's benefit, he said, "Before I leave for school I shall go into the kitchen and talk to Rosine."

Suddenly, the cabinet doors stopped slamming.

"Tentative plans, you heard it."

"Yes, but I don't know any more than you do."

Colette strolled onto the balcony into the warm afternoon sun, and leaned on the heavy railing. March winds had turned to breezes and across the street sparrows pecked crumbs off the boardinghouse windowsills. On the boardinghouse wall, trellised wisteria buds swelled to palest lavender.

"Tentative plans—are we moving to America?" Colette asked the puffy clouds. But Marie-Claire saw only Juliette looking for Romeo who, far away to the north, encased in scratchy, woolen armor, was grooming his steed for battle. The soft, green tendril of a rose vine entwined itself around a balcony post. Soon the whole balcony would become a fragrant bower—the perfect trysting place. . . .

"Stop daydreaming, Claire. Why don't you say something?" Colette had eyes behind her back. "Have you noticed any letters from America lately?"

"Why me, especially?"

"You usually know what's going on, Claire. Aunt Renée thought you had a sixth sense."

"No, I don't!"

"You thought letters from America upset Mother," Colette continued.

"That was in Randonette."

Colette turned to face her sister. "Maybe the situation has not changed. Father could still be playing around, you know. Adults are guilty of such things. He wouldn't be the first—"

"How can you say that?" Marie-Claire cringed before the cynical look in Colette's eyes. She wore her hair in snoods now to match her dresses and looked like a maiden in a medieval tapestry about to challenge the unicorn. This was a style Marie-Claire, with her large nose, could never emulate.

"Father thinks Mother is the prettiest lady in the world," declared Marie-Claire, "and you heard what was in the suicide note."

"Rather ambiguous, if you ask me."

"Well, I know Father is innocent of any wrongdoing. I know the letters from America have nothing at all to do with what happened in Randonette."

But Marie-Claire went downstairs anyway to wait for the postman to appear.

Susan was standing outside the gate when the postman unstrapped his leather pouch and handed her a packet of mail.

"This one is for your sister," said Susan to Marie-Claire.

Marie-Claire took the stampless, yellow envelope postmarked *aux armées;* on the left side Jean-Paul had inscribed his name and rank. How many times she had seen Colette tearing open similar envelopes. There was no way of knowing where he was stationed, of course. On the back of the envelope the local post office had stamped, twice: CALDAQUÈS CURES ALL RHEUMATISM—a desecration. What crude employee had dared do such a thing?

Marie-Claire ran upstairs, but when she reached the landing, she slipped behind the bathroom door and waited for her mother to appear. She knew she would. There had been a letter from America in the packet; red, white, and blue stripes on the envelope had given it away. Through the crack in the door she observed her mother's flushed face as she passed by on the way to her room.

Marie-Claire then removed her shoes and tiptoed into the corridor—as if all the world knew she had been spying, instead of merely relieving herself—intent on delivering Jean-Paul's letter to Colette. All alone in her room, her mother was sobbing.

*Oh God, what should I do?* Marie-Claire asked herself silently, standing there holding her shoes. She had caught a flushed look and wrinkled brow on a face that was normally as smooth as a lily, and now she felt like a thief.

*Mother is a cupboard expressionist,* she reminded herself, *a cupboard expressionist.* But she had never heard her mother cry before and the sound frightened her.

*Oh, would that I could go in there and put my arms about her, and press my cheek to hers and ask, "Mother, what is bothering you?"* Marie-Claire prayed for assistance. *Oh, if only there wasn't that great distance between us.* For one crazy moment Marie-Claire wished their roles had been reversed, that she could have been the mother of the sobbing child; she would never have allowed her to cry her heart out that way.

She took three steps in the direction of her mother's room. Again, she stopped, overwhelmed by timidity and awe. She couldn't go in there barefoot. Only gypsy girls walked around barefoot. So she sat down and slipped on her red espadrilles. The sobbing ceased, just as suddenly as it had begun.

She picked up the letter and walked into her own room. Colette was sitting cross-legged on her bed. "Well, it's about time," she said.

"I'll turn my head to the wall while you read it," said Marie-Claire, settling into the cane chair. She had to have time to collect her thoughts.

The bed springs groaned. Colette had jumped down. "Jean-Paul is coming to Caldaquès!" she shouted. "He will either come here, or I'll meet him in Paris at Pentecost."

Marie-Claire's insides turned over. She looked for solace on her mind's poetry shelf.

How do I love thee? Let me count the ways.
I love thee to the depth and breadth and height
My soul can reach . . .

She heaved an internal sigh. Spouting all this poetry was mere rote comfort, empty inspiration.

Colette danced around the room, waving the letter like a flag.

"What's this?" Colette was leaning against the basin now. "Listen, Claire, he wants us to be godmothers to an orphan soldier who's so poor his socks are full of holes and he has to beg cigarettes off the other men. His name is Badin, but behind his back the men call him Boudin, because he has black teeth—as black as blood sausage, poor thing. And he never gets any mail."

"What did he do before he was drafted?" asked Marie-Claire, clinging to a shred of hope that this ugly man might at least be a poet or an artist.

"He was a blacksmith from Normandy," replied Colette.

"What does a godmother have to do?"

"Write letters, send socks, cigarettes."

"I see. . . . " Marie-Claire consulted her watch. "I've got to get over to Latin."

"It's Saint Eustache's Day," Colette said.

"I know."

"You must have a crush on Mr. Dreyfuss."

"Col, he's an old man! I just think he is very interesting. He wants me to come today because he has to go to Bordeaux next week to see his editor." Marie-Claire packed her briefcase and poked her head into the hall.

Mercifully the door to her parents' room was open, the room empty. From the kitchen arose the melody of a popular song, in Rosine's gusty falsetto: *"La mer"*—Rosine scrambled for the high note and Marie-Claire winced—*"a perdu mon coeur pour la vi-e."*

"The sea has stolen my heart for life" went the words of the song. Marie-Claire sighed. Here they were wintering in the country of the Andes, like Caesar's soldiers before them, and she was yet to see the ocean.

*Buck up old girl. At least you had the good sense not to ruin Colette's happy moments. You didn't tell her about the letter from America, thank goodness.*

# *26*

"Do you like blood sausage?" Marie-Claire asked Dreyfuss.

"It all depends on how it is made."

She nodded her head in agreement.

"I don't like the kind you usually get in the shops," he said, "and prefer to make my own sausage meat and put in my own spices—" He turned abruptly towards her. "Why this sudden interest in sausage making, Marie-Claire?"

She told him of Jean-Paul's letter and he listened attentively, puffing on his pipe. Today he wore a dark polo shirt that covered his stringy neck and made him robustly younger.

"I also received something in the post today," he said.

"When I opened the package, my first impulse was to throw it in the dustbin, but here it is." He picked up a little red book off the fireside table and when he turned around his face was grim. "This is what the Nazis are exploding all over Alsatian fields—in wooden bombs; disgusting propaganda. Just because we Alsatians look Germanic and speak gutturally like the people on the other side of the Rhine the Nazis think they can play on our emotions." He flushed slowly, to the tips of his angular, scrawny ears, which on that bony skull usually looked like superfluous appendages. But today he was all warm flesh and blood. "They forget we have been French since the seventeenth century, and that the 'Marseillaise' was composed in Strasbourg for the Army of the Rhine."

Marie-Claire stood beside him as he turned the booklet's pages, revealing neat charts for the production of raw materials: the annual production of wheat and coal in France and Great Britain as compared to the Reich. The Reich produced more than the sum of the two western nations. And so it went for iron ore, steel, and chemicals.

"When it comes to steel and chemicals, they may be approaching the truth," said Dreyfuss, "and you know why, Marie-Claire? When Hitler took over Czechoslovakia, he acquired the most prosperous industrial nation in Central Europe, a nation famous for its manufacture of armaments and heavy machinery. However, these impressive little charts do not overwhelm me, and as for the pictures," he snapped the book shut, "so much for them."

"Oh, please," said Marie-Claire, "just let me have a peep."

He dropped the booklet on the table and fumbled in his pocket for his tobacco pouch; after he lit the pipe bowl, he removed the stem from his lips and wiped his mouth.

Marie-Claire could taste his bitterness, but she couldn't resist picking up the booklet.

Here were the same, neatly groomed little boys in shorts and knee socks she remembered from the bulletin board at Saint Ethelred's and big banners—bigger than those used in Corpus Christi processions.

"I think I know what *guter Vater* means," she said as she gazed at photographs of a little, uniformed man kissing babies and receiving bouquets from young girls in dirndl skirts. She continued to flip the pages. Now the little man was facing a sea of outstretched hands and adoring faces.

"Good father." Dreyfuss snorted with indignation. "Good father, who expands his family's living space by trampling the bodies of his neighbors and exterminating all non-Aryans—including those children of his own countrymen who happen to not be Christians—on his way to world domination." Dreyfuss puffed so hard on his pipe in the emotion of the moment that he choked, and Marie-Claire wondered whether she should pat him on the back. But she dared not. Dreyfuss inspired more awe than affection in her.

"Could you see Hitler writing the *Commentaries?*" he asked when he had recovered. "Trying to get into the mind of his opponents and making such a statement as this: '. . . all men are naturally bent on liberty and hate the state of slavery.'

"Let this booklet be a lesson in philosophy as well, Marie-Claire, for you who have never come in contact with victims of Nazi wiles, and, with your British convent upbringing, have no idea what it is to be totally without ethics."

So her father had not told him about Franz. Dreyfuss knew nothing about the little boy whose father was assassinated by the Nazis in his own country. She decided to keep this knowledge to herself and walked deliberately toward the card table and opened her books. "I would also like to study German," she said.

"The grammar is not easy."

"No matter," she said.

"I'm going to study German, Col."

"Good, Claire. Did you know Mother wasn't feeling well?"

"Well, not really."

"All right, Claire, what do you know this time?"

"There was a letter from America this morning."

"And you waited till evening to tell me?"

Marie-Claire shifted her weight from foot to foot. "It was such a beautiful day I didn't want to ruin it for you."

"Well, it's ruined now."

"What do you mean, Col?"

"I was downstairs in the smoking room writing a letter and Mother and Father were upstairs in their room when suddenly Father yelled, 'I shall not abandon my motherland in time of crisis. Where is honor?'

"Rosine scurried around the hall with her apron up over her ears and finally ran downstairs to the basement, like a mouse running into its hole. Then Father came charging downstairs. He didn't even notice me he was so mad. He grabbed his walking stick and pretended to parry an imaginary foe. Then he hooked his hat with the end of the stick and plopped it onto his head. 'I'm going for a walk,' he said."

"I think I hear him now," said Marie-Claire, as the garden gate squeaked on its hinges.

"Well," said Colette, "I'm going into the kitchen to prepare a tray for Mother."

"Where's Rosine?"

"She left early today. I suppose she couldn't take it." Colette tucked a golden wisp of hair into her blue hair net. Snoods made her look awfully pompous; she was taking on airs like a film star, carrying her head high on the end of her long neck. "Good luck," she said as she pushed open the kitchen door.

Marie-Claire posted herself near the archway. That way she would have to fight the lion; there would be no escape into the catacombs.

When Victor entered, rosy from his walk, he pecked her on the cheek as if he had just returned from a day at school. "Did you have a good Latin session?" he asked.

"Yes, Father." She dared not tell him yet she was about to study German, too.

"We'll have to write your uncle and tell him what good progress you are making."

He hung up his walking stick and hat and smoothed his hair. Silver streaks accentuated a perfect widow's peak. Her father, unlike most men, only used a dab of brilliantine to groom himself. Growing from a center part, those luxuriant waves of his settled into place of their own accord.

"Jean went to the seaside today," he said. He scratched the back of his head, as he usually did when pondering, and Marie-Claire listened respectfully, waiting for him to tell her something of import. When he let his arm fall, she sensed he was withholding information. But it had nothing to do with her mother; she was as certain of that as she was that the tie Victor was wearing today was maroon with grey stripes.

She followed him into the dining room. "Spring has come early this year," he said at last. "Yes, the cherry trees will soon be blooming."

# 27

The Phantom War became a reality again even before the cherry trees bloomed. In one day the Nazis acquired Denmark. They were in Norway before nightfall.

"April ninth, Saint Mary of Egypt, another day that will go down in infamy," said Victor. "Do you realize it is six months since they invaded Poland? The weather was pleasant then all over the world. But April. In the north, especially . . . I don't understand it. Why, in Randonette the cattle are still in their stalls, Maurice tells me. There isn't a leaf on the bushes or any fresh grass worth chewing."

Marie-Claire could see Uncle Mo spending all his free time in the parlor, among archeological papers and books, his long nose quivering with delight over the prospects of uncovering his villa's household gods some day.

In Caldaquès the old men were out bowling in the park, rolling metallic balls from circles they had scratched in the dirt. No concerts for the duration. Still, the men were painting the sides of the octagonal bandstand so it gleamed like a wedding cake. They fed the pigeons. They fought old battles. They walked around the arena, testing closed doors with their cane tips. Spring had come early, as always. It took cinema newsreels to jerk everyone back to the larger reality.

Peeking between high-crowned hats during a Sunday matinee, Colette and Marie-Claire watched grim German soldiers riding open boxcars on mountainsides blanketed with snow, stolid black firs bristling in the background.

In those black forests Norwegians could hide out and harass the enemy, although on the first day of the Scandinavian invasion the enemy had already secured the principal ports and cities in the south and west.

Elbowing her way through the silent crowd after the show was over, Colette asked Marie-Claire, "Do you realize Pentecost is less than a month away?" She looked as grim as those soldiers, despite the fact she was not carrying a gun. "Most probably all leaves will be canceled, shortened at the very best. I must go to Paris soon."

"How?" Marie-Claire asked.

"By train, of course," Colette replied.

"Where would you stay?"

"At Aunt Monique's, now that François has been drafted."

"Col, you can't travel alone," Marie-Claire protested.

"I'll appeal to Father."

Colette had decided to appeal to her father's patriotism. Naturally that was something everyone could count on. But what would her mother think of a trip like that?

"No problem," Colette told Marie-Claire later, feeling mighty pleased with herself. "Father and I are leaving the first week in May."

*When the chestnuts and the lilacs bloom,* thought Marie-Claire, *and the tulips on the Rond Point are a riot of orange and yellow; the fishermen are lined up on the banks of the Seine; the lovers stroll under the trees in the Bois; and that waffle-maker's sweet dough can be smelled a kilometer away. . . .*

To placate Marie-Claire, Susan and Victor decided to spend part of the family's gasoline allotment on a landscape painting trip, now that the cherry blossoms had exploded.

Colette and Marie-Claire carried the easels, the canvases, the palettes, knives, brushes, rags, turpentine tins with little handles that could be attached to the easels, and the large, wooden box that contained the tubes of paint. Rosine scurried out with the loaded picnic basket. "What a beautiful day," she sighed, "a day to drive the sheep into the hills."

Colette ran back into the house and returned with a thick book under her arm. "While Father and Marie-Claire analyze the scenery, I'm going to start on *Autant en Emporte le Vent*."

"I wish it were in the original," said Susan. "Somehow I can't visualize a colored mammy speaking French. But you can't find *Gone with the Wind* in Caldaquès."

"Perhaps we could get it in Paris for you, *chérie*," suggested Victor. "All aboard. We want to work while the light is right."

They drove south into the foothills of the Pyrenees, where amid many small vineyards a cherry tree blossomed—a glorious, white standard above the tender green of the vines. There, near a lonely farmhouse in an empty pasture, Victor and Marie-Claire set up their easels and arranged their palettes, from warmest reds to coolest blues.

Marie-Claire stood behind the master, where she could observe his deft strokes. Still lifes of flowers she had attempted at home in Paris, but never before had she been confronted with living nature.

Victor selected a brush from between clenched teeth and sketched the overall design with thin blue pigment. The sky and the earth became one, like a tapestry, and the marvelous white cherry blossoms were lost.

"Give a lot of thought to where you will place that cherry tree," said Victor, "and sketch only the trunk and branches now. Look for the skeleton under all that froth.

Just like painting a portrait; you look first for the thrust of the arm and leg through the cloth. There is much you can express in your composition by what elements you choose to emphasize. You cannot possibly include all the eye takes in. Nature is an embarrassment of riches."

Marie-Claire wished she could include somehow the sunshine's warmth, the fragrance of the cherry blossoms, the silkiness of the new grape leaves uncurling over stringed trellises, delicately rubbed by her fingertips.

Deep in the woods a cuckoo called. He should be in the picture, too. The embarassment of riches was overwhelming and the selective process cruel: omitting a feathery bush here, a knotty branch there. By lunchtime Marie-Claire was so exhausted she was ready to curl up on the ground with her head in her arm to block out all shapes and colors. It was all too marvelous. No wonder God had to rest on the seventh day of His creation.

Colette and her mother spread the red-checkered cloth on the grass under overhanging branches, snowy white. "Looking at this pastoral scene, it is hard to believe there is a war on," said Susan, "and we seem to be light years away from frigid Norway."

"Yes, and there are not many cars on the road to Spain. But who wants to go to war-ravaged Spain?" said Victor.

Colette bowed her head.

Marie-Claire sensed that despite this beautiful day her sister was on the verge of tears. Colette had to read a war novel to exacerbate her own feelings of separation. *Is that the real condition of being in love?* Marie-Claire wondered.

They feasted on ham cured by Rosine's cousin and served on crusty bread, warm from a village bakery; buttery paté; plump, fresh white asparagus, succulent in vinaigrette; four varieties of cheeses; and for dessert, tiny, fragrant *fraises des bois*, nestled in violet leaves that Colette had picked in the woods. Victor insisted they accompany the meal with rosé wine.

"My beautiful ladies, how can I thank you enough." He looked straight at Susan and Colette as he raised his pink glass. "To the glory of France and to eternal spring."

They drank accordingly, then basked in the warmth of satisfied stomachs. Victor filled his glass again and downed the contents rapidly. He twisted the cork into the neck of the bottle. "Up, up, Marie-Claire. Back to work," he urged.

*When one is not beautiful, one must learn to paint beauty*, thought Marie-Claire, with more than a twinge of envy. She rubbed her bare arms. "Don't look around, Father, but I think we have visitors," she said.

"Caterpillars and ants, you mean," laughed Victor.

"Two old people. I wonder what they want."

"Just curious, I suppose," said Victor as he struggled to his feet. "When was the last time they met crazy artists?" He placed an arm around Marie-Claire's waist. "Smile, *chérie*," he whispered, "some day you will be a very attractive girl, but you must learn to smile."

Together Victor and Marie-Claire greeted the old couple—a farmer and his wife, as wrinkled as dried prunes.

"You are making the photo of the vine?" ventured the old man.

Victor nodded.

"My Julot planted it."

"Ahhh, very neat work."

"Yes, monsieur, *qui sait quand reviendra*." Husband and wife touched shoulders.

"*Qui sait quand reviendra*," Who knows when [he] will return. Marie-Claire recognized the peasant's words as a line from an old folksong, a mocking song about Marlborough, the proverbial English enemy, going off to war.

"Julot is your son, grandson?" Victor queried.

"Grandson," muttered the old man between toothless gums, "the only one."

"The only one." The old woman spoke up for the first time. Her head shook. Then she began to tremble all over. She trembled so, she had to cross her arms to contain her fluttering hands.

"Let's go, Mother." Gently the farmer turned his wife away from prying eyes.

*She looks older than he does,* thought Marie-Claire, although she realized "mother" was just a term of affection.

"Adieu." The old man respectfully bowed his head.

"Till in heaven we meet," Victor replied.

Colette came up behind her sister. "I don't see how she can walk at all," she whispered, as they watched the old couple make their way slowly, painfully, back to the farmhouse.

"Adieu," called Marie-Claire. She wanted to say more, but the words stuck in her throat.

She trudged to her easel, shivering despite the warm sun, and furiously applied gobs of white paint to the skeleton of the cherry tree. Sparkling white blossoms smothered the branches—a celebration of life. She wanted to forget about the darn war, which interrupted every pleasure, which affected everyone's existence, which poisoned relationships . . . Dab, dab, dab; brush paint was so thin. She took the palette knife and smacked the paint on.

"*Eh là*, Marie-Claire," cautioned Victor, "stop for a moment. Take a deep breath. Observe, observe. Painting should be more looking than doing. Before we pack up, I advise you to make a pencil sketch of your composition and note the colors you would use on your painting. Normally, we would return here every day until we were satisfied. But with wartime restrictions we are denied that luxury."

The evening was as bright as the day had been, the sky speckled with stars, and the moon so full you could read a book outdoors. Colette and Marie-Claire sat on their balcony, an eiderdown quilt about their shoulders, content to respect each other's private thoughts.

Suddenly a siren blasted the evening calm, notes ascending and descending in chilling waves that crashed over the roof tops. Instantly, all over town, the lights were extinguished, like candles snuffed out on a birthday cake.

"The masks." Colette dashed to the armoire.

"Listen to the cats," said Marie-Claire, "darting into the bushes as if the devil were after them."

"Where's your mask, Mother?" Colette asked.

Draped in a loose, blue robe, Susan stood in the doorway, like a pale madonna in a ray of moonlight. She was speechless—from terror or surprise, the girls could not tell.

"To the cellar," boomed Victor, a regal figure in his maroon silk robe. But the gas masks dangled from his wrist like heads of futuristic monsters.

"I'll run the water in the bathtub," said Colette on the way down. "We must have a supply of clean water."

"No, I shall," insisted Victor. "You ladies go on down to the larder." The larder was in the cellar, near the wine racks.

The siren had ceased howling and the neighborhood was unearthly still, flooded in moonlight. Through the cellar window the cherry tree in the garden appeared ghostly white. The Lavalettes huddled under the cellar steps, straining their ears, waiting for the explosion that would shatter the quiet.

When the All Clear sounded its long, insistent note, Victor exclaimed, "God be praised! It must have been a false alarm, or perhaps the prefect was testing all citizens." He hugged the girls. "To bed now, you moonstruck damsels."

Marie-Claire and Colette departed like horses at the gate. They closed their shutters, slicing the moonlight into pale strips, then jumped underneath the covers and lay staring at the ceiling. "My God," Colette exclaimed, "I didn't realize until now how frightened I was."

"I was petrified," admitted Marie-Claire. "This wasn't Saint Ethelred's; this was the real thing. Col, when you go to Paris, don't forget Teddy Bear. You are going to the house, aren't you? Aren't you, Col?"

But Colette had already fallen asleep.

*The Numbered Days*

# 28

The birds woke Marie-Claire, squabbling over the rose pods on the balcony railing. The whole house was sheathed in blooms and Colette wasn't even there to experiment with the rose beauty creams they had read about in the magazines.

No need to consult the clock. Now that she was awake she could hear the silver peals of the Angelus behind all that squawking. "Squawk, squawk." Would they ever stop? In a fit of anger she unlatched the heavy shutters and slammed them against the house. There was a sudden whirring of wings, and off they flew. Good riddance!

With Colette and her father gone, every awakening brought fresh loneliness. Marie-Claire took Colette's letter out from under the pillow and reread it.

Paris,<br>Monday, May 6, 1940

Dear Claire,

You should be glad you didn't have to ride the train to Paris with us. I had to sit with my knees twisted the whole way because the man across from me was so huge his feet touched the bottom of my seat. And that night he snored. Father prodded him, but it was like prodding an elephant. I don't think he had any feeling in those big legs of his. The coach was lit by a tiny purple light, hardly bigger than the tip of a lighted cigarette.

Wartime safety measures. When I finally dozed off, I dreamed I was being chased by the giant down the beanstalk.

I forgot how chilly Paris can be in May, especially coming from Caldaquès. Aunt Monique made Father pay for the gas meter when I took a hot bath. Of course, she grumbled at having to remove all that storage from the tub. You know, those hatboxes, camp stools, Grand-mère's shawls, et cetera. She hasn't changed. She's still just as stingy as ever. I don't think anybody in that family takes a bath more than once a month. Was Didi jealous when I got to take one right away. Sponge baths aren't much fun, as you and I both know from Saint Ethelred's. Besides, Didi is quite statuesque now.

Not much news from François. He's in the artillery.

The chestnut trees are blooming and the lilacs. But Paris is so dim at night. They've painted most street lights blue. Car headlights are also blue. The shop windows are taped, and you should see some of them. There are whole scenes made with tape: sailboats riding on waves, birds flying, palm trees—lots and lots of those.

There aren't many buses running. When we went to Notre Dame yesterday, Father and I had to take the métro and walk the rest of the way.

Jean-Paul stayed with a cousin on the Rue de l'Université. He had only three days' leave and went back to his regiment this morning. I'll tell you more when I get back.

Father and I are at the house sorting things. (We have not forgotten your old teddy bear.) Guess where I am sitting right now? At the Louis desk. I've been looking over our stamp albums. I can't bring those back, of course, they're too heavy.

Aunt Monique says that when you live in a house you accumulate too much rubbish, and we should live in an appartment, like she does. But I don't like staying on the top floor. During dinner last night, we could hear antiaircraft cannons booming in the distance. Then two policemen from Civil Defence came upstairs and fined Uncle Georges fifty francs for not properly covering his windows. Aunt Monique was furious. "We are not in mourning," she said. "Do you expect me to go to the undertakers and get black and white curtains with our initials on them?" Uncle Georges got red in the face. You could tell he was afraid they would be fined a hundred francs. Didi sat very straight, batting her eyelashes. Jean-Paul kicked me under the table. "Gentlemen," he said, "couldn't you be a little more lenient in honor of this happy occasion?" "What? what?" blustered Uncle Georges, and Jean-Paul winked at him. Didi blushed and tried to suppress a giggle. I know the officials saw that, but they reduced the fine to twenty-five francs anyway and wished us a good evening.

Everybody, including Didi, sends their love.

Hugs and kisses,<br>Col

Three days leave, how many hours did that make? Seventy-two, an enormity of time. In three days Colette could have gotten married and no one would know until she confided in her sister one morning that she was going to have a baby. Hadn't Colette asked her not to tell anyone about the scene in the barn eons ago?

Marie-Claire stuffed the letter into the envelope and slipped it inside her pillowcase next to the mattress. She flopped down on the bed and closed her eyes. Never before had Colette and she been so far apart. Infirmary stays at Saint Ethelred's were only an arch and a turret away, a walk along the cabbage patch.

Cabbage patch, ugh. She chased that image out of her mind and concentrated on her room in Paris: the walnut armoire with carved, stemmed roses; the dressing table on which Colette's and her silver brushes rested; the pink muslin curtains at the window and matching pink bedspreads; Teddy Bear on the pillow; and the enameled music box on the night table. "Lullaby and goodnight" . . .

The yearning for her childhood home filled Marie-

Claire so she felt she was drowning in a pool of nostalgia. She sprang out of bed and reached under it for her violin case. Balls of fluff scooted like dandelion clocks, and she rocked backward onto her heels to contain a sneeze. *Someone should tell Rosine to sweep under there,* she thought. The next sneeze sent her running to the armoire for a handkerchief.

The armoire shelves were half bare, as if the wind had blown jumbles of petticoats, panties, blouses, and hose to one side, exposing scratched wood on the rod next to the three spring dresses her mother had had made for Easter and Pentecost.

Marie-Claire glimpsed herself in the mirrored door: bushy eyebrows and a long, red nose. When would her mother allow her to pluck those brows? But her pajama top revealed peaks and valleys. Proudly she stuck out her chest and pushed in her shoulder blades. She turned to check her profile, admired her pointed breasts, and sighed. *Back to the violin, little one; music will surely bring consolation.*

Closing the window, she considered applying a mute to the strings. No. Thin, wispy notes did not a choir make, and today she would sing out her feelings. Marie-Claire fanned her music sheets on the bed and chose Kreisler's "Liebesleid." Love's sorrow suited her mood. "Don't slide in staccato," Sister Teresa had written at the top of the page. "Keep it crisp. In Vienna even love's sorrow is treated lightly, always elegantly."

Violin tucked under her chin, Marie-Claire limbered her fingers on the board, then she raised her bow and drew out the beautiful sounds, swaying with the emotion of them, accentuating the notes in the slower, more nostalgic sections where it seemed to her the composer did revel a little in his sorrow. Why else would he repeat the phrase? Sister Teresa had missed the point. But the trill at the finale dwindled to the softest of sighs, ending in a light, high-note flourish, as if a nightingale had completed his song and flown away.

"Bravo, *Mademoiselle*, very pretty." Rosine's brassy voice cut through the melody. "If you don't mind my asking, what made you get up before the chickens?"

Marie-Claire pursed her lips.

"Aha! I see it's none of my business; none of fat old Rosine's business, eh?" Rosine cocked her head.

Marie-Claire nodded.

"Oh, *Mademoiselle*, I wish you would play that part again that goes da-deda-deda-da-dada a little faster this time. I want something I can stamp my foot to."

Marie-Claire laid the violin gently in its case.

"For Rosine?"

The case snapped shut.

"Very well, then, I shall be downstairs. Your coffee will be ready soon." Rosine shuffled away and down the stairs, her worn slippers slapping against the treads.

Marie-Claire closed the door and opened the window. She brushed her teeth, her loneliness renewed at the sight of the empty glass on the shelf above the basin, the glass a mute testimony to Colette's absence.

When the telephone rang in the downstairs hall, Marie-Claire rushed to open her bedroom door. She heard the clang of the receiver as Rosine clumsily unhooked it, then a loud *"allo, allo, oui?"* Then Rosine shouted from the foot of the staircase, "Madame, come quickly; it's Monsieur Dreyfuss." Marie-Claire smiled. Rosine treated every telephone call as if it were a summons from the firestation.

"Marie-Claire, your coffee is getting cold." Dressed for the day, combed and powdered, her mother presided over the breakfast table in lonely grandeur. They exchanged perfunctory kisses, her mother's smooth cheek like perfumed alabaster.

When Marie-Claire pulled up her chair, her mother said, "The Germans invaded Holland, Belgium, and Luxembourg at three o'clock this morning. That's what Jean called me about. He must have been up all night listening to the BBC."

"Oh no!" exclaimed Marie-Claire.

"He says it sounds like another '14, except for the fact that the Germans did not even bother offering an alternative this time. It is just like the Scandinavian invasion: we're coming in and you had better not stop us." Susan's voice was slow, too controlled, as if she were reciting the facts.

Marie-Claire's stomach tightened and she could hardly swallow her *café-au-lait*. *What if Belgium were still part of Gaul?* she asked herself, as she thought of page one, book I, of the *Commentaries,* which she had been obliged to memorize at the village school.

Gaul is a whole divided into three parts, one of which is
    inhabited by the Belgae . . .

The present situation was serious enough, though.

"Mr. Dreyfuss informed me the people of the Low Countries are neutral—they were neutral during the Great War, too—and they have not consulted with the French and British in case of attack," she told her mother.

"I thought only Victor and Jean discussed military strategy," her mother replied.

"Mr. Dreyfuss is always comparing Caesar and Hitler," said Marie-Claire, "They are both well organized and swift to act; but Caesar was a just man—and a great one," she added.

"Yes," said her mother. Without a clink she placed her cup on its saucer and pushed it aside. Then she crossed her arms on the white tablecloth and said nothing more, she merely stared into a distance that was thousands of miles away.

Marie-Claire lowered her eyes and took small sips of her coffee. Always she felt helpless when confronted by her mother's aloofness. The white polka dots on the dark sleeves remained stationary. Piqué crisp they were, as mother and daughter sat in a charged silence. Even the birds stopped twittering outside the window.

"You know," said her mother at last, "I heard you playing Kreisler this morning."

Marie-Claire put down her cup. "Oh, Mother, I'm sorry if I woke you."

Marie-Claire extended her arm in her eagerness to bridge the distance between them. But even before her mother's hands slid off the table and into her lap, she knew her mother would shrink from her touch.

"You didn't wake me up. I heard the Angelus, but you must consider the neighbors."

"You heard the Angelus? I did, too," Marie-Claire said.

"Wouldn't a prayer have been sufficient?" her mother asked.

"What do you mean?"

"I mean what possessed you to take up your violin at that hour, Marie-Claire?"

"I closed the window," she protested.

"You're not answering my question," Susan said.

Marie-Claire tightened her jaw. How her mother could be so uncaring and exhibit such little understanding was positively beyond her.

"Sometimes I don't understand you, Marie-Claire,"

her mother said. She sighed. She straightened the navy cording on her belt.

Marie-Claire wanted to say, Mother, don't you ever feel like going to the piano instead of crying when you are upset? Didn't you ever worry about your eyebrows when you were growing up? Didn't you ever have foolish impulses, period? But the words stuck in her throat. And in a crinkling of polka dots her mother rose and left the room. The kitchen door swung to. Voices droned from the other room.

Marie-Claire stuffed her clenched fist into her mouth and bit down onto it, leaving red toothmarks. When the telephone rang, she bounded into the hall and picked up the receiver before the kitchen door swung open.

"*Allo, allo, oui?* . . . Oh, Father!"

"Tell your mother we are taking the first available train back," Victor said.

"Yes, yes, the first train." She smiled in the direction of her mother's and Rosine's anxious faces. "It's Father," she told them.

"Sunday is Pentecost you know," Victor continued. "The weather turned unseasonably warm. Some people are already leaving the city for the holiday, and the stations are crowded I understand. The government is asking all citizens to pray to Saint Genevieve and there will be a special Mass Sunday at Notre Dame. People don't pay much attention to the government. Are you there, child?"

Marie-Claire nodded, too full of emotion at the sound of her father's voice to speak.

"Say something, Marie-Claire," her mother called.

"Yes, Father," she blurted.

"I will send a telegram when I have a train schedule. Can you hear me?"

"Father—"

"That's all the time we have, child. The government is limiting civilian phone calls. Kiss your mother for me. Wait, one last thing. I want you to go to the stationer's and buy a large map of France and the Low Countries—a large map. Can you hear me?"

The voice crackled and faded away before she could say, "Yes, Father."

# 29

"This is only the third day of the invasion and already the attacker has all the advantages." Jean Dreyfuss's voice was grim as he faced the Lavalettes in their parlor. Every afternoon now he joined them for the program "Current Events" and the BBC newscast. "Students of the *Commentaries*," he continued, "please take note: what you are challenged with now is another chapter of 'History in the Making.' "

Marie-Claire, unable to sustain the gaze of those eyes, pale as gas flames, stared at the map she had bought, which was affixed to the parlor wall. Britain's profile and torso were chopped off; only an arm and a leg showed as John Bull leapt westward in a huge broad jump. But across the Channel and the North Sea, France and the Low Countries massed in one great lump. Every house in Caldaquès sported such a map.

Marie-Claire had waited till the heat of the afternoon on Friday to ride to the stationer's. There, she had had to inch her way through the press of old men, redolent of garlic and sweat, cigarettes dangling from their mouths. They stood about in groups of threes or fours, nodding over their outstretched maps, flicking ashes off the paper with their yellow thumbs.

"Look at the length of the front," said Dreyfuss. "From the North Sea to the Ardennes in the south; one great vertical, so to speak."

Arms crossed, head high, Victor nodded. He sat between Colette and Marie-Claire on that Pentecost Sunday, just as he had sat in church during the sermon. "Crises make a believer out of me," he had muttered apologetically, and Marie-Claire understood. In town fewer men attended Mass than those who lived in the country.

"It's almost teatime," said Susan. She was leaning against the archway. "Excuse me, Jean, would you please?"

Colette rose, but Susan waved her down again before she rustled across the hall.

"The southernmost point of the German attack is dangerously close to the Maginot Line," said Victor.

"But the Maginot Line is impregnable!" chorused the girls. They were repeating what was common knowledge.

"Here are the German positions." Dreyfuss had payed no attention to their exclamation. He stabbed a line of tiny, black paper flags to the map. "We are going to run out of swastikas at this rate."

"God forbid!" Victor slapped his hands on his knees.

"French and British forces are here," continued Dreyfuss.

"The French flags look like poppies in all that green," remarked Marie-Claire. She was referring to the forested Ardennes region. "But Indutiomarus hid his men from Caesar in there, so it must be quite thick, and there wouldn't be any poppies growing among the trees, of course."

"Living in the past again?" Colette muttered to her sister behind their father's back.

"Indutiomarus concealed only those men who were unfit for military service." Dreyfuss's lips twisted into a semblance of a smile. "Yes, the Ardennes is still forested and mountainous—very rough terrain."

"Pardon, Jean," said Victor, "but this map with which you are instructing and enlightening us on Pentecost Sunday does not convey the whole situation."

"I know what you mean," said the lecturer. Outwardly his pale face remained composed, but the veins about the temples pulsed blue.

*He's like an illustration for physiology in the Larousse dictionary*, thought Marie-Claire, fascinated as always by her Latin tutor's bald head.

"I have not alluded to the enemy's tanks and planes," he now said, "fighter planes screaming death, disgorging troops behind the lines to wreak more havoc." His arms dropped to his sides. "What a depressing way to spend the afternoon of Pentecost, which, for you Christians, is supposed to be a joyful occasion."

"Don't go blaming the Holy Spirit, Jean." Victor wagged a finger at his friend. "Blame the disorganized, spineless and corrupt Republic, whose leaders rotate at the drop of a hat and therefore have little accounting to do to the people. A king has a lifetime to serve his country. Out goes Daladier after two radical years, and in comes Reynaud. Pouf! I am not talking about our military leaders; they proved themselves in '14."

"You cannot fault Minister Reynaud; he is brilliant. This is a war of a different sort."

"That is the truth," said Victor, voicing the opinion of everybody present.

When Susan carried in the tea tray, one pink rose in

a fluted vase standing above the cups, Marie-Claire sighed with relief. What a way to spend a Sunday afternoon: listening to a lecture, instead of going to see the American film, *Stagecoach*, at the Métropole Theatre and also enjoying one of those Eskimo icecreams the ushers sold at intermission.

Gallantly Jean Dreyfuss took the tray from his hostess and placed it on the cobbler's bench, which passed for a low table at *Mon Repos*. "How beautiful," he said, as he fingered a rose petal. "Have you ever seen such delicate color? Madame, it is only excelled by the bloom of your cheeks."

"Bravo, Jean." Victor clapped his hands. "Pure eighteenth century. Ah, a gentleman was truly a gentleman then."

"Lemon or cream, Jean?" asked Susan, after she had poured him a cup of tea.

The following evening, the evening of the fourth day of the invasion, the Lavalettes sat around the dining room table in stunned disbelief. German forces had pushed through the impenetrable Ardennes and captured the French city of Sedan.

"Columns of tanks, such as the world has never seen, are advancing through the countryside," said the BBC commentator.

Without a word, Colette rose and ran out of the room.

"Follow your sister, Marie-Claire," said Victor.

"Yes, go to her." Susan sighed.

"What can I do?" muttered Marie-Claire. She pushed back the heavy ladderback chair and tiptoed across the rug, avoiding the dirty yellow diamonds in the design. *Playing a game of hopscotch*, she caught herself thinking, *without the stone*. Reluctantly, she trudged upstairs.

Colette lay face down on her bed.

"I'll never see him again, never, never," she sobbed. "Do you realize all Jean-Paul's predictions about the French army and its outmoded weapons are coming true? I'll never see him and he didn't tell me what his orders were, so I can't even be with him in spirit on that map of yours."

"Father told me to buy that map," said Marie-Claire, standing helplessly by. Why did she always have to be in the middle? It wasn't fair. She prayed for help to Saint Servais, whose feast day it was. "The thick of the fighting is in Belgium and Holland, Col."

Colette raised her head. "Yes, but French troops are there, and you heard about the capture of Sedan."

Marie-Claire flopped onto her bed and stroked Teddy Bear's tattered ears. "Jean-Paul could still be in the line of defense," she proffered.

Colette sat up and blew her nose. "Oh, I hope so; I do hope and pray so. . . . Don't tell Mother this, but he promised we'd get married right after the war."

"Mother probably suspects that already."

"We're engaged."

"What?" Marie-Claire rubbed the bear's paw over her cheek to conceal her dismay. Speculating about what had gone on in Paris was one thing; hearing the truth was another proposition entirely.

Colette pulled out the gold chain she wore around her neck to reveal a signet ring next to her medals of the Virgin, Guardian Angel, and Saint Christopher. "This is what he gave me. It's been in his family for centuries."

Marie-Claire fingered the dark gold, sharply incised lily. "I thought only kings and top officials wore signet rings," she said.

"Sire Phillipe de Joux did not let that bother him."

"I suppose not," said Marie-Claire, remembering the

story of the hundred horses. She touched the cold metal again. "Why does the lily have four petals?"

"So as not to be a *fleur de lys,* which belonged to the king alone." Colette crossed her legs and placed her hands on her knees. "Sometimes," she mused, "I dream I'm the chatelaine of the castle at Randonette. The roof is covered with shiny, new slate. I'm presiding at a hunt breakfast in the great dining room, surrounded by lackeys with ruffled jabots." She laughed bitterly. "The roof is in danger of caving in, and the windows are stained and cracked. Jean-Paul says that after the war he will tear the place down, if no historical society is interested in restoring it. And why would they be? There are so many castles in France bigger and more important than Chabral, he says, all waiting to be restored."

"What a shame, castles are so romantic!" exclaimed Marie-Claire. "Oh, you shouldn't destroy it. How could anybody in his right mind do such a thing?"

Colette bowed her head.

"I didn't mean to upset you, Col, gosh, darn." Marie-Claire jumped off the bed and kissed her sister's hot, damp cheek. "What we really need to do, I suppose, is pray the Secret from the Mass for Peace." She wondered, though, just what Mother Genevieve would say if she were alive today. Would she have recommended instead the Secret from the Mass in Time of War?

"Get out your poetry book and read me a sonnet, Claire—something tender, beautiful, and loving," said Colette.

On the fifth day of the invasion, Victor stood before the map. "Heaven help us," he said, "the Dutch have surrendered." He ran his fingers through his hair.

"What else could one expect?" Dreyfuss asked, slumped

in his corner seat, "after the Nazis practically bombed Rotterdam off the map?"

"It's a terrible loss of civilian life," said Victor. "And now those Huns have broken through the French lines and are heading westward." Scratch went his hand across the map and Marie-Claire winced. "It's unbelievable."

*Invasion with a capital I*, thought Marie-Claire. Next to her, Colette's body stiffened.

"This map is one giant game of checkers." Victor moved the little flags. "The black men have all the pieces; every time I remove a red one I feel my life's blood draining from me."

"Victor, really, don't be so dramatic," said Susan.

"But, *chérie*, history has never witnessed such happenings; there are no parallels. . . . This is beyond—"

"Then, Victor, the time has come to set our plans in motion."

Marie-Claire turned abruptly toward her mother. It was now or never. "What plans?" she asked. She squeezed her sister's hand.

"Yes, what plans?" asked Colette. "We demand an explanation."

"Well!" Susan exclaimed, and her knuckles were white with rage. "Didn't they teach you girls manners at the convent?"

The words stung like a slap. Marie-Claire stared at her father for assistance.

Victor sighed. Quietly, very gently, he said, "Susan, can't you see the children are upset?"

"Upset? Of course, they're upset. You're upset. I'm upset. We're all upset. All of Europe is upset. If it were not for you, Victor, we could have left the country by now. It isn't as if we were poor refugees with no place to go, God knows. How many times does your father-in-law have to extend an invitation to visit for the duration? (Marie-Claire pressed Colette's foot.) Why don't you place your family's welfare before your damn French pride and come to your senses before it is too late and we are *unable* to leave? I'm sorry, Jean," she said, before she strode out of the room.

Without a word Victor accompanied Dreyfuss to the door.

Marie-Claire escaped to the kitchen, straight into Rosine's welcoming arms.

"*Ma pauvre petite*," murmured Rosine, as she stroked Marie-Claire's head, "there, there. During these times one is not oneself."

"I came for a cup of tea for Colette," said Marie-Claire. She leaned her head against Rosine's ample stomach, soft and warm.

"Kind little girl, always thinking of her sister." Rosine patted her on the back. Then she took a large match out of the china wall box and struck it against the sole of her slipper. She lit the gas burner and put on the kettle. "Let's not forget madame. What I think madame needs is a good cup of camomille infusion. It calms the stomach, which is the seat of the nerves."

"Whatever," said Marie-Claire.

Rosine ran to the door and pushed it open a crack.

"Ah! there goes monsieur upstairs, ruffling his sickles. When the hen is upset, the rooster will not crow." Rosine shook her head. "After I take the tea up to madame, I'm going home. Cousins from the North just arrived—refugees, you know."

Colette sat there, like the last old lady after Mass, lost in her memories.

"Here, Col, drink this." Marie-Claire raised the cup to her sister's lips.

"I can't believe it," muttered Colette between sips, "Mother has gone haywire."

"You can say that again."

"She wants us to run away to America and leave everybody behind."

"Everybody?"

"Uncle Mo, Aunt Monique . . . You know who I mean."

Marie-Claire nodded, but she didn't think Colette cared that much for Aunt Monique.

She didn't much want to leave, either; she certainly didn't want to abandon Uncle Mo and the excavations. The prospect of leaving Europe, which alone existed in the temperate zone, and crossing a huge ocean frightened her. And America was a vast continent lately inhabited by wild Indians.

Colette squirmed. "Close the shutters," she said. She squinted as if blinded by the sun.

Marie-Claire rushed to the windows. Sunset tipped the roses with gold; across the street, the boardinghouse wall gleamed like mother-of-pearl.

"No, wait," said Colette, "closing the shutters might make people think there's a death in the family."

"Yes." Marie-Claire wanted to say, "Why don't you make up your mind." Instead she carried Colette's cup to the kitchen. *Everybody is going haywire,* she thought.

In the kitchen the cellar door was open, and on the floor next to the kitchen counter rested Rosine's wrinkled, cracked oilskin bag. Over it leaned Rosine, bare thighs shining white between ribbed socks and black-skirted rump, and into the bag were disappearing a hunk of meat, potatoes, onions, a half bottle of milk—all from the Lavalette larder.

"*Oh, là,*" Rosine whirled around with one hand over her heart, "you scared me so." She lowered her eyes. "*Mademoiselle* must not think I am a thief. I went downstairs to get provisions for my cousins, the refugees. I will replace everything tomorrow when I go shopping," she said, her hand already on the knob of the door to the garden. "Good night, *Mademoiselle.*"

"Good night."

Marie-Claire sat down at the kitchen table and buried her head in her hands. If she wasn't careful, she would go haywire, too.

# *30*

Carloads of refugees—the lucky ones—started arriving in Caldaquès even before the Belgian surrender, on the twentieth day of the invasion. Mattresses, cupboards, chests of drawers strapped to the roofs of their cars, they coasted in. Resting their bicycles against the curb in the town square, Marie-Claire and Colette observed the dusty vehicles and wondered how their tires could still roll under those monstrous loads.

Men and women on the front seats sat pale and bewildered, as if they had seen ghosts; in the back on top of suitcases next to cages of fluttering canaries, holding startled cats, the children were strangely quiet, blank looks on their little faces.

"They look so sick," said Marie-Claire.

"No wonder. How would you feel if you had been forced to flee your home and your country, too, perhaps?" asked Colette.

*Colette sounds a lot like Mother Eulalia,* Marie-Claire thought to herself, *that day at Convocation, before Franz's arrival.*

"Of course the heat doesn't help matters," Colette added.

Roses bloomed one day and dropped the next. May had become confused with August. Cherries ripened, camomile grew in shaggy rows, squeezing out the other herbs by the kitchen door at *Mon Repos,* and Colette and Marie-Claire picked armfuls of blossoms they planned to boil and use as a rinse to lighten their hair. "I can't use it all for tea," Rosine had said.

Old Jules Peyot sat behind closed shutters all day, so that nobody in the neighborhood knew whether he was dead or alive, except for the Lavalettes, whose dining room window faced his. Every day at thirteen hours, the dining room shutters of the Peyot house opened, and a woman in a straw hat shook out her tablecloth—every last crumb. Then the shutters were fastened again for the next twenty-four hours before anybody could ask, "How goes it, Madame?"

The blind fiddler changed his post to the town square, where refugees dampened their handkerchiefs under the lion-headed spigots to scrub their necks and their children's sticky faces. "The witches' cauldron," Colette and Marie-Claire heard an old man tell his tow-headed grandsons, as they pointed to the bubbling water. He dropped a copper into the beggar's bowl before he marched the little boys back to their car.

*Père* Dumas, who had slipped into retirement before

the outbreak of hostilities, dusted off his trumpet at the insistence of the mayor and resumed his job as town crier, exhorting all Caldaquois, "Come to the aid of your fellow Christians, who have been forced to abandon their domiciles before the enemy advance." These, the girls knew, included Belgians, Dutch, Luxembourgers, as well as the French. Every café owner slipped *Père* Dumas an ounce of wine, so by the end of the day he usually had to be carried home.

The same message was preached from the pulpit on Sunday. "Remember the glorious spirit of '14," thundered Father Tessier, himself a veteran of the Great War. "The spirit, too, of sacrifice, which should dominate the spirit of pleasure," and his fist struck the lectern so that the wooden angels on the canopy above him trembled.

On the previous day almost everyone in Caldaquès had listened to Premier Reynaud's radio speech. The Premier had announced the appointment of Marshal Pétain as Minister of State and Vice-Premier. "The victor of Verdun," said Reynaud, "the man thanks to whom the attackers of 1917 did not pass, thanks to whom the morale of the French army was reaffirmed in 1917 to make victory possible . . . is now at my side . . . putting all his wisdom and strength to the service of his country."

"I do not mean to sound irreverent," Victor had said, "but at eighty-four years of age Marshal Pétain will need superhuman strength. May God grant it to him."

Rosine, standing behind the master's chair, uttered a loud "So be it."

"My cousin brought with her the clock with the golden cherubs across the top," said Rosine, as she skimmed the foam off the boiling veal. "It's part of her dowry. She clutched it to her bosom all the way from Arras, carried it everywhere, even when she had to relieve herself. Ate with it, drank with it, and it ticktocked her to sleep at night. Since then, others have not been so fortunate."

"Why?" asked Marie-Claire.

Rosine pursed her lips. "There are things too horrible to relate to children."

"In times such as these one does not have a right to be a child anymore."

"Wherever did you hear that one, *Mademoiselle?*"

Marie-Claire smiled. "My grandmother told it to Uncle Mo twenty years ago," she said, "during the Great War."

"*Alors,* but we had better sit."

Marie-Claire pulled up a chair to the kitchen table and sat opposite Rosine's weathered arms, which rested on the green oilcloth like red oxen in a shorn pasture.

"The roads up north are crowded, very crowded," said Rosine. "Besides riding in automobiles, there are people pushing carts, wheelbarrows, and baby carriages; some ride bicycles, some motorcycles. The carts are full of household goods. You can get a lot into a cart: vacuum cleaners, sewing machines, fishbowls, rugs, portraits of ancestors. Ha! A lot of good your ancestor does you when you're running for your life. The old people sit on the rugs, holding those pictures like they were solid gold. And, can you believe it, some people just use their legs, carrying their parents on their backs like mules?"

Rosine shook her head. "It is so hot and dry, and a yellow dust covers everything. The cars can do no more than fifteen kilometers an hour, sometimes not even ten. What do I know? I've never driven a horseless carriage."

She sighed as she rose and shuffled to the sink, where she drained the water from the peeled vegetables then added them to the stew.

"Go on," begged Marie-Claire.

"In the country, the cows are lowing, poor things, standing there all alone in the fields with nobody to milk them."

"Nobody at all?"

"No one. Psst, all gone." Rosine's hand flicked the air. "Farmers, cultivators, landowners. What do I know? *Poilus* trudge along the side of the road. One takes pity on the cow's swollen teats. He grabs her by the tail. 'Come here,' he yells to a buddy, and they milk her."

"What were the soldiers doing on the side of the road? Why weren't they in the army?"

"They were running away. God's truth, so help me, miss." Rosine placed a hand on her heart. "This is what I have heard. The *Boches* have so many prisoners they cannot hold them all, so they just take the *poilus'* guns and say 'Scram.' Those poor *poilus* wander off looking for someone to fight, looking for their commanders. But the commanders have flown the coop."

"Is that possible?" asked a horrified Marie-Claire.

"But the worst I have not told to *mademoiselle*."

Marie-Claire turned her head. She did not want Colette to hear any of this. "What is it, Rosine?" she asked at last, satisfied that only the four walls could testify to what horrendous tale Rosine was about to relate.

Rosine leaned forward, then backed away. "No, it is too horrible," she said.

"Oh, please, Rosine," begged Marie-Claire.

"The *Boches* are machine-gunning the refugees on the roads. The sounds of the planes approaching is like distant thunder. People lie in ditches; they flop to the ground anywhere they can. The planes fly so low they can see the pilots grinning. *Pan, pan-pan-pan-pan* . . . Afterward there is smoke and confusion, children cry, and the air smells of burning rubber and singed flesh."

Marie-Claire shivered.

"The refugees bury their own dead—in the fields, with no markers. The mangled ones and the old people who have died of exhaustion or broken hearts . . . no markers, poor souls." Rosine dabbed her eyes with a corner of her apron.

"Don't cry," said Marie-Claire, "those souls are in Heaven now."

"What makes you so sure?"

"They're martyrs." Marie-Claire waited for Rosine to calm down. Then she said, "All refugees are martyrs."

"Oh no, *Mademoiselle*, some are thieves and murderers."

Marie-Claire stared at Rosine in disbelief.

"There are always thieves and murderers who take advantage of severe misfortune," said Rosine, with such assurance there was no questioning her.

# 31

"See what they want," called Susan from the rose garden.

Marie-Claire ran down the steps and pushed open the gate. She stared at the refugee car. The driver's head sunk onto her chest, her face veiled by a fall of dark hair; her arm still signaled—a dead weight of a plump, young arm, hanging out the window.

The woman threw back her head. "Just resting," she said, before Marie-Claire could open her mouth. "I would appreciate a glass of water, though."

Marie-Claire stared at the dark eyes, smudged with fatigue. "Certainly," she said.

"Look at my son." The woman pointed to a small boy huddled against her. She and the boy were the car's only passengers. "His hand is glued to the brake, poor *chéri*. We walked to the garage for my husband's car. I had never driven before. Five minutes' instruction from the garageman is all I got—all we had time for. So I told Jeannot to keep his hand on the brake and never let go. Sometimes he slept. I was not frightened. I knew his hand was still there and Saint Christopher would squeeze it, if necessary."

"I'll get you the water," said Marie-Claire.

When she returned with two full glasses, the woman was combing the child's hair.

"Bless you," she said. "Along the way some have not been so charitable. They charged five francs for a glass of water."

"Water?"

"Yes, plain tap water." She wiped the little boy's mouth. "Now, back to your post," she told him. "Goodbye, and thank you again, *Mademoiselle*. We're going to the hospital. They always need more nurses." A grinding of gears, the car sputtered, and off they drove.

*Plucky woman*, thought Marie-Claire, *I could never be that brave, driving all night and all day, then working with sick people.*

"*Villa Mon Repos?*" asked a bearded tramp, who must have crossed the street when she was talking to the refugee woman.

One look at him and Marie-Claire shrugged her shoulders. His gray eyes had trouble focusing, his face was so thin the sharp diagonals of his cheekbones almost cut through the flesh, and he seemed unsteady on his feet.

"I was looking for a Victor Lavalette," the man said, pronouncing Victor the English way. He rubbed his red stubble.

Marie-Claire hesitated. The man was not all that elderly. What if he were a thief or a murderer?

As if he divined her thoughts, the man gave her his name. "Thomas," he said, again stressing the first syllable of the word, "Thomas Wiggins."

"You are English?"

"No, American." He slurred the *r*.

"Wait here, I'll get Father."

Marie-Claire dashed up the front steps and burst through the door. "An American Thomas to see you, Father," she blurted.

"Why are you the messenger?" Victor was startled. "Why couldn't he inquire for himself this . . . this Thomas?" He grabbed his silver-handled cane. "Just a precaution," he said, "the only Thomas I know is painting in a Parisian garret."

Marie-Claire followed her father at cane's length.

When Victor glimpsed the bearded man leaning on the gate, he held out his arms and ran toward him, crying, "Thomas, ha ha! Oh, Thomas, old boy!" He clapped him on the shoulder.

Thomas's knees buckled.

"Put one hand under his armpit, Marie-Claire, the other around his waist, if you can. Rosine, Rosine!"

But Susan came running.

"Get Rosine, my dear, and fetch the cognac."

"Claire, did you hear that?"

Colette flung herself down on the bed. It was siesta time at *Mon Repos*. "Two hundred kilometers he walked. I'm exhausted just thinking about it."

"Two hundred kilometers," echoed Marie-Claire. "The man was drunk with fatigue."

The mattress creaked as Marie-Claire kicked off her espadrilles. She held her sides. Normally, two hundred kilometers would have been a lot of stitches. But Thomas looked as if he had not had a meal in weeks.

"It goes to show what one can do when one is desperate," said Colette. Miraculously, despite the siege of Dunkirk, she had received a letter from her fiancé and was in much better spirits. "Jean-Paul tells me you wouldn't dream what people will do then: march for hours on an empty stomach, lift a prone horse, sleep on prickly hay all night—"

"Oh yes, I do," said Marie-Claire, who did not want to be reminded of prickly hay—the barn scene at Randonette still burned in her memory.

Marie-Claire stretched her lanky frame and tried to think cool thoughts. But excitement at the day's events had not yet subsided. An American artist was snoring downstairs on the parlor sofa, the courageous Belgae had surrendered, and the Allies were backed against the sea at Dunkirk. On the wall map in the parlor the area surrounding France's northernmost city was a battlefield bristling with flags. Armaggedon, Dreyfuss called it; it made his blood boil, he said.

She closed her eyes and yellow discs swam under her lids, as the sun streamed in through open shutters. Colette insisted on open shutters during the day, despite the heat. "A sign of life," she said, "that all is well in this house."

In his letter Jean-Paul had told Colette that whatever happened in this war, she should maintain a positive attitude; a positive attitude, he said, would act as mental telepathy between the lovers.

Marie-Claire returned to Thomas. "What I don't understand," she said, "is how could anybody be so wicked as to steal his car when he was helping the wounded by the bombed-out bridge."

"Again, desperation."

"It's criminal."

"Yes, now please hush," Colette drawled.

"There are thieves and murderers who take advantage of every calamity," continued Marie-Claire.

"Shut up."

Two minutes later Colette was asleep, a frown puckering her brow, her golden hair spred awry. The Allied forces were backed against the sea at Dunkirk, bridges were being blown up, refugees were collapsing everywhere . . . and Colette slept.

Marie-Claire tiptoed onto the balcony. The sun disappeared between fleecy clouds and a breeze rustled the rose vines. She spread her arms to let the coolness flow around her. Her mousy brown hair streamed like a naiad's. Then an inky cloud covered the sun. A wind blew up, flattening leaves and the ears of a stray terrier pattering along the sidewalk. A weather vane atop a church spire swung crazily. Swirls of dust rose from the gutters and she could taste the grit. A sudden clap of thunder, and Marie-Claire retreated to the threshold.

"What are you doing out there, Claire?" asked a startled Colette.

Lightning zigzagged across the sky, followed by another thunderclap. When the first raindrops pelted the balcony, Marie-Claire held out her palms to feel their sting. A whiff of damp earth from the garden was more refreshing than eau de cologne.

"Get inside and close that window," ordered Colette.

She had no sooner done so when the rain turned to hailstones the size of marbles. They bounced off the balcony railing and ricocheted across the balcony floor. Colette and Marie-Claire pressed their noses against the windowpane.

"Hail in a heatwave!" exclaimed Colette. "I can't believe it; the devil is playing pool out there."

"Another sign," said Marie-Claire, "like the snowfall." *Like the monkey puzzle tree's demise,* she thought. *A bad omen.*

The storm ended as suddenly as it had begun. Clouds floated away. The sun appeared in a wash of blue, melting the hailstones so that only shattered rose petals remained as testimony. Next to a shutter lay a dead sparrow.

In the parlor, Thomas slept on, so the Lavalettes hovered over the radio for the BBC newscast. When the commentator announced the successful evacuation of besieged Allied troops from Dunkirk, Colette listened, transfixed. Marie-Claire thought, *That quirky storm was not such a bad omen after all.*

But Rosine kept shaking her head. "Hail in June, sign of doom," she muttered. "Let's not awaken the redheaded vagrant, who sleeps with closed fists."

"He's no vagrant," protested Marie-Claire, "and June has only just begun."

"June is June," insisted Rosine. "*Pauvre rouquin*, he looks like a dessicated corpse. Besides potatoes, carrots, and leeks, I'll put lentils in the soup for tonight, for extra fortification."

# 32

"Please answer the door," said Susan, carrying in a full soup tureen.

The American leaned his freckled hands on the table to get up, but Victor restrained him. Without excusing herself, Colette flung down her napkin and rushed to the peephole.

"Uncle Georges!" exclaimed Colette as she opened the door.

Hesitantly, hat in hand, Uncle Georges stepped over the threshold. Despite the warm weather, he wore a gray vest under his gray pinstripe suit, which was so badly wrinkled the stripes descended to his shoes in crooked rows. His face, fringe of hair, mustache, deep-set eyes, all were variations of gray, so that he looked like a newspaper photograph of himself.

"Here we are," he said, and in stepped Aunt Monique and Didi to take their places on either side of him. Aunt Monique, still stately despite her rumpled, dark brown suit, wore a feather-trimmed hat in shades of brown, which complemented her salon-blonde hair. Didi slouched in a crushed, rose linen shift.

Uncle Georges turned toward Colette and kissed her loudly on both cheeks, followed by Aunt Monique, whose feather tickled Colette's nose. Didi giggled before she followed suit.

"Didn't you receive our letter?" asked Aunt Monique, as she surveyed the assembled diners.

"What letter, Sister?" asked Victor.

"The letter announcing our arrival, of course. You didn't expect us to just drop in, did you?"

"These days one doesn't know what to expect," Victor replied.

"Everybody is leaving Paris," Uncle Georges hastened to say. "The insurance business is off; doctors and lawyers have abandoned their practices."

"Calamitous!" Victor exclaimed, throwing up his hands.

"You can say that again." Shy Uncle Georges twiddled his hat. "Soldiers had to help the policemen. And some of the exits were closed, you know."

Victor got up and put his arms around his brother-in-law's shoulder. "Glad to see you and the family made it safely, Georges."

"Sit down, everybody, you're just in time for soup," said Susan.

"I'll fetch more bowls," Marie-Claire offered.

"Aren't you going to kiss me first?" Aunt Monique plunked herself down on the nearest chair and Marie-Claire dutifully brushed her lips over the artfully rouged cheeks. She could detect a trace of her aunt's perfume, *Femme, de Patou*, and it was comforting. Some things never changed.

"What a trip!" said Aunt Monique, leaning back in her chair. "I won't bore you with the details. . . . We slept on café tables one night and left at four in the morning, two hours before the Germans started machine-gunning refugees. Next night, it was benches in a hotel lobby. My back is killing me. Before I forget, here are our food cards, Susan." She opened a voluminous brown bag and slapped three booklets on the table.

"Pardon, Monsieur," she said to Thomas.

"This is Mr. Wiggins," said Victor, "an old friend from Paris who is passing through on his way to America."

When Thomas rose and extended his hand, Aunt Monique looked him up and down as if she had never before seen an American. Uncle Georges shifted his hat as he waited his turn to greet the stranger.

"So much to do before we left," complained Aunt

Monique, settling back in her chair, "draw the curtains, cover the tub, put mothballs in the armoires, empty the larder, turn off the gas and electric meters—"

"She forgot her hatboxes," said Uncle Georges, with a hint of malice. "We had just stepped out of the elevator, when she let out a hue and cry. I had to go back upstairs after them."

Didi covered her mouth with two painted nails.

"Oh, my little Georges, I beg of you, don't start that," Aunt Monique admonished her husband.

"Let's all sit down and have some soup before it gets cold," said Victor. "Hang up your hat, Georges. Make yourself at home."

"If you don't mind, I'll leave mine on," said Aunt Monique, "I don't even have the courage to wash my hands. I'm so tired you could scrape up what's left of me with a teaspoon."

"We'll excuse you," said Victor.

"Of course," Susan added.

When each had consumed a bowl of Rosine's nutritious soup, thick with potatoes and flavored with green onions and sautéed giblets, the travelers leaned back in their chairs, while Victor poured the wine.

Suddenly Uncle Georges said, "The British have abandoned us." He put down his glass and wiped his mustache. "First, the Dutch capitulate, then two weeks later the Belgians, and now the British pull out of the continent at Dunkirk and leave us alone to fight the *Boches.*"

Silence. Then Victor said, "Did you hear the latest news? Reynaud has appointed de Gaulle as Under Secretary of State for National Defence. With patriots like de Gaulle and Pétain in the government and with the resources of our great colonial empire, how can the French cause lose?"

"I wish I had your faith," said Uncle Georges.

"You don't have a son at the front, Victor," Aunt Monique hastened to add. "We haven't heard from him in days."

"The British evacuated a lot of French soldiers from Dunkirk."

"I knew it. The British, the British!" exclaimed Aunt Monique. "Victor, you're always defending the British, as if they were ancestors of ours." She pulled out her handkerchief. "Pardon, Monsieur," she said to Thomas, as she started to sniffle.

Colette looked at her aunt with such compassion that Marie-Claire had a revelation: the war was drawing people of opposite temperaments together in a common bond; Colette and Aunt Monique suffered because of loved ones at the front. Once again, Marie-Claire felt she was living on the periphery of love. She was moved, yes, but not as yet committed. A secret participant, she was too timid to acknowledge her anguish.

"How about something nice and light now?" Susan suggested. "I have some country ham and could make an omelette to accompany it."

"Very good," said Uncle Georges.

"I'll help you, Mother," offered Marie-Claire.

"What happened to the maid?" asked Aunt Monique. "Is she just a cleaning woman? I thought maids were cheap down south."

"Rosine is all things," Victor affirmed, "not much on cleaning, but very loyal—a jewel, really. However, she lives in the outskirts and it's a long bicycle ride home."

"She leaves early now because of the refugees at *her* house," said Marie-Claire.

Aunt Monique wagged a finger at her niece. "You haven't changed a bit, my little one; no, not one bit."

Without a word, Marie-Claire got up and removed her parents' soup bowls and carried them into the kitchen. *Anything to get away from that stinging woman,* she thought, as she rinsed the dishes and stacked them in the sink.

"Don't let her upset you," Thomas whispered in her ear. Marie-Claire jumped. She hadn't heard him come in she was so busy smarting.

"Where do you keep the Flytox?" he asked.

"Under the sink."

"I've been given instructions—in English, of course—to go upstairs and fumigate the empty maid's room." He grinned. "Your relatives will probably have to sleep downstairs tonight."

Didi bounced in with two more plates. "What a huge kitchen!" she exclaimed. "Two doors?"

"Over here is the herb garden," said Marie-Claire, as she propelled her cousin toward the east corner so that Thomas could get away with the Flytox. "We have tons of camomile you can use on your hair."

"Ooh," said Didi, "I've been using tea to rinse mine." She smoothed her dark locks. "Tea gives it red highlights. What do you use on your face? Crushed cucumbers?"

"Rose paste. Look out there. See all those rose bushes?"

Colette and Susan came in with the rest of the plates. "We don't usually stack things this way," she said, "but my helpers disappeared," said Susan. "Marie-Claire, would you go down to the cellar and fetch all the eggs you can find in the larder. Here, take this bowl."

"I could pick cherries, too," offered Marie-Claire.

"No, not tonight, thank you."

After dinner it was too late to disturb the neighbors, and the boardinghouse across the street was already filled beyond capacity, so the rollaway bed was set up in the Lavalette's dressing room for Aunt Monique. Uncle Georges agreed to sleep on folded carpets on the parlor floor, Didi on the sofa, and Thomas moved to the smoking room.

"Tomorrow we will remove the map," said Colette to Marie-Claire as she climbed into bed. "We'll pull out the flags and roll it up."

"Roll up 'History in the Making'?" Marie-Claire was aghast. "Why?"

"Father says it is useless now. Military censorship is so strict we don't know the exact location of our troops." Colette tried to sound matter-of-fact.

*She's too calm. Poor Colette*, thought Marie-Claire. "Is that the real reason, Col?" she asked.

Colette did not reply, just adjusted her top sheet.

"It's really because of Uncle Georges and Aunt Monique, isn't it? He doesn't want to upset them. We'll probably have to discontinue listening to 'Current Events' on the BBC, too."

"I never thought you would be sticking up for the British, Claire. What happened to change your opinion?" Colette slyly asked. "As if I didn't know, after what happened at the dinner table. I was only teasing, Sis. Keep your chin up." Colette lay back and clasped the ring that hung about her neck next to the holy medals.

Marie-Claire closed her eyes and said her evening prayers. During her examination of conscience, she berated herself for uncharitable thoughts toward her aunt and uncle. Then her mind wandered.

Things were really crazy now around Caldaquès. Educated nuns had to prepare hot meals for refugees. They served them daily in the covered market on tables once reserved for fowl and livers, in season. And you couldn't ride through the square at midday anymore. Down the hill by the river, the once tranquil convalescent home was now an army hospital. The lawn, no longer green, was littered with chairs. Shutters stayed open on the side facing the river, and hairy men in undershirts and khaki pants perched on the sills. You couldn't ride by without running their gauntlets of jeers and vulgar exclamations. Not that they seemed unfriendly, but they must have noticed her blush because they laughed, the laughter ringing in her ears long after she had turned the corner and started pedaling furiously up the hill.

There was a light knock at the door, and without waiting for an answer, Didi walked in. *"Sainte Marie!"* she chirped, "have you kids already gone to sleep?"

Didi plunked herself down on the foot of Marie-Claire's bed. She held a sheaf of toilet paper, and now she proceeded to roll her hair with it. "I love your house," she said, "I just had a hot bath downstairs, and Aunt Susan let me fill up the tub. She gave me one of those huge sea sponges. Have you been to the shore yet? Biarritz is so elegant, I hear. Princes and dukes go there, and photographers walk up and down the beach." She stood up and strutted across the room to the washbasin. "Now I sprinkle my curls with water, like so—"

"Don't forget to brush your teeth," said Marie-Claire. She deliberately turned her head and plumped her pillow, and the gargling she heard next was sweet music to her ears.

# 33

" 'We're through with the *Commentaries*,' he said. I can't explain exactly, but he made it sound so final, as if he were leaving us." Marie-Claire leaned against the trunk of the cherry tree.

"Oh, you're just imagining things," said Colette.

"Time school's over anyway," Didi snorted.

"I suppose so," said Marie-Claire, still unconvinced.

Although today was Monday—and you never ate pastry on Monday—the adults had sent the girls into the garden to pick cherries for a tart for dinner. It was just to get rid of them, but still Rosine's basket sat empty on the grass.

"Do you realize we haven't seen Mr. Dreyfuss at the house lately?" asked Marie-Claire.

"Still at it?" mocked Didi.

"That's because we don't have 'Current Events' anymore," said Colette.

"Hum . . . " muttered Marie-Claire, sliding her back down the trunk to sit cross-legged on the grass. She was glad Didi hadn't picked up on the words "Current Events." Didi was standing beside her, blowing through a blade of grass, emitting shrill, barbaric noises.

"He was sorry we did not have time for book seven and the great revolt of the Gauls," continued Marie-Claire.

"I bet you weren't," said Didi. She reached for a cherry branch, and the leaves rustled like silk.

"Book seven had Vercingetorix."

"First French hero and all that," said Didi.

Was Didi really that flighty, or was it all an act? Marie-Claire couldn't decide. "The Gauls always did have a hard time uniting for defence against their enemies," said Marie-Claire.

"Listen to her," Didi mocked again.

"Mr. Dreyfuss told me that at one glorious point in book seven the Gauls were unanimous in their desire to fight to maintain their liberty." Marie-Claire looked up at blue strips of sky through laced branches, the same sky that had stretched over Gaul centuries ago. "He said to me, 'Don't forget, Caesar always recognized people's strong desire for liberty.' "

"No more Latin, no more German, no more listening to Jean's sermon," chanted Didi. She hung a pair of cherries behind each ear lobe. "Look fellows, edible earrings."

"*Zum, zum, zum, die Esel sind recht dumm,*" retorted Marie-Claire.

"You're showing off. You know I don't speak German." Didi popped a cherry into her mouth.

"It's just a little nonsense rhyme," Marie-Claire explained, "Zum, zum, zum, donkeys are very stupid—that's all."

"Thanks!" Didi shook with laughter.

"German might come in useful," said Colette.

"Such pessimism," muttered Didi. She picked up Rosine's basket and dropped in her earrings. "I bet you I can fill this in no time," she bragged.

"You'll have to climb the tree," chorused Colette and Marie-Claire. "Go ahead, we'll boost you."

While Didi heaved and slipped and exclaimed over so many tantalizing branches, they cradled her plump buttocks in their hands until she wedged herself and the basket in a promising fork. Colette and Marie-Claire sat guard under the cherry tree.

"Glad someone's happy," muttered Colette.

"Know what you mean," replied Marie-Claire.

The adults had sent the girls into the garden to pick cherries as a distraction from the bad news on the radio.

All morning the men had sat around their coffee bowls. Monday, June 10, Saint Edgard's day, and Mussolini had invaded southern France, had "stabbed France in the back," Victor said. "A Catholic country fighting another Catholic country. What is the world coming to?" he'd asked. The government was leaving the capital.

"Shades of '14," said Uncle Georges.

When the Paris Stock Exchange closed down, Uncle Georges pronounced France in a state of panic and returned to a game of Solitaire. That was the signal for the girls to exit. Cards, checkers, games of chance with dice and little wooden horses that the men childishly dubbed *dada*, they tried anything to while away the time between newscasts and to avoid continuous political deliberations among people of different temperaments now drawn together by political circumstance.

"Imagine how Mother must feel," Colette whispered to Marie-Claire, as they continued their vigil under the cherry tree. "She's trapped. We couldn't leave the country now if Father agreed to it. Thank goodness," she added.

Marie-Claire stared at her sister's smudged eyes, green in the shade of the cherry tree. *Colette must be counting sheep at night*, she thought. Colette hadn't heard from Jean-Paul since the evacuation of the Allied troops at Dunkirk.

"Coming down now," called Didi from her perch, "watch out."

First came a rustling and a creaking before the basket thudded the ground, spilling red cherries onto the grass. Miraculously, the basket tipped upright. Then Colette and Marie-Claire caught sight of Didi's dangling legs. Plummeting, Didi flung her arms around her cousins' necks on the way down, and all three tumbled to the ground.

"I haven't had such fun in ages." Didi laughed.

Friday, June 14, at *Mon Repos,* they learned the Maginot Line had been captured. On the same day, to the accompaniment of fife and drum, German soldiers marched into Paris. The inexorable thunder of marching feet, amplified by the radio's sound waves, pounded their brains, and Uncle Georges echoed everyone's thoughts when he said, "Our days are numbered now."

"Thomas, you had better contact the consulate in Bordeaux to make sure your passport is in order," said Susan.

"I'm very concerned about Jean," Thomas replied.

"Jean can take care of himself," Victor assured them. His assurance astonished Marie-Claire. Again, she sensed her father was withholding information, as on that spring day in March—after the terrible fight.

"Why doesn't Mr. Dreyfuss come here anymore?" she asked.

Silence.

"Little one, if it's any consolation, I don't know either," replied Aunt Monique. "The men are purposely keeping us women in the dark, I think." This she said with provocative glances in their direction, but in their present mood the men were inflexible. "Why don't you, girls, go for a bicycle ride," Aunt Monique said then, smiling at Didi. "Get a change of ideas."

"Agreed." Didi jumped up. "I want to go down to the river bank," she said.

Reassured by her sister's regular breathing that she was asleep, Marie-Claire sneaked past a snoring Didi. The bedroom was set up dormitory style but without the veiled privacy of a convent cell. If you wanted to be alone now at *Mon Repos,* you had to feign a daytime headache. Didi was never sick; she was so delighted with the company of her female cousins that every day was "visiting day" for her, a "perpetual Sunday."

Marie-Claire knew which hall boards, which stair treads creaked, and she slowly navigated toward the kitchen where she could sit at the table and meditate on history.

Only two days after the occupation of Paris, Prime Minister Reynaud, in whom her father and Dreyfuss had placed such confidence, had resigned, and the aged Marshal Pétain had taken his place. Today, June 17, all *Mon Repos* had listened to his noonday speech, Rosine wearing her Sunday dress and amber beads "to honor Monsieur le Marèchal."

At the foot of the stairs Marie-Claire paused. A low humming sound, interrupted by crackling, indicated the radio was on in the dining room. There Susan, Victor, and Thomas—his red hair glinting silver in the glow of a tiny lamp—huddled like creatures in a storm over the beehive monster, intent on every word. It seemed as if their very lives depended on what the voice inside the hive had to say.

Without fear of reprimand, Marie-Claire tiptoed into the room and joined the group. She strained like the rest to catch the commentator's words. English. They were listening to the BBC.

"Prime Minister Pétain's speech today," said the commentator, "indicates that France has rejected the Proposal of Union."

*What proposal?* wondered Marie-Claire.

Victor smote his forehead. "Too late, too late! A lifeline extended too late! Why did the British wait until the enemy was at our gates?"

"Inside the gates," Thomas corrected him. "Think of Paris."

Through his maroon silk robe, Marie-Claire could feel her father sigh.

"Anyway, Victor, you know the French would never agree to a union with a centuries-old enemy; they're too chauvinistic," Thomas said.

"Not even when they are in danger of falling prey to a system that reduces mankind to a life of robots and slaves?" asked an indignant Victor.

Marie-Claire leaned against her father's shoulder and closed her eyes. But not for long.

Victor hissed, "Pétain is a defeatist, telling us we must cease hostilities. Where is the spirit of '14?" Marie-Claire could sense the blood boiling inside of him, his body as tense as plated armor, like a knight raring to go into battle.

"If it's any consolation to you, Victor," said Thomas, "remember Baudouin's words earlier today: '. . . there can be no question of accepting terms without honor; that if the enemy sought to impose such terms, France would prefer to go on fighting.' "

"Paul Baudouin is merely Foreign Minister," Victor retorted.

"Come on, Victor," said Thomas, "even Pétain talked about honor."

"Please lower your voices." Susan placed a finger on her lips. "Marie-Claire, you should be really sleepy by now; it's past eleven."

Victor pecked his daughter's cheek. "Go back to bed, little one," he whispered. "I promise to get you if there should be any important developments." He winked.

"Good night, Marie-Claire," said Susan wearily.

Impulsively, Marie-Claire put her arm around her mother's shoulder and hugged her before she made her way back upstairs. The Proposal of Union still puzzled her. She had heard nothing over French radio, seen nothing in the papers. If she'd missed it, Uncle Georges would have had something to say, she was sure of that. He always had something denigrating to say about the British. As she crossed the landing, a board creaked. In the absolute stillness it sounded like the snapping of a twig. *Stillness. Thank goodness, Didi has stopped snoring,* she thought.

The next day Victor had the whole family listening to a radio speech over the BBC. Opposite him at the dining room table, Marie-Claire sat tall, proud of her father—the Great Persuader.

"Believe me," said de Gaulle, "nothing is lost for France. The same means that vanquished us will bring victory some day. For France is not alone . . ."

Uncle Georges stroked his mustache. "What—what does he mean by that?" he muttered.

When de Gaulle announced France could "make common cause with the British Empire, which holds the seas and is continuing the fight," Uncle Georges squirmed. Aunt Monique conferred on him her imperious gaze, blue eyes glowering under carefully penciled brows. Uncle Georges crossed his arms then and leaned against the back of his chair.

"This war has not been ended by the Battle of France," de Gaulle continued. "This is a worldwide war. All the mistakes, all the setbacks, and all the suffering do not alter the fact that there are in the universe all the necessary means some day to destroy our enemies. . . ."

Uncle Georges and Aunt Monique raised their heads; even Didi sat tall through the close of the speech and de Gaulle's stirring admonition, "Come what may, the flame of French resistance must not be extinguished. And it will not be extinguished!" At this everyone applauded.

Then Uncle Georges shook his head. "He's reaching

for the moon, that de Gaulle. Pétain is already negotiating for an end to hostilities." He shrugged his shoulders. "Beautiful words from that de Gaulle. They come from a place that is far from the smoke of battle. De Gaulle has sided with the British, and the British abandoned us at Dunkirk, remember? Even the president of your great country, Susan—What's his name? Roosevelt? Yes, Roosevelt. Even he denied our desperate appeal for help." Uncle Georges pushed back his chair and stomped out of the room.

Aunt Monique raised her hand, then dropped it in a futile gesture of apology.

"Let him be, Sister, we are all on an emotional roller coaster," said Victor.

He was echoing the common sentiment. One day they were listening to the French premier, the victor of Verdun, tell them that hostilities must cease; the next, a relatively unknown French general in London was exhorting them to resistance.

When, on the twentieth of June and in a shaky voice, Pétain confirmed he had asked for a cessation of hostilities, no one at *Mon Repos* uttered a word. "I was with you in the glorious days," the old marshal reminded all citizens, "I shall be with you in the somber days. *Vive la France*."

"*Vive la France*," shouted Rosine, standing behind the master, "*Quand même, Messieurs, Dames . . .* " She reproached them for their lack of patriotism.

The German armistice was signed on June 22 and the Italian armistice on June 24, but hostilities on both fronts did not end until after midnight, June 25. Near the Franco-Italian border, the French repulsed all attacks and even staged a successful counterattack before midnight.

June 26 was proclaimed a national day of mourning

in France, and for the first time, the terms of both armistices were published in the newspapers. On that day Marie-Claire learned from her father that Jean Dreyfuss had left for England from Bayonne in a fishing boat, with one of his editors and five cartons of books.

"He left you this volume of German poetry," Victor told her, handing her a slim, green, leatherbound book, "to make up for all his boring discussions of military strategy. And everyone is to go over to *Reine Hortense* to pick the raspberries in the garden before the Nazis get to them."

# *German Time*

# 34

"One of you girls should stay behind to keep Georges and Monique company." Victor's muffled voice issued from the bowels of the old Peugeot, which was parked at the curb in front of *Mon Repos*. "Rosine is taking care of that refugee blackfoot that's eating all the hay around her farm. She's gone to the newspaper to place a notice in the lost and found column. How a Breton cow ever made her way down here is beyond me." Victor chuckled as he closed the hood.

"Same way we all did," said Thomas, "panic, then sheer determination to survive. She caught the refugee spirit."

"Her owners abandoned her, poor beast."

"Marie-Claire could sit on my lap," said Didi, who had perceived the real reason behind Victor's remark. Four in the back seat of the Peugeot was beyond capacity.

"I'll stay," said Colette.

"No, definitely not." Susan was adamant. "The change of scenery will do you good."

*Agreed*, thought Marie-Claire. Colette's light eyes were cloudy with fatigue. She still hadn't heard from Jean-Paul. At night that regular, even breathing of hers was a clever coverup for her insomnia, Marie-Claire had discovered when it was interrupted by staccato sniffs.

Suitcase in hand, Thomas confronted Victor once more. "I wish you would just drive me to the bus station."

"And deprive us of a little outing? I won't hear of it." Victor grabbed Thomas's cardboard suitcase and deliberately placed it in the trunk of the car. "Besides, who knows whether the bus will leave on time. You might not reach the Spanish border till midnight. I've changed my mind; we'll all go."

"I wish we could open some shutters before we leave," said Colette, "the house is so depressing."

"Where's your patriotic spirit, girl?" Victor scolded his daughter with a smile. You couldn't get cross with Colette in her present condition. "The mayor decided we had to observe a whole week of national mourning, remember?"

"That was his idea, not the government's," said Colette.

Certainly it had been the mayor's idea. Yesterday, the newspaper headlines had read, "TODAY, NATIONAL DAY OF MOURNING: TOMORROW, EACH FRENCHMAN MUST BE AT HIS POST READY TO BUILD A NEW FRANCE." And the mayor wanted all government offices closed!

"The mayor happens to be one of those fiercely independent Basques," said Thomas, "like the editor of that Bayonne newspaper who has suspended publication until France is a free country again."

"If only there were more people like him!" exclaimed Victor. *"En voiture,* everybody. Come on, Colette."

The women squeezed into the back, Marie-Claire perched on the edge of the seat, as was her skinny prerogative, like a piece of camembert popping out of two slices of bread. Victor drove slowly, solemnly through the shuttered town. There flags drooped at half mast, and the cathedral portals were still draped in black curtains edged in white, with the white initial *F*, standing for the collective deceased, centered over the main portal.

Yesterday, June 26, had been the official day of mourning. All Caldaquès had attended the special service for the country and for all Frenchmen who had died in her defence. In black stole and cope, short enough to reveal the blue cuffs of his old military uniform, Father Tessier had celebrated the daily Mass for the Departed.

During the sermon the Father's voice grew hoarse. From his eagle eyrie in the cathedral pulpit, he leaned so far forward he got red in the face and Marie-Claire thought he would have an apoplectic fit. "Now, more than ever," he rasped, "citizens must work with courage and a spirit of self-sacrifice to rebuild the country. Above all," he said, and here his voice regained some of its former power, "what the country needs is faith in God."

"God is dead," Colette said, from the depths of her despair, and no one contradicted her.

They were driving across the deserted square. Cafés and souvenir shops were closed, as was the pastry shop. (Pastry was a frill and a cause for celebration.) But water still flowed from lion-headed spigots, and the stolid Roman arcade rose in defiance of pestilences, sieges, and wars.

Marie-Claire thought of Uncle Mo. *How did he observe the day of mourning*, she wondered. *Was he able to drive to the excavations?* She could see him standing alone in the middle of the field—bare-headed, out of respect for the village men, gold watch ensconced in his waistcoat pocket—contemplating the grass-covered furrows in which lay the heating system of the Roman pool.

Once out of town and on the open road, Victor let the car run full throttle, and Marie-Claire grasped the top of the front seat. She wasn't going to ask her father to slow down on her account, but Susan made him do so anyway. At the first sight of the ocean, with the sun glinting on white caps, car windows squeaked all the way down and everyone inhaled great gusts of salt air. Like the wind, their spirits lifted.

Marie-Claire had a wild desire to leap out of the car, run onto the open beach, and mark footprints in the sand. Next to her, Didi's thigh twitched. She was probably itching to do the same. But they had to get Thomas to the Spanish border, so he could return home to America. Ships were not sailing there from France anymore. Thomas had to go clear across Spain into Portugal, to Lisbon, to board one.

"Don't forget to write us when you get to Lisbon," said Victor. Thomas was boarding an American cargo ship there bound for New Jersey. "And pay no attention to the sultry brunettes on the plazas."

"No way," said Thomas. "I shall be thinking of you all wherever I go, and I mean that sincerely."

"What kind of cargo will your ship be carrying?" asked Colette.

"Cork and wine, most likely, so we'll always stay afloat, won't we?"

"Indeed you will," said Victor. "I can just see you, Thomas, tippling bottle after bottle of port, reclining on a sea of cork."

They all laughed at the vision.

Thomas turned around. "I shall write you, Susan, as soon as I have contacted the Sterlings."

"My father is the one who needs reassurance." Susan sighed.

Suddenly Victor said, "Thomas, do you see what I think I see in my rearview mirror?"

Thomas stuck his head out the window. "By their

uniforms I should say they were Nazis. That young orderly is driving awfully fast."

"*Les Boches!*" exclaimed Didi and Marie-Claire.

"Keep your voices down," shouted Victor.

As the open car sped past them, they glimpsed two officers in the back seat. Everyone knew they were officers because they had caps with visors and an air of complete assurance; their arms rested on door tops as if they were reclining in desk chairs on the beach, basking in the sunshine of their newly acquired glory.

Colette paled, clutched her stomach, and made a retching sound. Marie-Claire ducked so her sister could stick her head out the window and throw up. Then Victor stopped at the next café, where Susan sponged Colette's sweaty forehead. They sat at round tables, while Colette sipped water through a straw.

"I have only lemonade or wine to offer you," the proprietor told them. He was polishing glasses behind the bar; from the light bulb above him hung a sticky fly trap, black with victims. "Those gentlemen in green took all my beer," he said sneeringly.

"Never mind," said Victor, "give us all another glass of water."

When they reached the international bridge spanning the little river that separated France from Spain, the occupying forces were nowhere in sight, strangely enough. A lone civilian stood by the raised barrier on the French side and Thomas identified him as the American consul from Bordeaux. His presence had elicited a glum, French crowd, so that he had cordoned himself off from it. *Like a museum exhibit,* thought Marie-Claire. Across the bridge, on the Spanish side, an official in a three-cornered hat paced the entrance to the tree-lined avenue.

The consul shook hands with smartly dressed travelers about to cross into Spain and the crowd watched the spectacle: gray-suited men carrying briefcases behind the luggage carts, behatted ladies jangling gold bracelets. Marie-Claire envied the women their tanned legs and faces.

The consul shook hands with Thomas. Thomas sauntered across the bridge, swinging his flimsy case. Next to the Spanish official he stopped and turned to wave to the Lavalettes, his red hair blowing in the wind like a ragged halo. Then he disappeared into the Spanish customs house.

The consul held up the cord and beckoned to the Lavalettes and Didi. "Why aren't all of you leaving?" he asked Victor. "The Germans are closing the border tonight. Who knows what will happen after they are in control; I can't guarantee safe passage anymore."

Wide-eyed, the French spectators followed the consul's speech.

*They don't understand English, but they comprehend what's going on,* Marie-Claire thought, and for the first time she was seized with apprehension. Cold shivers ran down her spine.

"We can't leave now," she heard her father say, "family obligations . . ."

"I'm sorry," the consul said.

Victor shepherded his family to the car. *"En voiture,"* he said, with false gaiety. "Colette, *ma chérie*, sit up front with me this time."

Solicitous of Colette, Victor drove cautiously. All feeling of elation had disappeared. Normally bouncy Didi stared glumly out the window, and Susan, hands clasped in her lap, seemed deep in meditation. Colette dozed on her father's shoulder, removed from the real world for a little while.

Their small circle of Caldaquès acquaintances was dwindling. *Another bird has left the cage,* thought Marie-Claire of Thomas's departure. She had never dreamed she would envy anybody leaving France, her native country; but the consul's words still echoed in her mind, *"The Germans are closing the border tonight."*

"My God, here they are!"

The avalanche of opposing traffic startled her father so, he pulled over to the side of the road. Marie-Claire could not believe what she saw: Truckloads of enemy soldiers careened around the curve. Then soldiers on motorcycles and in sidecars wearing goggles like frogs' eyes. Then more trucks packed tightly with men whose blackened jaws chewed constantly, whose eyes pointed straight ahead under camouflaged helmets. A contingent of rifle-bearing hussars passed through. Hussars of death, they proclaimed themselves, skull and bones emblazoned on their black berets.

No, it couldn't be. She was watching a filmstrip of some faraway country. All she had to say was "abracadabra," and the scene would disappear. But the rumble of trucks, the roar of motorcycles continued, and Marie-Claire was numb with horror and surprise.

When the last motorcycle and sidecar rounded the bend, a goggled soldier leaning perilously out of the sidecar, Victor drove off in a cloud of dust through the deserted village streets. But on the wide beach below were two army trucks, and around the enemy soldiers flocked some French girls—who else could they be?

Victor forestalled any exclamations of dismay. "Women of the night," he said. "They haven't seen an able-bodied man in weeks."

In Caldaquès the swastika flew over the Majestic Hotel. Shutters were flung open, curtains billowed, up the front steps soldiers carried portmanteaus and chests.

"The new tourists are quick to make themselves at home," Victor observed wryly. "Next, I suppose, they'll open the mud baths."

On the square in front of the hot fountain, soldiers darted about like schoolboys on holiday. "Many of those Huns have never seen a Roman monument before," said Victor. "Caesar never made a province out of their territory; he just crossed the Rhine now and then to teach those marauding barbarians a lesson."

Victor's disdain turned to anger when the car passed the cathedral. Parked on the flagstone watching soldiers scurry up and down ladders in the removal of the funeral curtains, a Nazi officer sat arrogantly smoking a cigar, while Father Tessier paced the court. "If he were in uniform," said Victor, "Father Tessier would punch him in the nose, I'm sure of that. I feel like doing so myself."

"God forbid!" exclaimed Susan.

Colette spoke up, as in a trance. "I was told the Nazis have the words *Gott mit uns*—God with us—inscribed on their belt buckles."

"Fanatics always imagine God is on their side," Victor said assertively.

They crossed the square of the covered market, where aproned nuns scrubbed the long, wooden tables on which refugees had eaten their noonday meal.

The shutters remained closed at *Mon Repos*. Birds twittered. Roses continued to bloom. Across the street, the boardinghouse manager swept her front porch—scratch, scratch, scratch. The sign on the boardinghouse door, however, shattered the residential tranquility of the little street. NO VACANCY it announced, in big, vulgar letters for all the world to see. The manager was no longer relying on the advertised list of guest houses at the Bureau of Tourism, nor on word of mouth at the neighboring tobacco shop.

Victor threatened an altercation with the woman, but Susan grabbed his arm. "She must have her reasons," she said. "Times have changed."

*They've changed in the space of a few hours,* thought Marie-Claire, *though none of us realized it. It's as if the swastika flying over the Majestic were just some boy's kite caught in the wind.*

# 35

"Claire, I didn't really mean it when I said God was dead." Colette squeezed her sister's hand, her fingers as cool as the grass under the cherry tree, where they were sitting enjoying one of those now rare moments of private companionship. Didi had gone shopping alone for once.

"I wouldn't blame you if you did." Marie-Claire spoke with such assurance that Colette withdrew as if stung by nettles.

"I wouldn't blame you if you believed God was dead," insisted Marie-Claire.

Colette's mouth dropped open. Wide-eyed, she stared at Marie-Claire. Her eyes, green in the shade of the cherry tree, seemed too large for her face.

"We prayed the Secret from the Mass for Peace and Mass in Time of War," continued Marie-Claire. "I even prayed to the newest saint I know, Saint Manfred. What good did all those prayers do us? I wasn't going to tell you this, but I think the monkey puzzle tree's demise was a bad portent after all . . . and the snowstorm . . . the hail. Rosine was right there. They say that country people have a kind of folk wisdom."

Marie-Claire couldn't sustain Colette's gaze, so she turned her face to the garden wall. White stucco dazzled in the noonday sun. She blinked. She would probably burn in Hell now for being such a pagan.

"The smell of so many overripe cherries must be making you tipsy," said Colette.

"I wonder what Mother Genevieve would think if she were alive today?"

"She would be in a state of shock, like the rest of us." Colette sighed, then she hugged her knees and retreated into meditation. Marie-Claire closed her eyes and waited.

"Why doesn't Jean-Paul write?" lamented Colette. "Everyone else has." By everyone else she meant Cousin François, who had notified his parents he was being mustered out. The news had so overjoyed Didi that, in a fit of generosity, she had volunteered to get today's luncheon *baguette* at the bakery.

"Perhaps he's in England with the others who were evacuated at Dunkirk," ventured Marie-Claire.

"I still would have heard," Colette replied. She didn't mention the unthinkable, what was listed in the newspaper under the column, "The Glorious Dead": "With deep regret we learned of the decease of Lt. Jean-Paul de Joux, killed on the field of honor during a reconnaissance for which he volunteered. His horse was shot from under him. . . ."

"Lunch everybody." Didi sprang out the kitchen door. She took a giant leap and landed at Colette's and Marie-Claire's feet. "Guess what?" she whispered. "On my way home I saw two *Boches*. They're ringing door bells."

"My God!" exclaimed Marie-Claire, crossing herself fervently.

Didi jumped up and disappeared indoors again. But not for long. When she reappeared, like a pink tornado, she announced, "They're trying to find out if anyone in this neighborhood has an extra bedroom for their officer. That's what I heard. You should see the women around here. They're standing on their doorsteps. Want to know who's going to harbor the enemy . . . oops." She clapped a hand over her mouth as if the cherry tree had ears. "They're on the way to *Repos* now," she said through her fingers.

"Lunchtime!" called Aunt Monique.

She waited for the girls inside the kitchen door. "We must go about our business as usual," she whispered, as they looked inquiringly past her. "I'm sure we have nothing to hide." But she sounded unconvinced. Upstairs, German soldiers were clomping all over the house, opening and closing doors. "To the dining room," she said, propelling them past Susan, who stood at the foot of the stairs polishing the newel post with a nervous hand.

Rosine had stationed herself behind the master's empty chair, hands folded over her stomach; her eyeballs rolled with fright and her mouth moved ceaselessly. By the dining room window, Uncle Georges pretended to admire the scenery.

"Sit down everybody," said Aunt Monique, and the girls did as they were told. "Come on, Georges *mon petit.*" Uncle Georges moved as in a dream.

*My heart's in my throat,* thought Marie-Claire. *I couldn't swallow a thing, even if they force-fed me, like a Caldaquès goose.* When she stared at her plate, the revelation came to her that if there were a Nazi officer in this house they would be caged in. No longer could they listen to the BBC, Rosine would be as quiet as a church nun, and what would happen to their tentative plans?

"Sit down, Susan," admonished Aunt Monique, "there is nothing you can do."

When Victor came downstairs, soldiers following close behind, Marie-Claire turned to watch them in spite of herself. The two young men were blonde, lean. Twin boys in identical green uniforms, with the same upward tilt of the chin as their boots hit the floor and they said to Victor, *"Danke, mein Herr."*

The front door was open so Victor didn't bother to see them out. With simultaneous gestures the soldiers doffed their caps, carefully closing the door behind them.

Victor blew out a giant breath. He patted his pockets and nodded, as if reassuring himself. Then he strode over to Susan and kissed her on both cheeks. "Don't worry, darling," he said, "their officer doesn't want to sleep on a rollaway bed. I didn't tell the *Boches* that Georges was taking his family home. You may serve now," he said to Rosine.

Over the tomatoes vinaigrette and the salami, Aunt Monique and Uncle Georges discussed their travel plans. "I got my extra petrol allotment," said Uncle Georges. "No problem. I just went to the prefecture and registered, like the other homeward-bound refugees. If only I hadn't had to register, though, it made me feel like a foreigner in my own country."

"But we are foreigners now, Georges, aren't we?" said Victor, laughing sarcastically.

Uncle Georges raised his thin, gray brows.

"Never mind that polite stuff you just witnessed," Victor said. "Those boys were just following orders."

"What are you trying to tell us, Victor?" Aunt Monique narrowed her eyes.

"Well, for instance, we set our clocks ahead to German time. And have you thought about the curfew and the blackout? They, meaning the *Boches,* pay us in *Reichsmarks* for all our butter, eggs, and cheese. Incidentally, did you see that swine licking a whole stick of butter the other day, as if it were an ice cream cone? Goes to show what the BBC said, 'The Nazis, in the build up of their war machine, were substituting guns for butter.' They tell our pastry chefs they can't bake cakes anymore. Got to send that butter home to the Reich. The best vegetables and fruit go to the *Feldkommandantur,* while our women have to stand in line for what is left. I've heard they are going to take our wheat and ship it to the Reich."

Victor pounded the table with his fist. "You know what galls me the most? We can't even stand on our bridges and admire our own scenery; that is called loitering. We cannot even honor our parents' sepulchres, because parking at the cemetery is forbidden. I am using the editorial 'we,' you understand. Pardon, I should have used *verboten.* Better speak German now, that ugly language one used to use to speak to one's horse."

"A little dignity, Victor, *voyons,*" said Aunt Monique.

"Don't you dare speak to me of dignity. The word has been overused by our paltry statesmen and newspaper reporters. 'In dignity France lived her National Day of Mourning.' 'Paris is dignified under the occupation.' Never mind that every time a Frenchman enters his post-office he licks his stamps under that monstrous slogan they have posted on our walls: *Heute Deutschland, Morgen die ganze Welt,* today Germany, tomorrow the whole world." Victor raised his arm in mock salutation.

"Just a minute," said Uncle Georges. "How would it

look to the British if every Frenchman lost his dignity and ran around tearing his hair out, *hein?* You know who would be the first ones to laugh at us. The British, of course. The British didn't even have the decency to express one word of pity for us on June 26. The Dutch did, the Belgians did, the Swiss—"

Victor held up his hand, but Uncle Georges would not be dissuaded. "Instead, that Churchill gave his ally a dressing down, after allowing him to negotiate a separate armistice. And you know why he agreed to a separate armistice? His country did not make the supreme effort. It had not put all its available manpower into the fight, while France had to draft men of forty-five. We could have been drafted maybe, just think of that. How does that strike you, *hein?*" He drained his wine glass.

"Careful, Georges, *mon petit*," said Aunt Monique, "remember your blood pressure."

Uncle Georges squeezed his empty glass, as if he wanted to crush it. "And then the day the armistice was signed," he said, "that very day the British had the nerve to announce that their country was now mobilizing all its forces and putting all its men into the fight."

"How do you know that, Georges? You don't listen to the BBC!" Victor exclaimed.

"I read the papers." Uncle Georges's mustache trembled. "Don't speak to me anymore of the British. They sold the French down the river."

"That is exactly what the Germans would have us believe," Victor said, in such a gentle voice it took Uncle Georges by surprise. He loosened the napkin about his neck and cleared his throat. At his wife's urging, he forked up the last soggy piece of tomato. Rosine would never have tolerated leftovers. The tomatoes were from her garden.

Throughout the next course, a *cassoulet*—light on the meat, heavy on the beans—the men retreated into silence. But Susan and Aunt Monique exchanged banalities about dress styles and how short the skirts were getting this year, exposing the knees, also how skimpy they were and how shoulders were losing their femininity.

After the *crème caramel*, Didi chirped, "Let's go for a bicycle ride. May we be excused, Aunt Susan?"

Before Susan could put in a word, Aunt Monique said, "Just a short promenade, there is still packing to do."

# 36

The notice above the service entrance of the Majestic read, *Juden Verboten* (Jews forbidden) in black and white letters, like a sign above a stationery shop advertising newspapers, *Paris Soir* sold here.

"I can't believe *they*'re putting a label on people," said Didi.

"Just what I was thinking. You read about this kind of thing happening in faraway countries like Poland," Marie-Claire said, shrugging her shoulders.

"But you don't believe your eyes when you see this at home," Colette was quick to add, and Didi and Marie-Claire nodded.

"It's horrible," asserted Marie-Claire. "You know, it's putting people in the category of animals. It's as if *they* were saying 'Dogs are forbidden in the dining room.' Now I know why Jean Dreyfuss was so anxious to leave."

"Did you think of Mr. Dreyfuss as a Jew?" asked Didi. "I don't mean his name. I mean, was he all that different? How do *they* know a person is Jewish?"

"*They* go to City Hall, I suppose, and look up birth records," Colette suggested.

"What if someone just moved here?" Didi asked. "If he were a Jewish deliveryman with a crate of poultry, would he have to say, 'Pardon, *Monsieur*, I'm Jewish. I'll have to leave these chickens on your doorstep.' Ridiculous, if you ask me."

The girls claimed their bicycles from the rack in front of the Majestic and rode to the park. There pigeons strutted around empty benches. Where did the old men congregate now? the girls wondered. The Germans had taken over their white bandstand and substituted oomaph, oompah, oompah-pah for happy hunting horns and clarinets; loudspeakers in moving cars replaced *Père* Dumas's trumpet and resonant voice. You only heard the very beginning, or the tail end of an announcement. *Just as well*, thought Marie-Claire.

The latest announcement, which no Caldaquois claimed to have heard in its entirety, had to be printed in the newspaper the next day. The *Kommandant*, if you please, requested the people to attend band concerts in the park. *Hah! You'd have to drag them out of their houses first*, was Marie-Claire's thought. Caldaquois were as independent as their mayor, who every morning ran up the French flag next to the swastika. Caldaquois turned their backs on the *Kommandant* and his prancing horse at the head of the Sunday parade; they stuffed their ears as his band crashboomed through their narrow streets.

In a sudden whirring of wings the pigeons flew to the alleys. "See," said Didi, "the pigeons are picking grain out of the horse dung." For a city girl she had come a long way.

"I knew I smelled something when we entered the park." Colette wrinkled her little nose.

The swastika hung from the portal of the arena, and over it a large Gothic banner proclaimed: *Tritts du ein Pferd hieran, ruf er schnell bei seinem Nam.*

"It rhymes," said Marie-Claire. "It means, 'If you should walk a horse in here, call it quickly by its name.' "

"So," said Colette, "I told you German would come in useful."

Soon a string of horses clippety-clopped down the alley, led by a dour, red-faced soldier; the pigeons scattered before it. The girls wheeled their bicycles in the opposite direction to that of the enemy horses.

"Now that the alleys are no longer clean and raked," muttered Colette, "the old men no longer have a place to go bowling."

"Little do *they* care," hissed Marie-Claire.

"Farewell to the park," chanted Didi, "and the bullfights. Shucks, when will I ever see one? Well, we'd better go back to *Repos.*"

Mindful of enemy traffic, the girls pedaled Indian file, close to the curb. A driver stripped his gears as his car passed Marie-Claire. Freshly painted flags of all Nazi-occupied countries decorated the trunk of the car; the French flag was displayed in the center of the group deliberately putting all Frenchmen to shame. *How arrogant and cheeky of him,* Marie-Claire thought, her blood boiling; she could feel it flush her cheeks. She was truly the daughter of Victor, a real Lavalette, oh yes. How well she understood their emotions now, the principles they stood for.

A truck suddenly roared so near Marie-Claire the noise was deafening. When the brakes screeched, it was upon her; she could feel the heat of the exhaust. Next thing she knew, she was down on the sidewalk. She had leapt off her bicycle, grazing her knee, while the soldiers in the back of the truck laughed at her. Gravel stung the open wound and brought tears to her flushed face, but the insulting laughter burned even more. Those Huns had deliberately squeezed her against the curb.

"*Ça alors,*" muttered an old woman as she trotted past. She disappeared through the rectangle of a *porte-cochère*.

Colette, who had evidently heard the loud guffaws, looked back over her shoulder. *Oh, if looks could kill,* thought Marie-Claire, hugging her injured leg, *Colette would massacre them all.*

She watched her sister signal to Didi, who squeezed the brakes so fast she almost lost her balance. They lifted their bicycles over the curb and leaned them against the flaking stucco of the old woman's house that adjoined the *Kommandantur*. The soldiers leered. Through a fringe of tears, Marie-Claire watched them vault out of the truck, hands grasping the side, knees bent neatly behind them—just like a gymnastics' class: one, two, three, one after the other, without interruption or hesitation. Looking neither right nor left, they marched through the archway into their headquarters.

A man in a black beret and striped vest ran out of the old woman's house. "*Ah, ces sales Boches!*" he exclaimed, shaking his fist in their direction.

"Be quiet, sir; you'll have us all shot," Colette warned him.

"Let me carry her to the pharmacy. Pagnol must be open today."

Marie-Claire blushed as she struggled to her feet. "No thank you, sir. I can manage with my sister and my cousin to help me." She flung her arms around their necks.

"Take my handkerchief," the man said, profferring his.

"Thanks."

"Wait, let me tie it around your knee," he added.

"Thank you very much."

"Too tight?"

"No, no."

"I think it is."

"It's all right," Marie-Claire assured him, as she started to hop away.

The man picked up her bicycle and examined the dented fenders. "Let me repair this for you," he offered.

"You are very amiable," said Marie-Claire, standing on one leg.

"It won't take long," he replied. "A little blow here, a little blow there. Have no fear, girls," he said to Didi and Colette, "I'll watch over your bikes, too. You just attend to her."

*"Ma pauvre petite,"* said the pharamacist, as Marie-Claire hobbled into his shop. He ducked behind the counter and came up with three bottles of perfume.

"We're not here for that," Colette said indignantly.

"I know; I have not lost my head."

"Well, then—"

"Permit me," he said, as he dabbed each girl's wrist with a different perfume stopper. "So much the less I have to sell those gentlemen in green. You know who I mean." He winked. "Now." He came out from behind the counter carrying a chair. "Sit her down while I get the peroxide."

The pharmacist opened a cabinet marked with a red cross and removed an amber bottle and a package of cotton. He took the cotton out of its box and laid it on the counter. "Just one more minute, girls," he said. He turned to the perfume shelf, grabbed four little bottles and swiftly concealed them in the cotton box. Then he placed the package in the red cross cabinet and closed the glass door. "Now I am all yours," he said, assuming a professional smile.

"I didn't just fall off my bicycle," Marie-Claire told him, mindful the pharmacist might consider her downright clumsy.

"Just superficial," he said, examining the wound, "but I must remove all foreign matter."

Soft as the cotton was, the pressure on the open wound caused shivers of pain, and Marie-Claire jerked. "Hang on," he said, as the peroxide foamed.

"I jumped," Marie-Claire said.

"I know. You'll also have a bruise."

"I jumped—" No, she decided, she shouldn't tell him why. She might have jumped out of fright and not necessity; surely no one in his right mind would deliberately try to run her over.

Heavy boots scraped the doorsill and Marie-Claire winced. *"Keine, keine!"* shouted the pharmacist, without looking up. "No perfume!" He waved the soldiers away, and they grumbled before they marched off. "They act as if they have never before smelled perfume," he muttered. "The Egyptians had it, the Romans . . . Keep this gauze and bandage dry for a couple of days before you change the dressing. Now, they're sending it home to the Reich."

"How much do we owe you, sir?" asked Colette.

"Nothing, ladies. You help me; I help you. That's a fair exchange, don't you think?"

Didi began to giggle, then put a hand over her mouth. "Come on, Cousin," she said to Marie-Claire, "I'm going to carry you home on my handlebars."

"We've got to get our bicycles first," Colette reminded her.

"What about mine?" asked Marie-Claire.

"Papa and I will drive over to pick it up after we get you home," said Didi. "Come on, Colette." She grabbed her cousin's hand.

"Keep your chair, *Mademoiselle*," insisted the pharmacist, when Marie-Claire tried to stand. Her knee throbbed and ached, so she diverted herself by concentrating on the contents of the shelves opposite her; cans of baby food, which in Randonette were kept in the storage room. Uncle Mo had told her one day, "Once the child has left the breast, he prefers fingers of bread dipped in a soft-boiled egg." He had chuckled then.

Aware the pharmacist was staring at her, Marie-Claire looked away. She was glad when Colette and Didi reappeared. Didi helped her onto the handlebars, and they wended their way home through the narrowest streets. There one's main concern was observing red and white directional signs, since the old town had not been built for modern traffic. Old men and women on their stoops clucked sympathetic tongues at the sight of her bandaged leg, and Marie-Claire felt a resurgence of self-esteem. Perhaps, after all, she was a *blessé de guerre*, a civilian casualty.

Before they crossed the square of the covered market, Marie-Claire changed her mind again, and she swore Didi and Colette to secrecy about the presence of the German truck and its mocking occupants. "Just say I fell somewhere. It was probably my fault anyway; I jumped, you know."

The night before she had dreamed that a carrier pigeon had flown through the bedroom window with a message in its beak, a message from Jean-Paul at last. What else could it possibly be? She must be psychic, after all. Back in Randonette Aunt Renée had said there must be another clairvoyant in the family, although Marie-Claire had not believed her at the time. If her parents thought the *Boches* responsible for the accident, Colette and she would no longer be free to go out on their own. Life was restricted enough now, with all the *Boche* regulations.

When they stopped to open the gate at *Mon Repos*, Marie-Claire was not astonished to see her mother standing on the porch and Rosine behind her, grinning like the cat that swallowed the canary. Naturally they both voiced their concern at the sight of her injured leg and Rosine and Didi helped her upstairs, but not before Marie-Claire heard her mother say, "Colette come into the parlor." At that, Rosine chuckled and made signals to Didi, which Didi could not understand, of course. But they both tightened their grip on her arms and after they released her she had three sore limbs to contend with.

Marie-Claire lay down on her bed to ease the throbbing in her leg. If only the pigeon in her dream had opened his beak. What kind of a psychic was she, anyway? The pigeon just stood there on the windowsill and strutted back and forth.

# 37

The minute Colette poked her head through the bedroom door and smiled at her, Marie-Claire knew what had happened. Those shining eyes, those pink cheeks—only news from Jean-Paul could have transformed the melancholy maiden into the fairytale princess again.

"Where's Didi?" inquired a cautious Colette.

"Packing."

"Good, I'm going down to the river and I don't want her following me."

Marie-Claire's heart thumped like bird's wings beating against cage bars as she waited for more information. Time became suspended, a pendulum that had ceased to swing.

"Do you remember the young refugee woman who stopped at the house and asked you for a drink of water?"

"Yes." *Why can't she come straight to the point?* Marie-Claire wondered.

"She came by the house while we were out riding." Colette sat gingerly at the foot of Marie-Claire's bed. "She's a nurse at the army hospital."

*I already know that*, thought Marie-Claire.

Colette took a deep breath. "Jean-Paul is a patient there. Can you believe it?" Her face was radiant, as if she were beholding a hundred angels. "He's here, Sis, here in Caldaquès."

*Alive*, thought Marie-Claire. There need be no more sneaking into the kitchen in the evening for the newspaper; no more running a trembling finger up and down the page, searching for "The Glorious Dead" column.

"What I didn't tell you," said Colette, suddenly grim, "is that he's recovering from combat wounds."

"How serious?"

"That's what I don't know," said Colette. "Mother wouldn't say."

Marie-Claire thought her heart would stand still. Quickly she searched for support. "I feel like spouting some Shakespeare again," she said.

"Go on." Colette urged her.

> O! never say that I was false of heart,
> Though absence seem'd my flame to qualify—

> As easy might I from myself depart
> As from my soul, which in thy breast doth lie.

Colette chimed in. "I'm so fortunate!" she cried. "I've found him at last. You know how many columns of notices there are in the paper concerning refugees who are searching for news of family and friends? Almost a whole pagefull the other day."

Colette ran to the basin and peered into the mirror above it. "Gosh, I look terrible." She leaned over and splashed water on her face. "Do you think I should take off my snood? It's too dark, isn't it?"

Without waiting for an answer Colette stripped away the confining hair net, shook her golden hair, and smiled at her reflection. She dabbed vaseline on her lids to make them shine and smoothed her delicately arched brows. Carefully, she applied a light film of the lipstick her mother had allowed her to purchase for her seventeenth birthday, then pinched her cheeks. "Bye Claire," she said, already at the head of the stairs.

*The princess sallies forth, and she has me to thank for this liberty,* thought Marie-Claire. *If I hadn't told them to keep their mouths shut about the accident, we'd all be quarantined.*

In her mind's eye Marie-Claire followed her sister. *She's rounded the corner, and now she's flying down the avenue. French soldiers in the hospital garden suck idly on blades of grass. They smile at the girl on the winged bicycle. The nurse waits at the door. "How is your nice little sister?" she asks Colette. They hurry down the white corridor, past haggard men shuffling along, into a dormitory of groaning cots—*

> *O du süsse, kleine Erika*
> *Tralalah, lalah, lalah.*

The distant but clearly audible words of the German marching song startled Marie-Claire's reverie. Young voices sang in perfect unison:

> *O du süsse, kleine Erika*
> *Tralalah, lalah, lalah.*

"O you sweet little Erika," they intoned, the voices growing louder as they came down the avenue to the percussion of marching feet. One. Two. One. Two. *Heil!*

> *Tralalee, tralalah,*
> *Tralalee, lalee, lalah.*
> *Wenn ich wiederkomm,*
> *Bist du mein . . .*

"If I come back," they sang cheerfully, "you will be mine. . . ."

Didi ran into the room. "What is that all about?" she asked anxiously. "It's just a marching song," Marie-Claire answered.

"Oh! Papa and I are going to pick up your bike now," she said. She winked at Marie-Claire, mindful of their pact of secrecy. "Wish me luck."

The girls had not reckoned on the man in the vest and beret who lived next door to the German headquarters.

"That fiery *Basque* let the cat out of the bag," Didi told Marie-Claire. "He recounted the accident as if he had been a witness to it. He had you stretched out on the sidewalk, and the *Boches* laughing over your unconscious body. Papa looked at me as if I were a spy or something."

*What am I going to do now?* thought Marie-Claire. But to Didi she said, "Sorry if I got you into trouble."

"Doesn't matter," said Didi, good-naturedly. "I made Papa promise not to tell your parents anything. But you know the adults. They don't understand our motives; they're suspicious of us."

"Yes," agreed Marie-Claire, thinking to herself, *Don't they know by now that in times such as these children do not exist anymore?*

"Do you think perhaps it was your fault you fell off your bike?" asked Didi, "that perhaps the soldiers were just teasing you?"

*Teasing?* Marie-Claire had not thought of that.

"Because they wanted to scare a dainty little French girl? Well, I've got to help load the car now, since we're leaving at the crack of dawn tomorrow."

"A dainty little French girl," the epithet pleased Marie-Claire. Now, arms and legs receded to graceful proportions. Even brows appeared less menacing. In other circumstances Didi's admission would have been cause for celebration.

She hobbled onto the balcony to wait for Colette. But when Colette came home and did not rush upstairs to see her, Marie-Claire sensed something was terribly wrong.

Stiff-legged, Marie-Claire ran to the bedroom door and opened it. Downstairs Colette was chatting with Rosine who, in her gusty voice, was dispensing gems of folk wisdom—certain cheeses had to ripen in the conjugal bed under the pillow where the temperature was just right; pears must be picked by the light of the waning moon. "Let me tell you a good one," she heard Rosine say before they disappeared into the kitchen . . . That must be the one about the steer they slaughtered at the farm one night, then hung the carcass in the pantry and sold the meat surreptitiously to the neighbors because they'd heard the

*Boches* were going to requisition cattle for their own butchering.

Marie-Claire clenched her fists in self-directed anger. The pigeon in her dream would not open his clenched beak and release his message, and she feared she would have to wait until Didi was gone before Colette would tell her more about Jean-Paul.

During dinner she watched Colette chase croutons around her soup—again, carrots and turnips mostly, because the newest vegetables were snapped up by the *Boches* for their field commander and his staff. The noodles that followed Colette forked as if they were eels. *Don't stare,* Marie-Claire reprimanded herself. *You'll only add to Colette's embarassment.*

"Do you consider it prudent, Victor, to allow the girls to circulate freely in the city now?" Uncle Georges asked, breaking the silence, "I mean with all those *Boches* about?"

"The *Boches* are highly disciplined," said Victor. "That is their only good quality."

"I wouldn't count on it," said Uncle Georges.

"Really?" Susan queried. Marie-Claire flinched.

"What do you mean, my little Georges?" Aunt Monique fixed on her husband her imperious gaze.

"Er, er . . ." spluttered Uncle Georges. The girls were glaring at him. "Just what I said, I wouldn't count on it, that's all." He picked up his knife and fork and attended to his noodles.

"Thank you for your advice, Georges," said Susan. Which meant she was taking it into account, Marie-Claire realized. Uncle George's admonition would soon be the topic of family consultation. Delay tactics were in order.

When dinner was over Marie-Claire proposed to Didi and Colette a game of Great Men of France, in the smoking room, where card tables were set up. Uncle Georges grudgingly became Colette's partner. But he warmed to the task. Lavoisier, Pasteur, Curie—he knew all the great chemists. "I memorized them before any of you were born. I also know about germs." He winked at Marie-Claire. "Take good care of that knee, little girl."

# 38

"Jean-Paul's recovery is a miracle," said Colette to Marie-Claire, after they had waved to Didi for the last time, standing at the curb in their bathrobes in first light. Shutters up and down the street remained closed. Roof tops were etched against a milky sky.

"If I hadn't heard it from Jean-Paul himself, I would not have believed it," said Colette. "Come."

She took her sister's hand and led the way, just as she used to do when they were small children and had secrets to impart to each other. Only then the anticipation of revelation had been a delicious feeling for Marie-Claire, one that made her feel warm inside—rather like hot chocolate. Now, as she allowed herself to be pulled upstairs to the reacquired privacy of their bedroom, Marie-Claire felt she was climbing the gallows; there was a sinking feeling in the pit of her stomach.

"Sit," ordered Colette, pointing to the cane chair with the tattered pillow, and Marie-Claire willingly complied; her legs were wobbly.

Colette plunked down on the foot of her bed and faced her sister. "He was evacuated with the rest of his platoon at Dunkirk—"

"See, I told you so," cried Marie-Claire.

"But his ship was torpedoed and thrown onto a sandbank. Jean-Paul was rescued by a British yachtsman, but Badin was drowned."

"Oh no!" exclaimed Marie-Claire.

"The poor man couldn't swim. He wasn't the only one . . . rescued, then drowned."

The sisters bowed their heads.

"The yachtsman who rescued Jean-Paul and the other survivors calmly smoked his pipe while he steered his boat to port—they weren't too far from the English coast at the time. The noise was deafening, Jean-Paul remembers. Screaming planes overhead, booming antiaircraft cannon, shells exploding. But the Englishman went right on smoking his pipe and kept his hands on the wheel as if this hulabaloo were just a big Fourteenth of July celebration.

"When they landed, the cheerful English Red Cross girls in their frowsy smocks plied them with tea."

Marie-Claire smiled at the image.

"Jean-Paul was quartered in Dover. He had time enough to dry out and get a new pair of boots. Four days later he returned to France to fight again."

Colette paused and rubbed her forehead, as if what she was about to relate was too painful for her.

Marie-Claire instinctively fingered the holy medals about her neck chain.

"He was on reconnaissance when the mine exploded. The earth in front of him shot up like a fountain, Jean-Paul says. He was carried through the air with such force he thought he was being blown apart, that his head had already come off his body and his mind alone was hurtling through space at a dizzying speed. Then he lost consciousness. He came to briefly when he landed and he remembers the feel of something cool and soft. But he was in so much pain he blacked out again.

"When Jean-Paul could keep his eyes open and focus on his surroundings, he says, he was in a hospital bed. A nun stood over him, coaxing him to drink through a straw. She had a kind, tired face. She told him his buddies had carried him to the hospital more dead than alive. He had landed in a pile of borax in a bombed-out glass factory, and it was most fortunate—no, incredible—the nun said. Incredibly, too, the borax was only deep enough to cushion his body, or he would have suffocated. 'Your guardian angel took marvelous care of you,' she told him."

Colette paused again. Marie-Claire gripped the arms of the chair.

"Listen to this now," Colette said, "One of France's top surgeons happened to be on duty when Jean-Paul was admitted to the field hospital. 'There were more holes in you than flesh,' he told Jean-Paul, 'I had to piece you back together.' The doctor marveled that no major nerves had been severed; it was beyond human understanding, he said. He predicted severe infection would follow, but it didn't. He thought, too, that the patient would not be able to stand the pain." Colette shivered.

"Then one day when Jean-Paul was lying there with his eyes closed, feeling so sorry for himself he wished he were dead, he overhead a conversation between two patients. 'Most of us are considered hopeless cases,' said the first man; 'only those strong enough to travel will be transferred to the Southwest.'

" 'I wouldn't mind that,' said the other, 'it's so noisy here I've forgotten what it's like to hear the crickets sing.'

"After that, Jean-Paul says he began to pray. He prayed to God and Saint Louis. He asked the nun for a rosary. She gave him one of wood from the Mount of

Olives. In the ward they began calling him 'the monk' because his fingers constantly worried the beads. He prayed for the strength to raise his head, to slide his foot. 'When you are a normal, healthy person,' he told me, 'movement is something you take for granted, like opening and closing your eyes or swallowing your saliva.' At the time it never dawned on him that his fingers were free to move as they wished. 'You can't imagine what it's like to be so weak it takes a conscious act of will to move a muscle . . . and then to fail, time and time again.' "

"At least he had the will power," said Marie-Claire. "You must have been transmitting positive thoughts." She reminded her sister of the pledge Jean-Paul and she had made.

A smile flitted over Colette's face, like a butterfly wing. "The day he was able to put one foot on the floor," she said, "although he was still flat on his back, he wanted to shout, to proclaim the news to the whole ward."

Then Colette turned solemn again. "He made a vow that when he was fully recovered—'I never considered "if," only "when," ' he told me—he would join de Gaulle. Now that France is beaten, he considers this his crusade."

"Fantastic!" cried Marie-Claire, who immediately thought of Saint Louis setting out to liberate the holy places.

"How can you be so unfeeling, Sis?" Colette stared at her sister.

*The accusation hurts because it isn't true,* thought Marie-Claire. She may have stopped *praying* since the armistice, but that didn't mean she had stopped *caring*.

"Jean-Paul and I have just found each other," continued Colette, "He wants to go off and join de Gaulle, and you call that fantastic!" Colette's eyes were dark with indignation. "Everything in life that happens to a body is on an intellectual level with you, Claire," she snapped. "You live in an ivory tower. When are you coming down to earth, for God's sakes?"

Marie-Claire turned towards the armoire and removed Teddy Bear. (He'd been concealed there during Didi's visit, for fear of ridicule.) *This will show Colette I'm no stone maiden*, she thought. She plopped the stuffed animal in her sister's lap. He was a one-eyed bear now, his face almost bald from too much affectionate rubbing. His right ear drooped, but his little, black, turned-up nose and curling mouth were so cunning he always evoked a smile from his beholders.

"Oh, Claire," said Colette, as she cuddled the toy, "he's so pitiful. Why don't you stitch up his ear?"

"Could I go with you sometime to see Jean-Paul?" Marie-Claire asked shyly.

"It's rather depressing, that hospital," Colette said.

"But I thought it was a convalescent hospital?" Marie-Claire said quizzically.

"Yes."

"Well, doesn't that mean they're all getting well?"

"Some patients have only one limb."

Marie-Claire suddenly had a sickening feeling at the pit of her stomach. "Do you mean . . . Does that mean . . . Jean-Paul has only one leg?" She played with the tassels on her sash.

Colette placed the stuffed animal on her sister's bed. "Calm yourself, Claire. Jean-Paul has two legs, like Teddy Bear."

There was a knock on the door.

"Marie-Claire," her father called, "your mother and I would like to speak to you when you've dressed."

# 39

Victor and Susan questioned Marie-Claire about her leg injury and were incredulous when she told them she had jumped off her bicycle.

"What for?" they asked. "You're not a child."

She told them the truck had passed so close she thought it would squeeze her against the curb and she got panicky. "They were probably only teasing," she said.

"Who?" Victor asked.

"The Germans, of course. They laughed at me."

Her parents shook their heads.

Hands clasped behind his back, Victor paced the master bedroom. He paused before a picture of the Blessed Virgin. "Postcard art," he muttered, "why not paint the roses in the garden?" And the pacing resumed. Clearly the accident contradicted his concept of German discipline, the one shred of reliability he was counting on in this period of adjustment to defeat.

"The *Boches* are drunk with victory," he said, pausing long enough to ponder this statement.

"Why would they try to hurt an innocent girl?" asked Susan, who, in contrast to Marie-Claire's agitated father, sat in an easy chair with her legs crossed. "Did you make a face at them, Marie-Claire, or insult them in some way?"

"Oh no, Mother. I was just riding along minding my own business."

"My dear," said Victor, "our little girl belongs to the ranks of the vanquished and they are the master race. *Eetlair*, in his book, *Mein Kampf*, emphasized the importance of physical terror toward the individual and the masses. Now it is becoming painfully clear. He said, if I remember right, that it was more honorable to be a street cleaner in the Reich than a king of a foreign state. To be a soldier fighting for the glory of the Reich, then, is truly heady stuff."

Victor smote his forehead. "How could I have been so blind to this? For instance, I heard that in Bayonne last week they paraded a half-dead Senegalese prisoner around town in the back of an open truck; he was covered with flies. They had accused his comrades of barbaric atrocities toward German soldiers—trumped up charges, you may be sure, because he was black, not Aryan."

"How horrible." Marie-Claire shivered.

"The day the *Boches* arrived in Caldaquès, the prefect told me one of their own soldiers fell out of his sidecar and the others ran right over him. *Immer vorwärts,* you know, 'Forever onward.' To hell with the individual; he's just a cog in their military machine. Everything must be sacrificed to the Reich's dream of conquest. *Heute Deutschland, Morgen die ganze Welt.*"

"Please, Victor—"

"What your mother is about to say is that I am getting off the point," Victor said, addressing Marie-Claire.

"Why did you keep this information from us in the first place? Why all this secrecy surrounding an accident in which you could have been seriously hurt?" Susan asked, leaning forward in her chair.

"Because I knew Colette would hear from Jean-Paul."

"Knew?" Susan queried.

"Yes, I'm psychic, I think. Rather like Uncle Mo."

Her parents looked at each other.

"Was that why you woke up early that morning at Randonette?" Susan asked then. "Did you have some premonition that Marie Langlos would kill herself?"

Marie-Claire flushed.

"Oh, my child," her mother continued, "I didn't mean to upset you. And you must forget all the foolish rumors concerning that tragedy."

Her father nodded.

"I had a dream about Colette." That sounded silly now, so she hunted for a better explanation. "I, er . . ." Forget about the pigeon. "I knew she would hear from Jean-Paul, and if *you* knew the *Boches* ran me down, I thought you would restrict Colette and me to the house and she wouldn't be able to see him."

"I'm going to the *Kommandantur* and ask to speak to the *Kommandant* himself," said Victor. "They are not going to treat our young people this way."

"You will do no such thing." Susan placed a restraining hand on her husband's arm. "Do you want him to deny us our exit visas?"

Marie-Claire stared at her mother. She had won out at last and tentative plans were now positive plans; they were leaving France after all. Although Marie-Claire had suspected this would happen, the room suddenly quivered. The blue satin draperies were slipping off their rods, the picture of the Virgin tilted perilously, as if the walls were about to collapse like a house of cards. *Jésus, Marie, Joseph,* she prayed silently, to calm herself.

"I think it's time we called in Colette," her mother was saying. "Stay put, Marie-Claire."

*Exits and entrances, that's what life's all about,* thought Marie-Claire as her mother left the room to fetch her sister. Colette isn't going to like *this* announcement. . . Her father was still in a frenzy. The room was not wide enough to accommodate his pacing. She closed her eyes, preferring not to see the expression on her sister's face.

"Visas, visas—we are applying to the *Kommandant*, all of us, for visas to leave this godforsaken continent." The whole of Europe Victor now considered benighted since the British had attacked French ships on July 3, although he understood the reason for their action at Mers-el-Kebir. "For you and me, the aliens," he pointed at the girls, then poked his own chest. "I have applied to Washington for visas to travel to A-mer-i-ca!" With grand gestures he flourished his arms, indicating the vast continent at the most exotic reaches of the universe. "Washington needs copies of police records, certificates of good conduct, can you believe it? Not for you, Marie-Claire, who are under the age of sixteen and in the eyes of the American law young and innocent."

Marie-Claire winced. She still would not look at her sister.

"That puritannical American government wants to know all about the morals of responsible adults, like Colette and me," Victor continued. "Let's see, what else does America require?" He cocked his head and feigned serious consideration.

"When are we leaving?" asked Colette. She might have been asking when was the next bus to the *Porte d'Orléans*. She was quietly accepting the reality of positive plans.

"That all depends on the Germans," said Susan, "when and whether they will grant your father his exit visa. But we must vacate these premises soon, the landlord says. He wants to return to Caldaquès. He's tired of the big city; Bordeaux is crammed with refugees, he says."

"But Paris isn't," said Colette. "Why can't we just go home, like everyone else?"

"The everyone else you refer to," said Victor, "have no other option. Why should we return to a captive city, when we have the opportunity to go to a free country?"

Colette bowed her head.

*"Liberté, Égalité, Fraternité,* I say. Those were pre-revolutionary slogans, you know, which the French Revolution abused."

"Where shall we go from Caldaquès?" asked Colette.

"To the border," said Susan, "to wait for the Germans to let us through into Spain. The Germans are free to go in and out as they please, but the French and foreigners must wait the German's leisure. Then on to Portugal, to Lisbon, where we shall board a ship for New Jersey—the Lord willing," she fervently added.

"Cheer up, *ma chérie,*" Victor reassured her, "there should be no problem. My profession cannot be of value to the German Reich." He smiled. "Now, if I were an engineer, or a physicist—"

"You planned all this without letting Claire or me know?" Colette was indignant, fighting back tears. When she turned her head away, she was crying very softly, and Marie-Claire handed her a handkerchief.

"Colette, I know how you feel," said Susan.

"No, you don't, Mother."

"You must think me very uncaring," continued Susan.

*Touché!* thought Marie-Claire.

"You don't understand, Mother." Colette cried out. "It was easy for you. You met Father one summer on your first European tour and came back and married him, and that was that."

"My child, if you think it was that easy, you are deluding yourself," said Victor.

"Who said anything about marriage in your case?" Susan paled. "You're only seventeen, Colette."

"Jean-Paul and I are engaged, and engagement usually means a wedding is to follow." Colette turned her head to blow her nose.

"Aren't you a little young to get married, daughter? To put the rope around your neck, as the old proverb goes? Consider the responsibilities involved." Victor rushed to his wife's defence.

"Especially during wartime," Susan added, "and when the young man has been seriously wounded." Her voice gentled. It had lost its sharp, brittle quality, the no-nonsense, keep-your-chin-up implication inherent in all she said.

"Jean-Paul is recovering fast," Colette assured her parents. "He plans to join the Free French when he is able. We would get married first."

"*Nom de Dieu!*" exclaimed Victor. His dark eyes flashed.

"And, darling, what would you do then?" Susan asked her daughter.

Before Colette could answer, Victor interrupted, standing in front of his daughter like an interrogator. "Last night the British torpedoed French ships, killed French sailors. Do you mean to tell me Jean-Paul wants to fight side by side with an ally who knifed France in the back?"

Marie-Claire gasped. Thank goodness, Uncle Georges had not heard the news before he left.

Colette did not reply. She just marched out of the room. Marie-Claire started to get out of her chair, but her mother clasped her wrist.

Victor leaned against the dresser. "What am I doing?" he said, wearily, "I'm falling into the trap. This is just what the *Boches* would have me say. De Gaulle is the only chance of salvation for France now . . . and the British had their reasons for Mers-el-Kebir. Although I still think there must have been some terrible misunderstanding. Go to your sister, Marie-Claire."

"Yes, dear," Susan urged her.

"Why can't Father console her?"

Before her astonished parents could reply, Marie-Claire limped out of the room, slamming the door behind her.

Why should she always be the middleman, the one whose duty it always was to comfort Colette? Why didn't her parents assume responsibility for a change? Well, let them do so now. She clung to the bannister and hopped slowly downstairs. Here she was disfigured and soon about to visit Jean-Paul. It wasn't fair for him to see her in this condition.

"Are you still hungry?" Rosine asked. She was peeling potatoes, and she wiped her hands on her apron before pulling out a chair. "Let me prepare you another *tartine*."

Marie-Claire nodded.

"Good butter, isn't it?" Rosine winked. "Fresh from the farm. Don't tell the neighbors. We wouldn't want the *Boches* to find out, would we? How about some cherry jam, too?"

# 40

"Tomorrow you and I are going to see Jean-Paul," Colette announced. She was standing on the balcony. "You said you wanted to go with me."

She sighed and Marie-Claire was seized with apprehension. Something in Colette's tone, the way she dressed lately—in dark navy, complete with navy snood—indicated a mourning, a grieving for something lost.

"He says I must leave for America as soon as possible," continued Colette. "Imagine that. We have just found each other, and he tells me to leave." She turned around and grasped the railing, as if she were already on board ship. 'France is now a prison,' he says."

*"No bars, yet prisoners in one's own country." That was the way Uncle Mo expressed it in his last letter,* thought Marie-Claire. *"The swastika has replaced the blue, white, and red; the village is still blacked out at night; and the pork butcher has to divulge the recipe for his very own pâté. No gasoline for excavations, of course. Jean is still a prisoner of war, Pierre has joined the glorious dead, and Jacques, the baker, is too busy since the Boches acquired a taste for French bread."* There had been no mention of Joseph, or Jean-Marie. *"My dear children, when you leave for America, do not forget the coins I gave you."*

Marie-Claire had smiled at the admonition at the time. In her mind's eye, Uncle Mo stood in front of her, in white smock and black beret, wagging a finger at her. She would sooner leave her poetry books behind: the volume of English poetry she had thought to pack when she left Saint Ethelred's; her French verse, which her Father had brought back from Paris; and now the still unopened German book Jean Dreyfuss had left her.

Oh, to smell the sweet odor of trampled grass in the field at Randonette, to see the men once more hacking at the dirt, which for centuries had remained undisturbed, and then to thrill to another shout of discovery . . .

Colette interrupted Marie-Claire's reverie. "We won't stay long this time," she said, "his energy must be saved for the final good-byes."

"Is he really going to be able to join de Gaulle?"

Colette placed an admonishing finger on her lips, as if the Germans were under their balcony. "When someone of his family and ancestry makes up his mind," she said, "anything is possible."

Marie-Claire tugged at the seams of her silk stockings. Silk stockings were imperative to conceal her knee patch. When she straightened, she held her head high and stuck out her chest—not easy, when one was wearing pumps.

For Jean-Paul and the poor convalescent soldiers she had put on her brightest dress, the red and white one with vertical stripes and short, puffy sleeves. Vertical stripes made her look taller.

Last night she had applied a face cream of rose petals and lard. Her mousy hair she had washed and rinsed in tea till it glinted with red highlights. In the privacy of a locked toilet, she had tamed her unruly brows with manicure scissors.

"Five minutes, that's all you'll get, Claire," Colette said.

In blue and white floral, resplendent Colette was parceling out Jean-Paul as if they were on a field trip to the Louvre, gazing at the magnificent Michelangelo's *Bound Slave*.

"Wait for me downstairs." Colette rushed back into the bedroom for her blue ribbon.

At the foot of the stairs waited Victor and Rosine. Susan was in the parlor, playing Chopin's Military Étude. Marie-Claire recognized the vigorous tempo.

"How radiant you look, *ma petite*," said Victor. He stretched out a welcoming hand, like a leading man in the films. "Just like Aunt Monique at this age, only a trifle shorter."

"Ah, *Mademoiselle!*" exclaimed Rosine. "Who would have known?"

When Colette came down, Marie-Claire heard Rosine murmur, *"Quelle beauté."*

The walk down the avenue was a nightmare of pebbles grinding Marie-Claire's thin soles like steel files. Her father grasped her arm. Surely he could sense the heaving of her ribs, her heart was pounding so.

"Wait a minute, child." He restrained her as she was about to step off the curb.

In front of the hospital the *Boches* were changing the guard. Goose-stepping, people called it, that stiff-legged, straight-out-in-front-of-you kind of marching. *Where did they get that name?* Marie-Claire wondered. *Geese waddle.*

Without hesitation, Colette handed the hospital *concierge* a note. Bits of blue paper littered the hospital desk. More notices were on the smudged walls of the corridor. But under a visitation schedule someone had drawn a jaunty Micky Mouse, with hands like boxer's gloves.

Marie-Claire sat down next to her father on a wooden bench, whose uneven legs rocked on the tile floor. Men in garments like potato sacks shuffled past, trailing whiffs of strong disinfectant. The eyes of all were upon her. She lined up the toes of her patent shoes.

A creaking board. Colette rose. The morning glories on the hem of Colette's dress flashed by in blue swirls.

An eternity later when she reappeared with a white-robed nun and beckoned to Marie-Claire to follow them, Marie-Claire took a deep breath.

*"Vas-y, ma petite."* Her father's low, soothing voice comforted her. "I shall wait here until you return."

Marie-Claire pitter-pattered down the corridor, past the raucous enlisted men's dormitory, reeking of disinfectant and ammonia; past the steamy laundry, where huge pots of linens were boiling on the stoves. A clatter of silver being sorted and put away announced the kitchen. In an alcove outside the kitchen door stood a blue and white Our Lady. Our Lady of Perpetual Help, read the gold inscription under the statue. At its base someone had squeezed in a jar of buttercups and Queen Anne's lace.

The corridor angled right, past a succession of small rooms, where, through half-open doors, emanated cigarette and pipe smoke and tones of male, yet subdued, conversations.

"*Par ici, Mademoiselle.*"

Marie-Claire followed Colette and the nun through an archway decorated with plaster ribbons and bows stiff as adhesive tape into a large sitting room, where prim, white antimacassars spotted the brown chairs. A round table centered on a faded, red Oriental rug, stood in the middle of the room, and on it a dark blue vase contained a bouquet of dried plumes.

Remembering to hold her head high, Marie-Claire walked as though on stage, repeating to herself lines from the sonnet Colette and she had lately recited: "If I have rang'd, like him that travels I return again . . ."

She passed three officers who sat reading by a cold, stone fireplace; they glanced at her, she noticed, then went on with their reading, except for one who followed her out of the corner of his eye, above the spread pages of a tattered magazine. *Where is Jean-Paul?* she wondered.

Alone, in pajamas and robe, he sat at the opposite end of the room, head turned toward the French windows, gazing at the purple blooms of a myrtle tree on the lawn outside.

The nun glided toward him, leaned over and whispered in his ear. Slowly he turned around and smiled at Marie-Claire, and—oh, horrors—she saw that the once handsome face, smooth as a painted statue, was now disfigured. The left side sagged as if a malevolent hand had pressed Jean-Paul's brow and continued down over the eye, across the cheek, and twisted the corner of his mouth. The once lustrous black hair was tinged with gray. Or was it simply the light shining on it through the window?

Marie-Claire wanted to run away. *Our Lady of Perpetual Help,* she prayed silently, as she advanced toward the invalid, *please help me not to show my dismay.*

"So kind of you to come and see me," Jean-Paul said, profferring a steady hand.

Marie-Claire, still sending up silent prayers like incense wafting over an altar, gingerly touched the cold fingers. She tried not to stare. The once merry gray eyes were dull, bereft of mischievous sparks; the face, under a black stubble, was pale as parchment.

"Ah, you can do better than that, little sister," he said, squeezing her hand, and Marie-Claire smiled in spite of herself. "So, are you ready to leave for America and the road to freedom?" he asked. His right eyebrow suddenly shot up; it had a will of its own. "Give my regards to Broadway."

Marie-Claire nodded. Now that she was in Jean-Paul's presence, still recovering from the shock of his transformation, she could think of nothing appropriate to say. She stared at the flaming myrtle tree. *A fitting background for this heroic man,* she thought, *who has been in the heat of battle.*

On impulse, she leaned forward and kissed him lightly on his injured side. Her hand brushed his knee as she steadied herself on the arm of his chair.

A slow blush suffused his cheek, as if she had imbued it with new life. For an instant she thought his gray eyes twinkled.

"Thank you, little sister," he said. "You know, love is the greatest healer of all."

Marie-Claire treasured his words. His twisted smile

moved her so that she wanted desperately to straighten his face with magic fingers, to make it right again.

Then they shook hands, and it was time for her to leave. *Lord, keep my eyes dry,* she petitioned.

As she turned, yielding her place to Colette, Marie-Claire found herself eye to eye with the officer across the room. He was watching her intently, a smile on his boyish face. When she walked toward the door, he reached for his cane, which lay on the floor, and struggled to his feet. She paused.

"*Mademoiselle*," he said, bowing before her, and she noticed his dark, thick-lashed eyes, the long, thin nose. "Lieutenant Gabriel de Meursac, at your service. You are like a breath of fresh air in this stuffy place."

Marie-Claire flushed. She was unused to such gallantry.

"May I escort you down the corridor?" he asked.

"I don't want to trouble you," she said, glancing at his rigid leg.

"No trouble. It's my pleasure. The exercise will do me good, and so will the company."

She was not convinced when she saw how he dragged his leg across the sill. But she adjusted her pace to his, and side by side they ventured down the corridor, he talking freely of his ancestral home set among the vineyards of the Gironde Peninsula.

"Pardon," he said, as he grabbed her arm and held his cane straight out in front of him. "There are vineyards undulating to the horizon. As a small boy I would follow the harvesters, pinching ripe fruit here and there." He laughed like a happy child. There was no bitterness in him.

Marie-Claire smiled at him. Never had she felt more comfortable in a young man's presence. When they reached the bench where Victor sat drumming his fingers, the man leaned on his cane, bowed once again, and then he was gone, tap-tap-tapping down the corridor tile.

"A perfect gentleman," commented Victor. "When will he be calling on you?"

"I didn't even mention my name." Marie-Claire sighed.

"Cheer up, Jean-Paul can give him all the particulars. Life in a convalescent hospital is like a boarding school in some respects." He winked. "Don't worry, little girl."

Marie-Claire winced. When would her father stop calling her "little girl"? Besides, the blisters on her heels burned, her toes were cramped, and the elastic in her dress sleeves held her arms in a vice. Now that her mission was accomplished, she wanted only to return to *Mon Repos* and strip off her finery.

When Colette appeared Marie-Claire jumped up.

"Wait for your poor papa," said Victor.

The day Colette visited Jean-Paul for the last time was the day Victor was granted his exit visa, the Paris *concierges* returned with their canary cages to their appartment lodges, and the Paris Stock Exchange opened—"discreetly," the paper had said, "having been asleep since June 10."

Marie-Claire occupied herself with emptying the pantry and giving Rosine what few packages of sugar, flour, and rice remained after the exodus of the refugees.

"I should buy these from you," said Rosine. "You know they would fetch a good price on the black market."

"Forget it," said Marie-Claire, "Mother would not hear of such a thing."

"Madame has a heart, as well as the gift of music. Just listen to her."

From the parlor came the sonorous, deeply religious

chords of a Bach prelude, and Marie-Claire and Rosine paused in their work and smiled.

When Colette returned from the hospital, face still flushed from all the tears she had shed, she handed Marie-Claire an envelope. "Lieutenant de Meursac asked me to deliver this right away," she told her sister. "Sorry it got crumpled."

Heart pounding, Marie-Claire ran upstairs to her room and closed the door. She flung herself onto her bed before tearing open the envelope. "Ah, what beautiful penmanship," she said aloud. "So this is how one writes a *billet doux*."

Dear Mademoiselle,

I would like to reiterate what a pleasure it was to make your acquaintance. It is not every day that one is granted such a favor. You remind me of my dear sister, Angélique, and I cannot wait to return to my family again.

Now that you are leaving France for distant shores, I wish you a safe journey and a happy return to us some day.

My respectful homage,<br>Gabriel de Meursac

Marie-Claire held the note to her bosom for an instant, then tucked it inside her missal, next to the Ordinary of the Mass. On second thought she removed it and placed it inside her diary, where it would be under lock and key. The envelope she placed in her handkerchief case.

# 41

Wednesday, August 21, Saint Chantal, the calendar said. Flushed with the noonday heat and the anxiety of the coming ordeal, filled, too, with hope of liberation at last, Marie-Claire sat on her suitcase inside the stuffy customshouse, waiting for the German official. She kept one hand on her violin case, which rested on her lap. *Why can't they open the windows on a day like this?* she wondered. *Do they think people will try to climb out and escape under their very noses?*

Her mother and Colette sat on their suitcases beside her, as did two other families further on down the line, all wrapped in silent cocoons. But Victor paced the floor.

Behind the counter the French official dozed in his chair. He had unbuttoned his jacket, and his cap perched on the back of his greasy head.

Marie-Claire watched a green botfly creep up the smudged windowpane, feeling for an exit. He dropped back in frustration and buzzed angrily to and fro, only to return to the same futile exploration. She patted her suitcase.

"Don't do that," whispered Colette.

Teddy Bear nestled underneath her, inside Marie-Claire's packed dresses. She had insisted she would be the one to carry him. Her mother had opened his crotch and in his straw innards concealed money with which to help pay for the family's trip to Lisbon. Five hundred francs were all the *Boches* allowed each departing head of a household. No securities. No precious stones or metals.

"Are you sure you can carry this off?" her mother had asked. "Going through customs under normal circumstances is harrowing enough."

"I want to do it," insisted Marie-Claire. If Jean-Paul and Gabriel could be so courageous, she would be, too. This would be her one, final, desperate act of valor, now that she was leaving France.

The Roman coins Marie-Claire had concealed inside a jar of cold cream, though this was not necessary, her father had told her. Roman coins were not living currency.

Inside Victor's cases Susan had packed the household silver—spoon, forks, knives—covered with soft cloth and wrapped in tidy bundles inside their shoes, like shoe trees; the knives, being straight, she packed among his paint brushes, in tins marked Sennelier, which everybody knew was Paris's largest art supply store. The *Boches* had better not try to lift those cases.

Marie-Claire closed her eyes on the frustrated botfly and concentrated on Saint Chantal, whose feast day it was. Jane Frances Fremiot de Chantal, born in Dijon, her missal said, spouse, mother, and widow—like the Blessed Virgin. A brave woman, too, she wrote with a red hot iron the name of Jesus on her breast.

Outside the open door, the thump of marching feet. Marie-Claire opened her eyes. The *Boches* were changing the guard.

One of the travelers down the line shivered, despite the heat. He had a long, thin face and aquiline nose—a Jew, no doubt. Not French, either; Marie-Claire was pretty sure of that. Who knows what he had already been through?

An extended boot came into her field of vision. For the last time, thank goodness. No more absurd, misnamed goose stepping. When the German officer called "Halt!" the French official opened his eyes, hurriedly buttoning his jacket. "Not long now," he reassured the emigrants.

The German officer strode in, and the travelers stood

up. "Be polite," Victor had warned, "but don't smile, above all. Do not appear coquettish." How could one? He was looking them over as if they were sides of meat hanging on hooks in the butcher shop.

The officer pointed to Marie-Claire's violin case, which she held tightly against her. Without a word she handed it over and he placed it on the counter as she stood helplessly by. "Open, please."

He pulled the handle of the rosin compartment and poked around inside, then gently lifted the neck of the instrument and looked in the voice box.

"You may close now," he said. "I, too, am violinist, you know." He said this with pride and some warmth, she thought, and she gritted her teeth so as not to smile.

"Are all these belonging to you?" He pointed at the six Lavalette suitcases.

"Yes, sir," she said.

"Sergeant," he corrected her.

"Yes, sergeant."

"You have your money declaration?" He turned abruptly toward Victor, who hovered next to Marie-Claire, and Marie-Claire held her breath.

"Passports, exit visas? *Nun.* Going to America. You're an artist, I see. First visit?"

"Yes." Victor mopped his brow.

"A little warm in here, isn't it?" The German officer smiled. Before Victor could respond, he waved him out of the hut and nodded to Marie-Claire, Colette, and Susan. *"Bon voyage,"* he said.

As she picked up her luggage, Marie-Claire noticed the look of envy on the faces of those about to pass examination.

It had been a long wait. Three weeks at the border, while the *Boches* made up their mind. Three weeks housed in a small, resort hotel that catered to the German civil police and their families and sweethearts. Walkyrien females, large wives and sweethearts, who treated French women with fierce disdain, ordering them off their path every time they crossed the park to go to the beach. Meanwhile their men sailed into Spain, to San Sebastián, to see the bullfights. In the hotel dining room they sat at long tables opposite the mirrored fireplace and consumed all the fresh vegetables the manager had to offer, while the French guests ate noodles and boiled potatoes. . .

Marie-Claire followed her parents out into the shimmering heat. Specks of mica in the sidewalk glittered like diamonds. They stooped under the frontier barrier and proceeded across the international bridge. The bridge to freedom, at last. But she was not free to rejoice yet. Conflicting emotions raged. Loved ones were being left behind as was all that was cherished and familiar. Newborn hopes, too, mingled with the humiliations of the recent past.

On the Spanish side, customs officials in three-cornered hats were pompously waiting. In the Spanish customshouse a huge photo of Generalissimo Francisco Franco papered the wall. Again came the demand for documents. Victor was informed he could exchange only the amount of money declared at the so-called "French" customs.

When the Lavalettes were told to open their suitcases, Victor refused. "We have exchanged one tyranny for another," he said, pounding his hand with his fist.

"During your terrible war, we French received your refugees with open arms," he reminded them. "How many of you drowned trying to swim to safety across this very river?"

"Communists," said an older official, his face long

and yellow as straw. He was so gaunt he reminded Marie-Claire of a picture of Don Quixote. The younger officials stood blank-faced; they had obviously not understood the French declamation.

"Victor, dear," muttered Susan in English, "I beg of you, don't get us involved in politics now, of all times. You know they have every right to open our luggage if they want to."

"I am a Catholic," Victor declared, "like your great general here." He gestured toward the huge photograph, "*Católico,* you understand?" He opened his wallet and waved a card at them, "*Croix de Feu,* Cross of Fire, you see? The membership card of the Conservative party."

The gaunt official saluted then. He motioned to a khaki-clad soldier, red tassle dangling from the front of his cap, to hand the Lavalettes their suitcases. The soldier bowed to them. *Ah, now we are being treated like visiting royalty,* thought Marie-Claire.

At passport control the official glanced perfunctorily at their documents, then handed them over with a smile and showed them where to go to exchange money. It was not until they reached the railway station that they realized the five hundred francs would not pay for enough *pesetas* to purchase tickets for the whole family on the Sur Express.

"If only Thomas had warned us," said Susan, "but he couldn't, of course, with the censorship of the mail."

"There must be a way," said Victor, glancing around the hall.

Not many people occupied the wooden benches. Doors opened onto the street. Marie-Claire uttered a silent prayer to Saint Christopher.

"Let's have a bite to eat, first," said Victor. "You can't plan on an empty stomach." He led the way to the lunch counter, where they munched on brown bread and salty cheese and sipped bottled lemonade, sickeningly sweet.

Through an open door Marie-Claire noticed a beggar sitting cross-legged on the street, shoes tied with rags. Behind him loomed the ruins of a tall building where, in gaping holes, rusty radiators were somehow suspended.

The stale bread stuck in her throat. Marie-Claire's stomach was queasy at the thought they might have to linger in this dirty place, devastated by war. The Battle of Irun, she remembered, had been a fierce one during the Civil War.

"Eat up," Victor urged her, "this might be our last meal before we reach Lisbon."

"Lisbon, eh?" asked a fat Frenchman, sitting two stools away. "You must have just crossed over. How are things in the old country?"

He got up and extended his hand to Victor. They could have been distant relations the way Victor greeted him, and Marie-Claire's spirits rose. What happened next she would remember for all eternity.

"I am returning to France," the man said. He pulled out a roll of bills. "See all those *pesetas*? I am returning, and I cannot dispose of them."

"Marie-Claire," said Victor, "come here."

*No need to explain,* thought Marie-Claire, as she climbed off her stool and picked up her suitcase. *This man is going to be the instrument of our salvation. I know it. I just know it.*

She laughed when, after a discreet interval, her father followed the man through the door marked *Caballeros*. Poor Teddy would have his crotch slit in the men's room, while the women outside offered silent prayers. *Forgive me, Lord, if I sound impudent*, Marie-Claire's prayers joined the others'. *I do not mean to be irreverent if I pray what was in the end of the Collect for today's feast—that by the help of Thy grace we may overcome all things that withstand us.*

The Frenchman emerged first, sauntering in the direction of the baggage room. Then Victor appeared. Still carrying her suitcase he headed in the direction of the ticket counter. When he returned, he waved four little pieces of paper as if he had won the National Lottery. *The unabashed hero of the family*, thought Marie-Claire. Ah yes, now Colette knew it and her mother, too. Her mother gazed at him with love and admiration.